Praise for Shannon Stacey

"Stacey's gift for writing easily relatable characters will hook readers and leave them eagerly waiting for the next installment."
—*Publishers Weekly* on *Heat Exchange*

"This is a series that I can already tell I'll love. You've written another winner, in my book."
—*Dear Author* on *Heat Exchange*

"This is the perfect blend of sweet and sexy for those who love a bit of firefighter action!"
—*Heroes and Heartbreakers* on *Heat Exchange*

"Stacey's engaging novel is pure comfort food...deeply satisfying."
—*Publishers Weekly* on *Controlled Burn*

"*Fully Ignited* was completely captivating, heartwarming and with a good dose of sensual sexiness making it a fantastic addition to Ms. Stacey's Boston Fire series."
—*Guilty Pleasures Book Reviews*

"The kind of story that kept my eyes glued to the pages. I read this one straight through and will probably find myself doing that again soon."
—*Book Binge* on *Fully Ignited*

"Don't miss out on this third book in Shannon Stacey's Boston Fire series.... I highly recommend this book."
—*Night Owl Book Reviews* on *Fully Ignited*

HOT RESPONSE

SHANNON STACEY

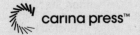

carina press™

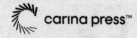

carina press™

ISBN-13: 978-1-335-47137-6

Hot Response

www.CarinaPress.com

Printed in U.S.A.

For Jaci Burton and Biker Dude.
I love you guys and not a day goes by I'm not thankful
we found each other in this big, crazy world.

HOT RESPONSE

Chapter One

"Change of plans, boys," Rick Gullotti announced from the shotgun seat of Ladder 37.

Gavin Boudreau sighed and kissed his plans for a sandwich stacked with about three inches of deli meats goodbye as the siren started wailing again. They'd just finished an overhaul, making sure there were no hot spots that might flare up again, and he was starving.

"PD's requested possible medical assistance and EMS doesn't have an available truck yet. We're closest, so we win," Gullotti continued because they'd been talking sports and he figured they hadn't been paying attention to the radio. And he was right.

"Possible medical assistance?" Jeff Porter looked at Gavin and shook his head. "They don't even know if they need help yet?"

"A woman screaming somewhere in the building is all they know, although a second caller reports there is a very pregnant woman who lives on the third floor and it sounds more like pain screaming than fear screaming."

Chris Eriksson, who did the driving, pulled to the curb while the LT was talking, coming to a stop behind Engine 59. There were several cruisers there already, and Gavin could see a couple of officers standing in front of the building. The firefighters gathered, looking for an update, and Gavin rolled his eyes at Grant Cutter, who looked as annoyed by this lunch delay as he was. They were the two youngest guys in the three-story brick fire station that housed L-37 and E-59 so, even though they hadn't known each other before they landed assignments there, they'd become the best of friends. They'd gotten pretty good at nonverbal communication.

They were held up at the front door until more information came through and the reason for the screaming was confirmed. Police officers had located a woman in labor in the hallway on the third floor and she was *not* happy about this detour in her birthing plan.

Gavin hustled up the stairs, the other guys on his heels—though some were closer than others. If they could get her down to the ground floor by the time EMS arrived, it increased her chances of giving birth in the hospital. Or at least in the ambulance, which wasn't ideal but was better than having her baby delivered on a floor by firefighters.

He reached the top of the stairs first, with Grant right behind him. Aidan Hunt and Scott Kincaid from E-59 were right there, too, but Gavin had the most advanced and recent first aid training, so he took the lead.

The police officer who had been talking to the woman stood as the firefighters approached, the relief so plain on his face it would have been comical under other circumstances. "Her name's Kelly. She wants us to take her to the hospital, but she can't move and she refuses to let us help her up."

The officer was young, and Gavin assumed he was still pretty fresh if he hadn't yet figured out that sometimes you couldn't let the terrified people in pain be the ones in charge. You couldn't make them do anything they didn't want to do, but there were ways of being persuasive and exuding calm and confidence helped.

Ignoring him, Gavin dumped his coat on the floor before kneeling next to the woman and taking her hand in his, giving it a squeeze. She looked at him, her eyes wide with fear and pain, and he gave her a warm smile. "My name's Gavin and I'm with the fire department."

"I should have…more time." She could barely get the words out through panicked breaths. "First babies are supposed to take forever. My husband. He's at work and…it'll take him almost an hour to get to the hospital."

He wasn't going to make it to the hospital in time. *She* probably wasn't even going to make it to the hospital in time, but he wasn't going to tell her that right now. He didn't need a cuff to tell him her blood pressure was jacked up, and that wasn't good for her or for the baby.

"I need you to calm down for me, Kelly."

"Calm down? I can *feel* this baby. I'm going to have my baby in this stupid, ugly hallway."

"You can feel the baby? Try to describe exactly how that feels right now." He felt like an idiot saying it, but feeling the baby could mean she felt increased pressure, or it might mean she literally felt the baby exiting the birth canal and that made everything a lot more urgent.

"Like if I stop clenching my muscles, a bowling ball will fall out of me."

"Okay, so the good news is that means the baby's probably still in there, but probably not for much longer."

Her fingers biting into his arm so hard he expected her nails to perforate his skin gave him a few seconds' heads-up before she wailed again. Gavin winced against the sound and the grip on his arm, wishing he'd kept the thick turnout coat on, but he did his best to keep his voice

comforting and calm as he gave her breathing instructions she either couldn't hear or couldn't follow.

When the contraction passed, he led with the important stuff. How far along she was. No gestational
diabetes. No preeclampsia, or any other complications
anticipated by her doctor.

Then another contraction hit her and by the timing
and the severity, he knew they were pretty much out of
time. Kelly was probably having this baby on the hallway floor, and he needed to make sure things looked
copacetic down below.

The wailing stopped, but the grip on his arm didn't
loosen. "I need to push."

"Pant through it and *do not push*." When she tried to
look away, he moved his head to keep his face in her line
of vision. "I need to look and see what's going on first.
If it's time, then you'll push. But we don't want to push
before the little one's ready."

"No," she said, shaking her head. "I do *not* want a hot
guy seeing my vagina like this."

He knew it would only be a matter of minutes before
she didn't care if her vagina went viral on the internet as
long as the baby came out. "I could put out a call for an
ugly firefighter to assist and see who shows up."

"Oh!" Scott Kincaid snapped his fingers. "That guy
from Haz Mat. What's his name? You know, the one who
looks like he did the Snapchat face-switch thing with an
English mastiff."

Kelly actually managed a smile, which Gavin took as
a good sign. The smile was a little pinched and he could
tell by her eyes she was still in a lot of pain, but at least
she wasn't in a full-blown panic anymore.

"I don't think we can wait anymore, Kelly."

She nodded, and in a matter of seconds, the other

guys were lined up, facing away and holding their coats up in an effort to give her some semblance of privacy. Somebody tossed him a blanket and he was able to help her roll so he could spread it under her before pulling on a pair of gloves.

"Do you know if you're having a boy or a girl?" he asked, trying to keep her distracted from the fact he was peeling her leggings off.

"No, we wanted to be surprised." She snorted. "This isn't exactly what we meant."

And, *holy shit*, they were about to be surprised. He looked up from between her legs, looking for backup or help or anything. Some of the guys had kids already, so surely they were more qualified to deliver babies. They'd probably cut umbilical cords and everything.

Where the fuck is EMS? He almost said the words out loud, but at the last second realized that wouldn't do much for Kelly's newfound and fragile calm, so he gave his mouth's filter a few seconds to kick in before addressing Gullotti. "Hey, LT, can you get an updated ETA on EMS?"

"They're one minute out."

"Hey, try not to push any firefighters down the stairs this time, okay?"

"It was one time, Tony." Cait Tasker reached between the seats to get a couple of blue gloves from the dispenser mounted on the back wall of the ambulance cab and snapped them on as her partner pulled up behind a fire truck. "And that was an accident."

"So you've said, multiple times. Hell, I'm pretty sure you said it twice before he even hit the landing."

"Funny." She grabbed her bag and headed toward the door of the building, leaving Tony Colarusso—her partner of four years—to grab the OB kit since it sounded like they'd probably need it. Dispatch was also sending a paramedic, but it was going to be a few minutes.

A police officer was holding the door open for her and she nodded her thanks as she passed through. The first flight of stairs was no sweat, but she felt the weight of the bag by the time she reached the second. Another officer was standing there, and he pointed off to his right.

Not that she needed any help finding the commotion. The reported screaming had stopped, but there was a gaggle of firefighters in the hall. Or a herd or a flock or whatever you'd call a bunch of guys holding turnout gear, standing around and doing nothing.

They parted to let her through, and she saw the back of the firefighter kneeling between the patient's legs. And his back was all Cait needed to see to know it was Gavin Boudreau.

That freaking cowlick.

They crossed paths occasionally, and there was something about the man that got under her skin. The first time they'd been on the same scene—a minor MVA involving a confused tourist going the wrong way up a one-way street—she'd gotten sucked in by his good looks and quick humor. She'd been working up the nerve to ask him if he wanted to grab a coffee or a drink sometime when he'd called her *ma'am*.

Not only had she not asked him out, but every time she saw him, she remembered the *ma'am*. It made her feel old and these days, she didn't need any help feeling older than her years.

Gavin glanced over his shoulder and as soon as he caught sight of Cait, he moved to the woman's other side and gave an update—including the patient's name and what vital info he had—as he moved.

Then Kelly grabbed a fistful of Gavin's shirt and pulled so hard, she almost yanked him down on top of herself. "Don't leave me."

"I'm not going anywhere. I just need to get out of Cait's way so she can take over. She's better at delivering babies than I am."

He knew her name. Why that should stand out to her in their current situation, she didn't know, but she noticed it and was surprised. "Kelly, he can stay by your head, but I need room for my partner."

"By my head, like a husband," Kelly said with a short, breathless laugh.

"You should at least buy me dinner first." He moved toward Kelly's shoulder without letting go of her hand.

Cait ignored him as she moved into the position he'd vacated. It was baby time.

"I want *my* husband," Kelly said, and her face began to crumple as tears welled in her eyes. But before the crying could begin in earnest, her face paled and her eyes widened. Her sharp intake of breath held a note of panic, like a sour musical tone, and Cait blocked out everything but the baby crowning between her patient's legs.

Tony was next to her, ready to take and assess the infant. It went as smoothly as unplanned labor on a hallway floor could go, and by the time the paramedic arrived, Kelly had a squirming, fussy bundle of baby boy on her chest. Though it was a busy day for EMS and there were a lot fewer paramedics than EMTs, they always tried to transport newborns with them in case they needed advanced medical care.

Phil had a rookie EMT with him, but Cait and Tony stood back and let them take over since they had to take care of the OB kit and somebody had to bag the mess.

Gavin was still holding the patient's hand as they put her on the stretcher, and Cait saw him smile at Kelly.

He really had a great smile.

"That's a good-looking boy you have," he was saying. "If you and your husband have trouble coming up with a name for him, Gavin's not too bad."

She laughed and said something Cait couldn't hear. Then Phil had the firefighters in motion, ready to carry mother, child and gear to the ground floor.

It was just Cait's luck that Gavin also lingered. She couldn't blame him for letting the other guys do the heavy lifting down the stairs, since they'd basically done nothing during the incident, but seeing him was a reminder she hadn't dated in a while and, considering how things were going at home, wouldn't be for a while. And that made her feel even older than the *ma'am* had.

"I feel like I should be handing out cigars," he said, and both he and Tony laughed.

Gavin's laugh made her even more tense. It was rich and deep and made heat curl through her insides. It was his laugh that had first turned her head, so every time she heard it, it reminded her of that day.

"Not gonna lie," he continued. "I'm glad you guys got here in time for Cait to play catch."

Play catch? "At least I took the situation seriously."

He'd been in the process of picking up her bag, and his head jerked up as if she'd slapped him. "What the hell is that supposed to mean?"

"Emergency childbirth isn't playing catch." She took her bag and slung it over her shoulder.

"Jesus, lighten up. It was a joke."

She was tired. She was hungry, and she wasn't in the mood. "Like I said, I take my job seriously."

"When I got here, she was laying on the floor screaming, and not just from the pain. She was in labor and in a full-blown panic. Her BP was through the roof and that's no good for her or the baby, so I did what I had to do to relax her."

She headed for the stairs before the conversation could escalate any further. If she really pissed him off, Tony might feel obligated to intervene and that wouldn't be fair to her partner.

"At least you're going down first," Gavin called after her. "I don't have to worry about you pushing me down the stairs."

"That was an accident," she shouted over her shoulder, and she might have been tempted to go back and explain it a little better, but she heard both men laughing.

Gavin was pushing her buttons and she'd let him get under her skin. Again.

After helping load mommy and baby into the back of Phil's truck, Cait and Tony took a few minutes to pack their gear away in their own ambulance before climbing into the cab. The firefighters were still milling around on the sidewalk, laughing and talking about who knew what.

Her gaze landed on Gavin because it always seemed to, whether she wanted it to or not. She wasn't sure how old he was. One of the younger guys in his house, but around her age—late twenties or so. There definitely weren't enough years between them to merit him calling her *ma'am*.

He was average height for a guy, but with a better than average body. Or maybe that was just her take on it. She liked guys who were in shape, but not such good shape they spent hours at the gym and expected applause when they flexed an arm. Physically, he definitely checked all her boxes.

And every time she saw him—which thankfully

wasn't *that* often—she wanted to smooth that damn cow-lick down. Maybe run her fingers through his hair a few times to help it stay. Then she'd invariably remember how close she'd come to asking him out, and why she hadn't.

He turned his head, looking straight at her, as if he'd felt her staring. Which he probably had. After a few seconds, he lifted an eyebrow and she looked away.

Dammit.

"I can't stand that guy," she said, not sure if she was making a statement or simply reminding herself of the fact.

"Why?"

Cait opened her mouth, but then snapped it closed again because she didn't want to tell him the real reason why. "He just rubs me the wrong way."

Tony gave her a sideways look before checking the mirrors and pulling away from the curb. "Maybe you're just mad because you want him to rub you the *right* way."

That was close enough to the truth so she wasn't going to discuss the possibility with Tony or anybody else. Gavin Boudreau was attractive, but the feeling wasn't mutual. Men didn't want to go on hot dates with women they called *ma'am*.

It was for the best, anyway. She was drowning in responsibilities and didn't have the time or energy to be fun and sexy with anybody, never mind somebody like Gavin.

"Shut up," she told Tony, "or I'll push *you* down the stairs."

He just laughed at her and took a left, heading toward their favorite coffee shop.

Usually, by the time the apparatus—Engine 59 and Lad-der 37—were backed side by side into the bays of the brick firehouse they called home, Gavin was starving. As the adrenaline rush faded, his appetite kicked in. Throw in being genetically blessed with a fast metabolism, and there was a reason the guys gave him shit about being a human garbage disposal.

Today, though, even the thought of the overstuffed sandwich he'd been thinking about for half the day couldn't tempt him. Childbirth might be natural and awe-inspiring, but it definitely wasn't pretty.

But by the time they'd finished up checking and re-packing their gear and gone up to the third-floor living quarters, he was starting to feel better. He figured he'd start with some chips and, if those went down okay, he'd follow up with that sandwich.

"What did you do to piss that EMT off?" Grant asked, taking the bag away from him and shaking some chips out onto a napkin for himself.

"I don't know. I think it pisses her off when I breathe."

"You guys have some kind of a history together?"

He knew what Grant was really asking. Had he slept with her and then cut it off badly? "No. The only time I've ever talked to her has been on the job, and it can't have been more than a dozen times, if that. She just doesn't like me."

"She's pretty hot."

"Yeah, she is. Not my type, though."

Grant snorted. "You don't have a type, other than women being susceptible to your so-called charm."

That wasn't true, and Grant knew it, since they'd been each other's wingman for several years. He had a particular weakness for women who were soft and super feminine. It wasn't so much about makeup and manicures, but women who liked having doors held for them and needed spiders killed and had soft hands.

Cait Tasker was abrasive and tough and there was nothing soft about her. He doubted she was afraid of bugs, and she'd probably give him shit about being able to hold her own damn doors, thank you very much.

But an image of her popped into his head and he decided maybe she had some soft parts, after all. Like her lower lip, which was soft and full and his favorite kind of mouth on a woman. And it was natural, too, since she didn't wear makeup. More often than not when he kissed a woman with a mouth like that, he had to put up with the faintly burning tingle of those fancy lipsticks that made their lips look fuller. Maybe they did, but they tasted like shit.

But while Cait's mouth looked like a perfectly kissable mouth, the words that came out of it were a serious problem.

And she'd crossed a line today. She could be annoyed by him. She didn't have to get his sense of humor. She could think he was an asshole and tell him so, if it made her happy. But to imply he didn't take his job seriously? That wasn't okay.

"You're thinking about her right now."

"Of course I am. We're talking about her."

"No, I mean like really thinking about her. You forgot I was even in the room."

"I guess I just can't figure out why she dislikes me so much." It was partly the truth, anyway. If he mentioned Cait's mouth, he'd never hear the end of it.

"Does she have any sisters? Maybe you hooked up with one of them and it went south and she has to hate you on principle now."

"I don't know if she does or not. I guess it's possible." At least that would be an explanation that made sense. "But I doubt it. What are the chances somebody dating a Boston firefighter doesn't mention her sister's with Boston EMS?"

"Good point. I guess she just doesn't like you." Grant grinned and reached for the chips.

Jerking the bag out of his reach, Gavin was in the middle of telling him where he could shove that suggestion when Jeff Porter walked into the kitchen.

"It's like living with a couple of teenage girls around here," he said, shoving his hand into the chip bag.

Danny Walsh, E-59's LT, was right behind him. "We've talked about this, Porter. Pour some chips onto a napkin or paper plate and stop groping around in the bag. God knows where those hands have been."

"Me? How 'bout where the kid's hands were today."

"Hey!" Gavin pointed at the pile of chips he'd shaken out onto the table. "I had gloves on. You could have helped but it takes an hour and half a bottle of baby powder to get gloves on those baseball mitts you call hands."

He ducked when Jeff tried to cuff him with one of those enormous hands because even in fun, those suckers hurt when they connected.

"This coffee tastes like dish soap," Walsh grumbled.

"For the hundredth time, LT," Grant said, "the new dish soap is super concentrated, so you're supposed to use less."

"What was wrong with the old dish soap?"

"Coupon from Mrs. Cobb."

Gavin snorted, knowing that would only escalate Walsh's grumbling. Their chief's wife got sick of him grumbling about grocery costs, even though they all had to contribute to the house fund, so she'd taken up coupon clipping. Now they had super turbo dish soap and a freezer full of Hot Pockets.

As they droned on about how embarrassing it was

to hold up the entire line while the cashier scanned the coupons Cobb's wife had sent in to work with him—all sorted into a pink wallet-type organizer with panda bears on it—Gavin's mind wandered.

Straight back to Cait Tasker and that mouth of hers. He couldn't stop himself from wondering what her reaction would be if he cut off the attitude-loaded words coming out of her mouth by kissing her and maybe catching that soft bottom lip between his teeth.

Knowing her, he'd end up in the back of her ambulance and she and her partner would stop for lunch on the way to the hospital.

Chapter Two

Cait stood in front of the small, shabby cape with dirty blue vinyl siding she was once again calling home, trying to brace herself before she went in.

She'd only lived in the house for a few years, between her mom marrying Duke—whose real name was John, which had inexplicably led to John Wayne jokes and the nickname back when he was a child—and moving into a shitty apartment with two broke friends as soon as she graduated from high school. She'd worked hard and eventually moved into a much smaller apartment with a similar level of shittiness, but without the roommates she'd come to like less than she had before living with them.

Then, almost eight months ago, Duke had a heart attack and he didn't make it. Her mom and her sixteen-year-old half-brother, Carter, hadn't handled it well. Her older sister, Michelle, was in Texas with her Air Force husband and had her hands full with a toddler. Cait had given all the help she could from arm's length, but she'd eventually had to come to grips with the fact her mom wasn't coping with being widowed a second time. It was a scared phone call from her brother that had been the final straw. Since she'd already been looking to lease or buy a less-shitty-than-her-apartment condo, she let her place go and *temporarily* moved back in with her mother.

Now it was six months later and it wasn't going well.

But it was too cold to stand outside all night, wishing she was someplace else. A nightclub with friends, dancing and drinking and checking out the hot guys would be nice. Or maybe she'd finally get around to stopping by Kincaid's Pub, which was supposed to have damned good food and was a favorite of the local firefighters. It was owned by a retired firefighter from Gavin Boudreau's house, actually, and the owner's son and son-in-law were on the same crew, too.

And she'd managed to circle right back around to the one guy she was trying not to think about anymore today. With an aggravated sigh, she walked into the house and almost ran into her brother, who was crossing the kitchen to the fridge. Carter's hair, as dark as her own, needed cutting again and one more thing got added to her to-do list before she even got her shoes off.

"How was your day?" she asked him as he sidestepped around her.

"Fine." He didn't stop walking or look up from his phone. The only indication he gave that he'd even heard her was the one word spoken in a flat tone.

On another day, she might have pushed him—forced him to put the phone down and have a conversation with her—but she was tired and not in the mood to get in a war of words with another guy today. Especially since she was already starting to feel guilty about the earlier exchange with Gavin. Whether he pushed her buttons or not, she shouldn't have taken her bad mood out on him.

Carter rummaged in the fridge for a few seconds before heading to the living room with a drink and his phone.

Her mom was at the counter, where she usually was when Cait came home. Every day, after her workday as a bank teller ended, Patty changed into one of Duke's old sweatshirts over leggings. "Hi, honey. I wasn't sure when you'd be home, so I didn't start dinner yet. It won't take long, though."

Cait had sent her a text message when she left the garage, but her mom rarely had her cell phone with her in the house. It was probably at the bottom of her purse, which was hung on the hook under her mom's heavy winter coat, chiming out reminders nobody could hear.

"I'll help," she said, but she wasn't surprised when her mom shook her head and told her to go relax.

Patty had always enjoyed cooking and they'd often worked side by side in the kitchen but, since Duke's death, she'd become adamant about doing it herself. Cait had figured out a long time ago that it was one of the few aspects of being the sole head of the household that Patty felt confident about—feeding her children was something she could handle—so she didn't argue with her.

Instead, she turned her attention to one of the household chores her mother definitely didn't handle well, which was dealing with the pile of mail tossed on the kitchen island.

And, oh, joy, it was credit card statement time again. One of the first fires Cait had to put out when she moved back in was stopping the auto-payments to the credit card company from Duke's savings account. The automatic withdrawals meant the statements could go unopened, to deal with another day. Her mother probably would have let it go on forever if Cait hadn't gotten pushy about her financial situation. Now, every month, Cait looked over every item on the statement, watching for problems and trying to keep a rein on the retail therapy habit her mom had developed. It was a double whammy because she got the retail therapy by buying things for Carter he didn't need—or deserve—just to make him happy for about two and a half minutes.

"Mom, we need to talk about this gym membership." *Again.* "Neither you or Carter have used it a single time since the last time we talked about it."

"I told you it was Duke's. He liked to go alone, and I think he went more to hang out with his friends than to work out. I won't use it, but it just keeps renewing itself."

So it was basically just setting forty of her mother's dollars on fire every month. "It needs to be canceled."

"I tried once. The gym has a website, but I didn't have the information to sign into his account. And I told you last time you asked that I've been meaning to ask Carter if he'd be interested in it, but I keep forgetting. I'll ask him."

Cait took a long drink of her coffee to drown the words she wanted to say to her mother. If Carter had any interest in going to the gym, he probably would have gone with his dad. He wasn't likely to be more interested now that his dad was gone. But she could tell by the way her mother ducked her head and lifted her shoulders a little that she wasn't feeling very strong at the moment, and Cait knew pushing the issue now would only end in her mother's tears and her own increasing frustration. Especially if they had to go through the grueling process of trying to guess the answers to her stepfather's security questions. That hadn't been fun and the only saving grace was that Duke seemed to reuse the same few passwords on a lot of sites.

Instead, she reached for the notebook that was never far from her laptop—which pretty much lived on the island with the mail since she rarely used it—and opened it to the page where she kept the list of credit card transactions that required further action. After writing down the company name and all the details, she finished scanning the statement and was relieved she didn't find anything else amiss.

Then she flipped to the most recent page in her never-ending to-do list and added *nag Carter about stopping at the barber shop after school.* That was a hard one because one Saturday morning of every month, Duke and Carter would go out to breakfast and then spend a couple of hours at the barber's, getting their hair trimmed and engaging in the male version of salon gossip. While most of Carter's acting out got on her nerves, since much of it was aimed at getting one over on their mother, she knew this one really hurt him.

"They're saying we might get snow later this week," her mother said as she snapped spaghetti in half and dropped it into the pot of boiling water. "We should hire somebody to shovel the driveway and the walk. One of the kids in the neighborhood, maybe."

"We are not hiring a teenager to shovel snow, Mom. You have one sitting in the living room."

"It's a lot for one boy. And you know he's behind on his homework. He needs to spend that time catching up."

"It's not too much for him. He just doesn't want to do it because *nobody* wants to shovel snow, and you need to stop babying him. He can shovel the snow and then do his homework."

"I know you think I baby him, Cait, but you're too hard on him."

With a weary sigh, Cait closed the notebook. Then she shut her eyes and breathed deeply for a moment, wondering what her life would be like if Duke hadn't died. She'd never been much of a party girl, but she'd gone out with friends. She'd even started dating again, after her last long-term relationship had gone stale.

But now, after an exhausting day at work, there was an exhausting evening with her mother and brother ahead of her. And the distance to her old neighborhood, where her friends and favorite stomping grounds were, was just far enough to require an effort she didn't have the energy for.

It made her feel old and tired, and the memory of Gavin's carefree laugh popped into her head. She could picture that boyish grin and that damn cowlick, so she opened her eyes. Thinking about him again wouldn't do anything but make her feel restless, and it was a restlessness she couldn't do a damn thing about.

She was willing to bet Gavin knew how to show a girl a good time, and—damn—she really needed a good time in her life.

But trying to date, even casually, while she was stressed out by her family would probably only lead to more complications and her plate was full of those. She'd be better off getting her mom back on her own two feet, finding herself her own place and *then* finding a guy who was actually her type.

It made a lot more sense than being frustrated by her inexplicable attraction to a guy who was very much *not* her type, and—as her mother often pointed out—Cait was always the sensible one in the family.

Gavin wasn't really in the mood to shoot pool, but they'd all come up with the plan to meet up at Kincaid's Pub while they were standing out on the sidewalk after the surprise childbirth incident yesterday, so he showed up. A night with the guys would probably beat sitting on his couch, watching TV alone. And even if it didn't, he could use the distraction.

He wanted Cait Tasker out of his head.

There were *zero* good reasons why the opinion of one

cranky EMT should not only matter to him, but matter enough to still be pissing him off over twenty-four hours later.

But it was, like a tiny sliver just far enough under the skin so he couldn't dig it out.

"You want in?"

Gavin looked at Aidan Hunt, who was holding a pool cue out to him, and then shook his head. "Nah, I'm good. Thanks."

He much preferred leaning against the wall, nursing his beer and his grudge against the sexy EMT with the big attitude problem.

The bar had a full house tonight but the crews from Gavin's house had pretty much taken over the pool alcove. None of the other regulars complained, though. The owner, Tommy Kincaid, and his best friend and fellow bar stool hog, Fitz Fitzgibbon, were retired Engine 59 and Ladder 37 respectively, so complaining about the firefighters to the management didn't do anybody any good.

And the bartenders didn't care, either. Lydia was married to Aidan Hunt and Ashley was married to Danny Walsh. And both were Tommy's daughters and Scott's sisters. It was a family bar and a firefighters' bar at the same time, and Gavin was part of that extended family.

Neither Jeff Porter nor Chris Eriksson were there tonight. Both were family men with kids and, while they occasionally showed up, they weren't big drinkers, either. Aidan would be in and out on any given night if his wife was working. And Ashley only worked the busiest nights because she was taking some online classes and because her and Danny's world had completely changed when their son started walking.

Jackson Kincaid Walsh might have his daddy's last name, but he was pure Kincaid. Stubborn, opinionated, hot-tempered and with enough energy to wear out his dad's entire crew during visits to the firehouse with his mom. Gavin thought he was one of the most awesome kids he'd ever met, but he might feel differently if he didn't get to give him back to his parents when he was exhausted, which usually took less than five minutes.

"Come on, Boudreau," Grant called to him from the other end of the pool table. "You gotta stop sulking because the pretty EMT was mean to you."

Gavin flipped him off.

"It could have been worse," Grant continued. "She didn't push you down the stairs."

That got a laugh out of him. He'd heard stories about the day Cait Tasker pushed Joe Grassano down a flight of stairs and, though he knew they were 90 percent bullshit, Gavin let himself imagine her cackling as Joe tumbled.

"Seriously, kid," Aidan said, and Gavin tried not to bristle. Aidan and Scott always called him and Grant *kid* even though there wasn't that much difference in their ages. Usually he took it in stride, because the other guys kind of were like the big brothers he didn't have, but he wasn't in the mood. "Is there something else between you and Tasker? It's not like you not to get along with somebody. Especially when that somebody's a woman."

"I don't know why she doesn't like me. And Grant already asked me if I hooked up with her and the answer is no. Nor have I hooked up with any sisters or best friends or anybody else that I know of." He took another swig of his beer. "She's not even my type."

"You have a type?"

"You guys are really a barrel of fucking laughs lately."

Aidan laughed. "Somebody has to pick up the slack while you're sulking."

He wasn't sulking, dammit. He was…brooding. "Whatever."

"You guys hardly ever cross paths and, when you do, it's on the job and you've got other things to focus on." Aidan took a sip of his beer and then shrugged. "I don't know why you're letting it get to you, anyway. Who cares what she thinks?"

Gavin shrugged because he knew Aidan was right. He would only go in circles because he knew her opinion of him shouldn't matter, but it did and he couldn't explain why.

The best thing he could do if he saw Cait Tasker coming was cross the street.

Chapter Three

"I'm out of my tea bags. Can you run to the market and grab me a box?"

Frowning, Cait walked to the pantry and rummaged around the shelves, searching for a box of the herbal tea her mother liked to drink before bed. "You shouldn't be out of them already. It's only been a week."

"I was talking about the tea at work and Del wanted to try it, so I brought a box in to her. They have it at the market and it'll only take you a few minutes."

Running to the store would be easier than listening to her mother complain in a few hours when she didn't have the tea she'd managed to convince herself was the only reason she was able to fall asleep at night.

It wouldn't be a big deal at all if it weren't one of the many small reasons Cait had decided to move back in for a while. Unable to cope with lists and planning and making a weekly trip to a chain grocery store, her mom and Carter had been living off almost daily trips to the corner market. They were throwing together quick, often unhealthy meals, while burning through crazy amounts of money. It had taken Cait a while to get them back on track, but now they limited trips to the market to cravings, her mom's lottery tickets and occasional half-

gallons of milk, the way convenience stores were supposed to be used.

"I'll go," she said, "but make sure you put the tea
bags on the grocery list so we don't forget them next
weekend."

Cait worked every other weekend, so on her off weekends, they did a "big" shopping trip together. On the Saturdays she worked, her mom did a smaller shopping trip
for meats and produce, shopping from a list she and Cait
kept on the fridge, but they'd had to work up to that. Not
due to a lack of ability on her mom's part. The woman
had raised three kids while working a full-time job. But
she and Duke had always grocery shopped together and
doing it alone had been too hard for her at first.

And that was why Cait had made the decision to move
back home—because it was temporary. She knew her
mom would get her feet back under her emotionally. It
was just taking longer than either of them had anticipated.

"Carter, we're going to the market," she said to her
brother, who'd been sitting on the couch, staring at his
phone for so long, Cait wasn't sure if she should go check
his vitals.

"Have fun," he muttered.

"No, I mean you and me. Let's go for a walk."

When he sighed and rolled his eyes, but got up and
slid his phone in his pocket without arguing, Cait was
surprised. It was the closest he'd come to admitting he
might not mind a few minutes of his sister's company.

"How's school going?" she asked when they reached
the sidewalk. Both of them had their hoods up against
the cold breeze, and his hid his face from her.

"Okay. Better, I guess. I didn't get to see my friends
much over vacation."

Christmas break had been tough on him, she knew. Not only did he have to navigate the emotional minefield that was their first Christmas without his dad, but his friends had all been dragged into their own families' holiday activities, so he hadn't had much online distraction.

She didn't ask him about homework. Or if his room was clean or he'd done laundry. Not only was she forcing her mom to handle the teenager wrangling—with blessedly fewer nudges each week—but she didn't want to butt heads with him right now.

"Is whatshisname still seeing that girl?"

He turned to give her a *seriously?* look and she laughed. After a few seconds, he laughed with her, before shaking his head and looking forward again. "Whatshisname and that girl broke up and now he's seeing that *other* girl. That girl's pissed and keeps putting bad pictures—like when she's looking down at her paper and has like three chins and shit—of that *other* girl on Snapchat."

She let the language slide, reminding herself her baby brother was sixteen and probably knew—and said—more curse words than she did. "What does that other girl do about it?"

The drama of whatshisname, that girl and that other girl lasted until they got to the market, and Cait was relieved to see glimpses of the funny, open kid he'd been before the teenage hormones and losing his dad doubleteamed him. But as soon as they walked inside, she heard the subtle buzz of his phone in his back pocket and, just like that, his attention was gone.

That was okay with Cait. They'd had a nice walk and she'd take the win, though she wished she'd worn gloves. Blowing into her cupped hands to warm them up, she headed off toward the aisle where the tea would be, assuming Carter would follow her by way of whatever smartphone sonar teenagers used to walk and stare at the screen at the same time.

She walked around the corner, going wide so she didn't bump into a display of poorly stacked soup cans, and almost collided with another shopper. Words of apology died on her lips when she realized it was Gavin Boudreau.

Of all the markets in all the world, or something like that.

His jaw tightened for a few seconds when he realized who she was. "Hey."

She wasn't sure if that was a *hey, watch where you're going* hey or a *hey, how you doing* hey. But she realized she was still standing there with her hands cupped in front of her mouth, staring, so she dropped them to her sides. "Hey."

"I don't remember seeing you here before."

With his brow furrowed almost to scowling level, it would have been easy to misconstrue his words as some kind of challenge. But she knew this was the kind of market that was frequented by the same neighborhood people, day after day, so the expression was probably more confusion than anything. "My mom lives a couple of streets over. I lived there for years and I don't remember seeing *you* here."

He gave her a sheepish grin. "I've lived in this neighborhood my entire life, but my sister usually got sent to the store for my mom because she didn't keep the change."

"Seems strange we haven't crossed paths before." She didn't really see any point in telling him she'd moved back temporarily. He'd probably assume she was visiting her mother and ran to the store for her, and there was no reason to disabuse him of the idea.

"Maybe we have, but didn't know it."

She was pretty sure she'd notice a guy like Gavin, whether they'd had words on the job or not.

Carter made one of those annoying teenage sigh noises, like an audible eye roll, catching their attention. But he didn't look up from his phone. He was just trying to nudge Cait along, and then he'd follow behind silently, because the sooner they got home, the sooner he could be back in front of his video games.

"Carter, this is Gavin Boudreau," she said, just to annoy him and force him to interact with another human being for a minute. "He's a firefighter. Gavin, this is my brother, Carter."

To her relief, he lowered his phone in his left hand and reached out with his right to shake Gavin's hand. "Nice to meet you."

"You, too." When the handshake was over, Gavin tucked his hands into the pockets of his coat. "I think I've seen you around."

"Probably. I'm here a lot." When Gavin nodded, Carter faded backward and Cait didn't need to turn her head to know he'd gone back to his phone.

When Gavin turned his gaze back to Cait, she saw that brow furrow again and, afraid he was going to pick up where they'd last left off, gave him an obviously fake smile. She might feel bad about the argument they'd had, but she didn't want to get into it now. "Good to see you again."

Since she was walking past him, she heard the muttered *yeah* under his breath, but kept on going. It was hard to chalk her slight breathlessness and quickened pulse to being aggravated by Gavin's presence, but she tried. She refused to believe she was still attracted to him. Not after the *ma'am*.

Or at least that's what she told herself while grabbing two boxes of her mom's herbal tea off the shelf.

"That guy was totally checking out your ass when you walked away."

She jumped at the sound of Carter's voice, then glanced around to make sure nobody was within earshot. "No, he didn't. Especially with you standing right there."

"Yeah, he did."

When he lifted his phone, she snatched it out of his hand and stuck it in her pocket, sick of watching him look at it. "I doubt it, since we don't even like each other."

"Whatever," he mumbled. Then he gave her a defiant look. "He might not like *you*, but he likes your ass."

"I swear, Carter…" She let the threat die unspoken, just giving him a stern look before heading for the register.

But, yeah, she couldn't help thinking about the possibility as she walked away. And it made her smile.

Cait Tasker had a great ass.

Gavin already knew that, of course, but only to a point. But he'd never seen that ass in worn denim that hugged her curves in a way her uniform pants didn't.

But since he was about two minutes from walking into his mother's kitchen, he forced himself to stop thinking about *her* ass and instead focus on what an ass *he'd* felt like when he turned and saw her brother watching him watch her. Feeling like a total creep, he'd given the kid an awkward smile and practically fled toward the register at the front of the store.

Real smooth, Boudreau.

He jogged up the back steps of the house he'd grown up in, waving to Mrs. Crawley next door. He wouldn't dare to guess out loud at her age, but she had to be pushing a hundred and twenty, he thought. She'd been old when he was three and she'd dragged him home by his earlobe for pissing on her petunias.

Hell, he couldn't even remember how many times over the years she'd caught him up to no good. His earlobe throbbed just thinking about it. But the day he'd gotten his first assignment with the fire department, she'd baked him a batch of the most disgusting maple cookies he'd ever tasted. And he'd eaten them and smiled because he'd been raised right and she felt as if she'd been a part of it.

He loved this neighborhood, which was a big reason he lived within walking distance. His big brick apartment building didn't have the charm of this row of single-family homes, but it was close enough so he still felt like a part of the community he'd grown up in.

The back door opened straight into the kitchen. His parents had talked for years about remodeling the kitchen, but once they had the money to make the plan a reality, they bought a convertible Cadillac instead. His mom didn't give a damn about her cabinets being outdated when they were cruising down the coast with the top down.

She was at the counter, preparing dinner, and he leaned around to kiss her cheek without interrupting the meatball-making process. "Are those the good kind or the bad kind?"

"The good kind." No onions, then, just for him and over his dad's objections. "Your sister said she ran into you and made you feel bad about neglecting me, so you might stop by. I was hoping."

He was the worst son ever born in the history of the planet. Maybe the history of the entire universe. And still she didn't put onions in the meatballs, just for him. "Ma, you know—"

Her soft laugh cut him off. "You know I'm just messing with you. If I ever feel neglected, you know damn well I won't be shy about picking up the phone. And if that doesn't work, I'll show up on your doorstep."

"But not at the firehouse, right?" Being the youngest on his truck was challenging enough without his mommy showing up to lecture him about not calling or coming to dinner.

She laughed again, though this chuckle had a far more maternally sinister undertone than the first. "I guess you should make sure I never feel neglected."

"I stopped at the market on my way." He pulled the container of coffee ice cream out of his pocket. It was the only flavor of ice cream his father wouldn't touch—practically the only *food* he wouldn't touch—so it had always been a special treat just for her. "I'll put it in the freezer for you."

"I don't care what anybody says, Gavin. You're a good boy."

He laughed and went through the doorway into the living room to find his dad. Taking down the wall and making the first floor more open-concept had been part of the kitchen remodel that became a Cadillac instead.

"Hey, Pops."

"Thought I heard you in there." He put out his hand for the fist bump that had replaced kissing his old man on the cheek around the time he'd starting growing hair in strange new places.

Gavin took his usual seat on the sofa, knowing based on the meatball progress that it would be a little while before it was time to help his mother with setting the table and serving the food.

"How's work?" his dad asked, turning the news down a few notches.

"It's good. Now that the Christmas insanity is behind us, it's mostly accidents and people trying to stay warm when their heat's out. How about you?"

"Just pushing papers." He'd worked for the water and sewer commission since Gavin was a kid, and rarely talked about his job. But since paperwork was Gavin's least favorite thing on the planet, he could only imagine his dad simply didn't find it worth talking about.

They talked sports for a few minutes, and then his dad turned up the TV again so they could watch the guy on the screen talk about sports. Other than a few derisive snorts, there was no talking during the sports segment so when his phone chimed a new text message from his pocket, it sounded loud.

He was just going to silence it and set it to vibrate so it wouldn't interrupt dinner, but the preview showed a tiny photo and curiosity got the better of him. His dad was engrossed in the news, so he pulled up the message.

It was a group text, to his entire crew. He opened it to get a better look at the picture of a phone in a bright pink case. And displayed on that phone was another picture.

Of him checking out Cait's ass.

And just in case none of the guys could come to that conclusion on their own, her brother had added a helpful caption. TFW a guy checks out ur sister's ass in front of you.

"Shit."

His father cleared his throat. "Problem?"

"Uh, no. Sorry." Obviously he was lying, since he knew better than to swear in his mother's house, whether she could hear him from the kitchen or not. "Just a work thing."

And by work thing, he meant that work was going to be a nightmare of ribbing about his interest in the EMT who clearly didn't like him. The text had originated from Jeff Porter. And Jeff had a daughter about Carter's age, and he'd bet that was her phone and that she was part of the circle of friends he'd sent the picture to.

The word *shit* bounced around his head again, though he was smart enough not to let it out of his mouth. Forget vibrate. He silenced the phone entirely because there was going to be a shitload of crap coming his way and there was a strict no-phones-during-visits-with-Mom rule. He'd rather catch up on the ribbing when he was home with a beer in hand, anyway. It was going to be a long time before he lived this one down.

Before he put the phone back in his pocket, he pinched the picture and zoomed in on Cait, though.

She really did have a great ass.

Tuesday morning got off to a slow start, so Cait and Tony lingered at the garage, socializing with others before climbing into the ambulance to go in search of good coffee, and to be ready to respond should a call come in.

"Bailey had a little bit of congestion this morning, so she stayed home," Tony explained as he responded to yet another text from home before stowing his phone in his pocket. "And I do mean a little bit, but she got to Rob first, so you know how that goes."

Cait laughed. His husband was definitely not the strict parent of the two, and their six-year-old daughter had him wrapped around her little finger. And four-year-old Riley was as smart as his big sister and would figure it out soon enough.

Cait didn't have a lot of experience with children, but Rob would bring them by the station sometimes if they were in the area and she thought they were probably the cutest kids on the planet. Along with her nephew, of course. Noah had been born in Texas and she'd only seen him in person a couple of times, but he was blood. And he also looked a lot like his auntie Cait had as a baby, so she couldn't leave him off the cutest-kids list.

"You better not give me Bailey's germs," she warned as she buckled her seat belt. "The last thing I need is to bring them home and get my mother sick. Or Carter. He's bad enough now. If he gets a man cold, I might have to smother him in his sleep."

It never failed. As soon as they were close enough to the best coffee in town to start looking for a place to park, a call came in.

A sidewalk fall with reported head injury. Tony flipped on the lights while Cait responded to dispatch.

"It's our buddy," Tony said as they pulled up at the address.

Cait rolled her eyes as she snapped on a pair of gloves. Victor worked the night shift, or so he claimed, so he did his drinking during the day. A lot of it. Based on the number of interactions they had with the guy, she doubted he was any better at holding a job than he was at holding his liquor.

"Victor," she said in a friendly tone to the man standing on the sidewalk looking confused while a Samaritan held a wad of napkins to the cut on his head. "How you doin'?"

"I told them not to call an ambulance," he grumbled. "Least they sent the pretty one, though."

"Thanks, Victor, that's really sweet," Tony said, earning a scowl from their patient.

"I don't need no help."

"There's blood, so you should let me look."

The laceration wasn't bad, and the helpful bystander told her he hadn't lost consciousness. She checked his pupils and he answered her questions to the best of his drunken ability. When sirens sounded in the distance, getting closer, Victor frowned and pushed her hand away.

"You call for backup?"

She laughed. "You won't even let us treat you properly. Why would we call more people to stand here and argue with you?"

In her peripheral vision, she caught sight of the approaching apparatus and turned her head.

It wasn't Ladder 37, though, and she was taken off guard by the strength of her disappointment. It was stupid to be bummed she wouldn't get a glimpse of Gavin, or maybe even a wave. Not that they were friends, but the man *had* checked out her ass.

And it was even more stupid to be so obvious about it in front of her partner, she thought when Tony cleared his throat.

Cait turned back to Victor as the truck that wasn't Gavin's rolled by, deliberately avoiding Tony's gaze. "You should probably have some stitches, Victor. Or a couple of staples."

"Shit, I got a staple gun somewhere."

"Different kind of staples." She poked her finger at his chest to make sure she had his attention. "Do *not* staple your own head."

"Ain't no difference," he mumbled.

"There's a *big* difference." Not the least of which was sterility. "No staples. No superglue. No epoxies."

"Let us give you a ride in," Tony said, using his compassionate-but-stern voice. "They can clean up your wound and make sure it doesn't get infected."

"I ain't giving those doctors money to wash my head. I can do it my own damn self. And I'll pour a little whiskey on it. That cheap shit my old lady buys will kill any kind of infection."

He probably wasn't wrong, but Cait wasn't ready to give up yet. "They have those warm blankets you like. You know the nurses will give you a couple straight out of the warmer while they patch up that cut."

Victor shook his head. "Just gimme the papers to sign. It's too cold to stand out here yapping with you two."

Tony took care of that, and Victor was in the process of signing his name to the statement he was refusing transport AMA when a shoe flew past Cait's face and bounced off Victor's jaw.

And there was the wife.

Cait took a step back as Tony bent to pick up the clipboard Victor dropped. She didn't want any part of a domestic.

"Get your ass in the house," Victor's wife yelled. "The kid down the street came running in, yelling for me and telling me you were layin' on the sidewalk with blood everywhere. I had to leave before she got my top coat done. My whole manicure's ruined because you have two left feet."

The injury probably had more to do with his blood alcohol content than a lack of grace, but Cait had tried to reason with Victor's wife before and it hadn't gone well. And the woman still had one shoe left.

"Did he sign it?" she asked, keeping her voice low while the couple yelled obscenities at each other.

Tony looked at the paper. "Good enough."

"You get yourself to the hospital if that cut doesn't heal up right. Wash it out. No staples or glue."

He waved a hand in their general direction as his wife tugged on his shirt, trying to drag him toward their house. They'd almost made it up the front steps when

Tony pulled the ambulance away from the curb and she heard him laugh softly to himself.

"What are you chuckling about over there?" she asked, assuming he was thinking about Victor and his wife.

"I'm imagining what might have happened if that had been Ladder 37 going by."

Immediately her brain coughed up the image of Gavin watching her ass that her brother had so helpfully sent her a screen cap of, as if just seeing it on *his* phone wasn't enough.

She hadn't deleted it, though.

Cait decided she'd try denial first. "I don't know what you're talking about."

"You might be a hard one to read, Cait, but I know you pretty well and you, my friend, have let a certain firefighter get under your skin. I saw your face when that truck went by. You were disappointed it wasn't Boudreau's."

"That's stupid."

"It might be stupid," Tony said, "but that doesn't mean it's not true."

"I don't even like him," she said, but then she surrendered to the inevitable. "Why the hell can't I get him out of my head?"

Tony limited his gloating to a quick, triumphant glance. "You don't really know him all that well, so my guess is pure chemistry. He's young and hot and, considering your dating situation of late, that makes him your type."

"He's cocky. That's the opposite of my type."

"Maybe your subconscious wants to shake things up a bit."

"Then my subconscious can add itself to the list of things making my life more difficult right now."

Truth be told, her subconscious was already on that list, thanks to the dream she'd had the night before last. She'd woken up overheated and yearning, with a quickly fading image of a very naked Gavin smiling down at her.

And that pissed her off. If she was going to have sex dreams about a pain-in-the-ass firefighter at night, the least her subconscious could do was let her savor them for a while. Maybe then she could spend a little less time during the day thinking about him.

Chapter Four

"So then she brings me her phone and tells me I'll never believe who popped up in her Snaptalk or whatever it's called."

Gavin rolled his eyes, wishing Jeff would tell the story of the Snapchat picture a little bit faster. As soon as he got upstairs and saw that some smart-ass had put a printed and framed copy of the photo on top of the table the television sat on, he'd known this twenty-four-hour shift was going to feel like days.

"As soon as I saw that hair sticking up, I didn't even have to zoom in to know it was Boudreau." They all laughed while Gavin self-consciously smoothed a hand over the crown of his head. Stupid cowlick. "I told her I wanted a copy, but she said she couldn't save it or whatever or the other kid would know, so I had to take a picture of her phone."

"So your daughter and the EMT's brother are friends?" Aidan asked.

"They have friends in common, I guess. He included her because he knows her dad's a firefighter, though he doesn't know who I am, or that I know the guy he's taking pictures of."

"She didn't tell him?" Gavin asked.

"Nah. She just sent back an LOL or whatever it is the kids say."

So there was a very small chance Cait didn't know he'd watched her walk away. There had been no *OMG, he's Ladder 37 with my dad* from Jeff's daughter to her brother. And maybe Carter didn't want his sister to know he was taking pictures of strangers—and her—and sending them to his friends to make fun of on the internet, so she might not even know the photo existed.

"I would have looked, too," Grant said, making a *yeah, I'd hit that* face toward the framed picture. "I mean check out—"

He let the words die when Gavin gave him a look, but the other guys laughed. "She's hot. I checked out her ass. End of story."

But it wasn't the end of the story, of course. They didn't miss even the slightest opening to crack a joke about pictures, asses, EMTs, markets or pretty much anything, since they didn't even care if the jokes made sense. He did his best not to give them a reaction, but it got old fast.

It was almost a relief when the tones sounded for a second alarm and they ran for the apparatus bay.

For some reason yet to be determined, a truck's engine had caught fire. The driver panicked and drove it into the corner of a house, and now the truck *and* the house were on fire.

They got set up and waited to see if they'd be sent in now, as relief for the crews already on it, or held for the overhauling. It didn't look too bad and he knew they'd already gotten the mother—who'd been knocked unconscious in the initial impact—out of the building, so Gavin assumed they'd go in after and poke around, making sure it was fully extinguished and no longer a hazard.

He glanced over to where they'd staged the EMS for fire standby. And, of course, it was just his luck to see Cait and her partner standing next to their ambulance in their turnout gear.

She was totally focused on the house, her profile to him. Her dark hair was pulled back into the ponytail she always seemed to wear and she had no makeup on, though he wasn't sure if that was by choice or she just didn't for work. Either way, he liked it. She was a beautiful woman, even if she was a pain in the ass.

"Do you think if you stare at her long enough she'll turn around so you can check out her butt again?"

Gavin tore his gaze away from Cait and turned to scowl at Scott. "You need some new material, Kincaid."

"I bet if we stand here long enough, you'll give me some."

They did end up standing around for longer than Gavin liked, especially in fucking January. But eventually the fire was knocked down and the building deemed stable enough for them to go in and make sure it was fully extinguished.

He glanced over to see if EMS was still on scene. The paramedic unit was gone but not the EMTs, and he caught Cait looking at him. Their eyes met and he wasn't sure what to make of it, so he gave her a cocky smile, since that seemed to annoy her. Sure enough, she rolled her eyes and turned back to face her partner.

They went inside and poked and prodded at the house, looking for potential hot spots. Gavin was pulling Sheetrock upstairs to check for fire in the walls when another call came over the radio.

Possibility of a second victim in residence. The six-year-old boy got sick and was dismissed to his mother be-

fore lunch, according to the school. His name is Hunter.
Current location unknown.

He froze for a few seconds, processing that information, and saw Jeff do the same at the other end of the hall.
The neighbor who'd told the first crew on the scene that
the mother was in the house must have seen the kids all
leave for school, but not noticed the mom leaving and
returning home with the boy.

"Okay," Jeff said calmly over the radio. "Likely lo-
cations for a sick kid would be the couch, his bed, the
bathroom or maybe Mom's bed. Listen hard and check
the usual hiding places."

They called out his name, listening for even the faint-
est cry for help. Gavin ran down the hall, glancing into
rooms until he spotted the decor of a six-year-old boy.
A quick look got him nothing, and Jeff was right on his
heels.

"I'll check under the bed and in the closet. Go to the
master bedroom but be careful because it's fucked up."

Hunter must have tried to get to his mom when the
truck crashed into that corner of the house because he
wasn't in the bed. Through the lingering smoke and
Sheetrock dust, Gavin saw a pale white hand sticking
out from a tall, heavy bookcase. Books and smashed
knick-knacks were everywhere, so as he updated the
others, he had to dig to find the boy.

His head was bleeding and he was so white—even in
the lips—that Gavin was afraid he was dead. He had an
open compound fracture in the leg and he'd lost a lot of
blood, but he had a pulse.

"I need a paramedic now," he told the others.

The paramedic had been released to a cardiac arrest call,
so Cait checked her gear and grabbed her bag. "I got this."

They never talked about it, but Cait always took the lead when a call involved kids about the same age as Tony's kids. He did his job, but it was tough on him and the emotional fallout worse for him if they lost a child.

"Be careful," he said, staying behind in case she needed something from the truck.

"Always."

Danny Walsh met her at the front door and guided her through the house to the upstairs master bedroom. It was like something from a carnival house of horrors. The floor was slanted toward the crumpled outside wall, and the ceiling was half caved in. A couple of firefighters were lifting a bookcase off her patient and she started to move, but Gavin—who was kneeling next to the boy— held up a hand.

"Let them out first. I want as few people in here as possible. It doesn't feel solid."

She stepped aside and let the two guys out. It only took them a few seconds, but they were valuable seconds and she felt her impatience growing. Finally, she was at the boy's side and she swept aside some books and broken glass to kneel beside him.

She radioed in to request the first available paramedic and then heard shouts from somewhere in the house, followed by a pounding of boots.

"What's going on?" she asked as she opened her bag.

"Reflash." She glanced up at him, and his mouth was set in a grim line. "The house is on fire again. Below us. They want us out."

"He can't be moved yet." If she didn't get a tourniquet on his leg, he was going to bleed out. And she hadn't even assessed his head injury.

"I'll pick him up and carry him out."

"If you do that, he'll probably die. I need a few minutes."

"We might not have a few minutes."

"Then go."

She didn't even have to look up from her patient to gauge his reaction. The *fuck* that echoed through the room was enough.

"I want you out of here." His voice was harsh, almost raspy. "Tell me what to do and I'll take care of him."

There was too much to do, and they didn't have the time for her to explain it. "I'm not leaving him."

"Get the fuck out of here, Tasker."

"I'm not leaving him, Boudreau, so if you wanna go, go. Don't waste your time barking at me."

His gaze locked with hers, his mouth set in a grim line. "I won't go without you."

For a long moment, she felt the weight of her decision being potentially life or death—*his* life or death versus the child's life or death. They'd been ordered out. If they moved the boy now he'd die.

They couldn't save everybody.

She knew the rules and she was prepared to break them, and damn the consequences.

"Please go," she whispered.

Not fucking happening.

Gavin gave a status report to everybody on the receiving end of the radio as he turned his back on Cait to assess the situation.

She could tell him to leave. The commissioner himself could get on the radio and order him to leave. Hell, they could get his mother outside with a megaphone, yelling for him to get his sorry butt out of there or she'd drag him out by his damn earlobe. He wasn't leaving without Cait and she wasn't leaving without her patient.

So all he had to do was keep them safe until the child could be moved or more help came.

Suddenly, the entire world seemed to shift and he threw himself at Cait and the boy. He was able to block most of the falling debris from hitting Hunter, but they were dropping and sliding. The noise was deafening, and then it went dark as the wall with the big window caved.

Then it was still and all he could hear was his breath and Cait's ragged cough. He took out his light and turned it on. The room they'd been in was now just a small box with no openings, because they'd all been crushed or were blocked by debris.

"You okay?" he asked.

"I think so." Cait nodded and then wiped at her eyes before turning all of her attention back to her patient.

They were yelling his name on the radio, so he told them they were okay, but they weren't going to get out on their own.

The smoke was a problem. It wasn't getting worse, but with no place to vent, it wasn't getting any better, either. And the Sheetrock dust didn't help. When Cait coughed deeply and then lowered her face to check the boy's breathing, he knew it was a *big* problem.

He knew the rules. He was no help to anybody if he succumbed to the smoke, so the mask stayed on his face.

It took him a few seconds to get out of his gear, and then he held the mask out to her. "Get a seal and take a few breaths. Then try to seal it on him for a few minutes as best you can."

She shook her head. "You can't get us out of here if you can't breathe."

"When I need to, I'll put it back on for a minute, then

you can. Then back to him." She still didn't move. "I won't push it. I promise."

She only took a few breaths before putting it over Hunter's face. Gavin knew it wouldn't be a good seal, but it was better than nothing. He listened to the chatter on the radio and could hear stuff happening outside. Occasionally they'd ask him questions he'd answer.

He and Cait each took a turn with the mask, and he gave her a reassuring smile. "I know his leg's bad, but it won't be long."

"It's not just the leg. I'm pretty sure there's internal bleeding." She paused and he watched her throat move as she swallowed hard. It was the only crack in her composure. "He doesn't have a lot of time."

Gavin heard what she didn't say. Hunter was going to die before they were able to safely extricate them according to protocol and he felt a rush of panicked helplessness.

But he pushed it down and gave her a sharp nod to acknowledge that he understood. Then he looked around the small space, taking stock of the situation before making his decision. They couldn't wait.

He dug his fingers into the cracked Sheetrock and pulled until a chunk broke off. He kept breaking off pieces until the insulation was exposed. After pulling that out and tossing it aside, he looked at the back side of the plywood sheathing.

It was either going to work, or he was going to find out the plywood was holding this corner of the room up. He looked over his shoulder at Cait and, after a few seconds, she nodded.

He didn't have a lot of room, but he got down on his side and kicked hard at the center of the plywood. It didn't give a lot, but he kicked again. There were voices outside and he heard the scratching sound of the melted vinyl siding being pulled free.

"We can't use the saw," Rick told him over the radio. "If we cut the studs, it'll collapse."

"We just need to cut out a big enough area to pass a board through. We'll strap him the best we can and send him out sideways."

"That's not—"

"It's his only chance," Cait broke in.

"Get the reciprocating saw and make a vertical cut through where I knock," Gavin said. "I'll tell you where you can cut."

It felt like a slow process, but he knew it was really only a couple of minutes before they had a rough cutout big enough to pass a board through the studs. And big enough to hand a little boy out.

"I'll get his torso," Cait said. "You get him behind the knees. Slow and smooth to the board."

"His leg is—"

"He's unconscious and the only thing we can do for that leg is get him to a surgeon."

They strapped him to the board from his head to his ankles, and then slowly and carefully tipped him sideways and passed the board through the hole. As soon as the guys outside had his head, Cait let go and stripped off all her gear, including her boots.

She put her arms and head between the studs and told the guys to pull. Gavin had no choice but to lift her by the legs and support her until they had her.

He didn't think he'd fit, so he tossed their gear through the hole and then had to wait while they figured out how to extract him.

"We can probably cut one of the studs out without jeopardizing the wall," Rick said finally.

"Probably?"

The LT grinned at him through the hole. "Almost definitely."

By the time they got him out, Cait was gone and he assumed she'd climbed in the ambulance with her patient. She would stay with them, relating what info she had and assisting the paramedic, until they handed the boy over to the doctors.

It was her partner, Tony, who snapped his attention away from her. "Let's check you out."

"I'm fine."

"You took your mask off."

Gavin didn't know if it was a guess or somebody—maybe Cait during the brief time they'd been extracting him from the house—had told him, but it didn't matter. He was okay. "I just need some water. Did you get all her gear?"

After Tony nodded, Gavin walked to where the volunteers had the canteen truck set up and turned down their offer of coffee or hot chocolate for a bottle of water. He was thirsty and having to call Tony back because he'd scorched his throat guzzling coffee wasn't his idea of a good time.

When they were cleared to return to quarters, it was a quiet ride. They were all a little subdued after a situation went sideways, when the should-haves and what-ifs ran through their minds. And they'd wonder about Hunter and his mom until they saw an update on the evening news or heard something through the grapevine.

He took a quick shower and sat on the couch, propping his stockinged feet on the table. His intention had been to turn the TV on and channel surf until he found something mindless to stare at.

Instead, he stared at the framed photo next to the

television. He knew it was just the luck of the draw, so to speak, that Cait's ambulance had been the closest to respond for fire standby. That she was the one in that room with him.

There had been no panic in her eyes. Tension. A little fear. But mostly what he'd seen on her face was determination. She knew the risks and she wasn't leaving the boy. He knew what that felt like, and he respected the hell out of anybody who could remain calm and focused in that kind of situation.

He shifted his gaze to Rick Gullotti, who was sitting in the recliner, watching him stare at the picture. "Hey, LT."

"How you doing?"

"I'm good. Anybody hear anything about the little boy yet? Or his mom?"

"Not yet. The news might have something. Don't take your mask off again."

Gavin nodded, because that was the right thing to do. He knew why he'd done it and Rick knew why he'd done it, but they both acknowledged it wasn't what he was supposed to do.

"Food's almost ready, so let's eat." He pushed himself out of the chair. "I'm surprised we haven't had to drag you out of the pantry yet, like a freakin' raccoon."

"I had a Snickers in the truck."

They got through the meal and the evening news—from which they learned both victims of the earlier incident were expected to make full recoveries—before the tones went off for a motor vehicle accident with entrapment. A couple hours later, they responded to a carbon monoxide alarm before hitting the bunks.

When an alarm went off and it was his phone rather than dispatch, Gavin was surprised they'd made it through the night without interruption. He'd slept hard and rather than go home and crawl into bed for a power nap, he'd probably find some breakfast and then get some errands done.

Grant popped his head into the bunk room as he was stowing his tablet and charger into his bag. "Hey, Gavin, there's somebody here to see you."

"Unless it's a supermodel with a sandwich in one hand and a beer in the other, I'm not here."

"Beer?"

Shit, it was morning. "Breakfast sandwich and a coffee, then."

"It's that EMT with the great ass who doesn't like you." Grant chuckled. "She said not to hurry. She'll wait while you finish up."

Gavin sighed and zipped the duffel bag shut. Screw the beer and screw the coffee. A nice shot of whiskey wouldn't hurt.

Chapter Five

Cait was pretty sure she'd hit her head at the scene yesterday and hadn't noticed it because that was the only way to explain the fact she was standing inside Gavin Boudreau's firehouse at a ridiculously early hour on her day off, waiting for him to appear so she could invite him out for breakfast.

She'd had a rough night. Her mother saw her on the evening news and totally fell apart. There was sobbing and anger and demands Cait quit her job, because who was going to take care of her if something happened to Cait? Then, when Cait had refused to give in, there had been sulking. Cait hated the silent treatment even more than the sobbing or yelling.

And she hated a night spent tossing and turning, trying not to imagine the emotional devastation losing her would have piled on her mother and brother. Carter had seemed okay, muttering a *good job, sis* and giving her a high-five when their mom wasn't looking. But even if seeing the news hadn't shaken him, their mother's over-reaction had to affect him.

She'd also thought a lot more about a certain firefighter than she wanted to. She'd accused Gavin of not taking his job seriously and, even before yesterday, she'd forced herself to admit it wasn't fair.

She owed him an apology, and what better way to apologize than over a cup of coffee and some bacon?

It was only a few minutes before he appeared, wearing jeans and a zip-up hoodie. He didn't look nearly as tired as she felt, and she felt her body doing its *omg, this man is so hot* thing, which she hoped didn't show. "Hi."

"Hey, how you doin' today?"

"Good. You?"

He shrugged one shoulder, making the duffel bag slung over it bump against his hip. "Just another day in paradise. What's up?"

"I wanted to talk to you about something, and I thought..." She paused, and then made herself say it. "Maybe over breakfast."

He looked confused for a few seconds, not that she could blame him. Nothing in their past interactions indicated she'd ever have an interest in sharing a meal with him, and the incident in the hallway after delivering the baby had probably made him believe she didn't like him at all.

"Or just a coffee or something," she said when he didn't respond right away. "It won't take long."

"I could go for breakfast right about now. I was going to go around the corner if you want to join me?"

"Sure."

They walked in silence to the tiny restaurant only locals would know was even there and took a table in the back. There were a few other diners, but nobody that she recognized as somebody she wouldn't want eavesdropping. Most of the firefighters probably went straight home to crash in their beds for a while, she thought. Or maybe Gavin hadn't given them the heads-up on the good food to be had. Cait had grabbed coffee and pastries there a few times, but she'd never sat and had a meal.

"This is a bit of a surprise," he said once they had their coffees and had ordered the veggie-filled omelets the place was famous for, minus onions for Gavin and both with bacon and wheat toast on the side.

She couldn't tell if he was pleasantly surprised or unpleasantly surprised. "Yeah. It was kind of a spur-of-the-moment thing."

After tossing and turning all night.

"You okay? From yesterday, I mean?"

"I'm good, really. But it's the kind of situation that gets you thinking about things, and I was thinking about the things I said after delivering that baby the other day."

He leaned back in his chair and grinned. "You mean the part where you implied I don't take my job seriously?"

Yeah, that part. And why did he have to have such a great smile? "See, you're doing it right now."

"Doing what?"

"That smile that probably makes women's pants fall off."

The eyebrow went up before he pushed his chair back a few inches. Then he bent over, as if he was picking up a dropped fork. A second later, he sat up and pulled his chair back in.

"What are you doing?"

"I was just checking to see if your pants fell off." The lift of his left shoulder matched the curve of his mouth. "I guess I'll have to try harder."

Oh, god, please don't. Cait had never been so thankful she wasn't prone to blushing because if she was, her face would be as red as the ketchup bottle. She'd come here to apologize for being a bitch to him and, before she'd even addressed her hostility toward him—or at least the part she was willing to admit to—he was implying he'd like to get her out of her pants.

It was obviously just a habit, she told herself. Gavin was probably just a natural charmer who never had to try. And if he did have to try harder…well, what man could resist a challenge?

She tried to focus on that assumption about his character so she wouldn't be able to focus on the fact he could probably make her pants fall off without too much of an effort at all. Of all the people she came across on a daily basis, she would have bet he was the last person who had a shot, but there was something about his carefree confidence that might grate on her nerves when they were at a scene, but was sexy as hell when he was sitting across a table from her. And between the added stress and reduced privacy that moving back home had brought, she was barely managing to have a social life, never mind a sex life.

She needed to get this conversation back on track, though, before he tried to up his game. "I want to apologize to you."

"There's no need for an apology. Believe it or not, the pants don't always fall down. It happens. Not *often*, but it happens." The expression on his face was almost as cocky as the words, and she was about to tell him to forget it—he was exactly who she'd originally thought he was—when he dimmed the high-wattage grin to a sheepish smile and shook his head. "I'm joking. And yes, I do that too much."

"Why?"

"Why not? I like to laugh. This is the only life I know for sure I'm getting, so I'm going to have fun while I'm living it." He looked at her, his expression more sincerely thoughtful than she'd thought him capable of. "Maybe sometimes I take it too far. I don't even know how many times in my life my mom's told me I don't know when to quit. But that doesn't mean I'm not doing my job."

Cait forced herself not to look away from his direct gaze. "That's what I wanted to apologize for. What I said the other day, when we delivered that baby, was out of line. You obviously take your job seriously and rumor has it you're good at it. I'm sorry I said that."

She half-expected him to make some kind of smart-ass remark or gloat in some way, but the smile he gave her was warm and genuine. "Thank you. I accept your apology. And I'm sorry, too. I might have pushed your buttons a little on purpose because you're so easy to rile up."

"I am not."

"You're getting riled right now."

He wasn't wrong, but he hopefully hadn't guessed on how many levels he got her wound up. She was going to say something about being sensitive to him pushing her buttons, but she couldn't figure out how to say it without the possibility of the conversation spinning into innuendo.

"So tell me something, Cait. Since we're on the subject, why don't you like me?"

"I don't know you well enoughback seatlike you."

"Okay." He fiddled with his coffee mug, turning it in his hands. "I'll put it another way. I've wondered why you react to me in a way that makes other people ask me what I did to piss you off."

"They do not." When he just stared at her, one eyebrow raised, she looked away first. "What did you say?"

"You mean what I tell them I did to piss you off? I breathed."

Ouch. But that was why she'd invited him to breakfast

in the first place—to apologize and talk through whatever their problem was. Whatever *her* problem was. "I don't know what it is about you that rubs me the wrong way."

So much for keeping the conversation innuendo-free, she thought, barely stopping herself from slapping her palm over her face.

"Pent-up sexual tension between us?"

She laughed, because she knew he was joking. Or she was fairly sure he was, at least. "You're cocky."

"I'm confident."

"Same thing."

He shook his head. "Nope."

She propped her chin on her hands. "Tell me the difference, then."

"Confidence is believing the guys I'm with and I have enough training and skill to go into a burning building and get everybody back out again. Cockiness is running into a burning building without fear because, hey, nothing's going to happen to me because I'm just that awesome."

"So fear is the difference between confident and cocky?"

"Maybe. I don't think I'd want to face a fire with somebody who doesn't fear and respect it." He shrugged. "That's really it, I guess. The difference between confident and cocky is respect. For the situation. For the people you're in that situation with."

They paused while the server—who was about her mom's age—set massive omelets in front of them. Her blond ponytail swung as she turned her head to Gavin and gave him a brilliant smile. "No onions for you, of course."

He returned that smile with a high-wattage one of his own. "Thank you, ma'am. I appreciate it."

When the server was out of earshot, Cait paused in the act of cutting her omelet to lean forward. "I hope she makes it back to the kitchen before her pants fall off."

He laughed, and Cait wasn't surprised when the other women in the room stopped eating to turn his way. She would have, too, if she didn't have a front-row seat to the way he threw back his head a little and his eyes crinkled. "I think I'm probably a little young for her."

"Calling her *ma'am* probably cued her in."

He shrugged one shoulder. "I call every woman *ma'am*. I can't help it and I blame my mom. Or rather, my dad, since he's the one who cuffed me every time I forgot."

She let that sink in for a moment. He called every woman *ma'am*. And the day it had been her on the receiving end of it was the first day they'd met. She was a stranger and he used the term out of habit. Not because he regarded her as some possibly older woman he had no interest in dating.

Then he put a forkful of omelet in his mouth and made a long, low sound that vibrated through Cait's body. Her mind offered up a dubbing of that sound over the fleeting memory of his naked body over hers from her dream, and she had to look down at her plate.

She had to admit that she'd found the Gavin who'd irked her sexy. And the intense, competent Gavin from yesterday was even sexier. This Gavin, relaxed and just being himself, was dangerously sexy, though. He was jacking up the attraction from *okay, he's hot* to *I want this man in my bed now.*

"So, your brother and Jeff Porter's daughter are about the same age, huh?" he asked between bites, and she needed a second to wrap her head around his question. She wasn't sure if it was her suddenly rampaging hormones or the abrupt subject change.

"Yeah, I guess. He doesn't talk about his friends much, so I don't know if they know each other." She knew Jeff Porter was on Gavin's crew, and she'd actually seen his daughter around a few times. "They must go to school together, I guess. Why?"

"Just wondering. This neighborhood's a small town in a big city, so I just assume we must know some of the same people."

They did, as they discovered over the rest of the time it took them to eat. Not many, since their parents had different circles of friends and went to different churches, which often made the difference in the who-knew-who game. But it was a light, engaging conversation and by the time she pushed her almost-empty plate away, Cait was feeling more relaxed than she had in a long time.

"I'm glad you stopped by this morning," Gavin said after wiping his mouth with a napkin and tossing it onto his plate. "Good food. Good company. Not a bad way to start the day."

"I agree." She reached for the check sitting on the edge of the table, but he was faster. "Gavin, I invited you. Hand it over."

"That's not how it works."

"That's exactly how it works. I invited you, so you're my guest and it's my treat." She reached across the table and held out her hand.

"I was raised to be a gentleman."

"Which means respecting the lady's wishes."

After a few more seconds, he handed over the check and grinned. "You've got me there."

She liked that he didn't push the issue and insist on

paying just because he was the man. And she knew this was the perfect opening for something off-the-cuff like *you can get it next time*, to let him know she wouldn't mind doing it again. But she chickened out and then the moment passed.

Once they reached the sidewalk, she realized they were leaving in opposite directions. "Thanks for letting me buy you apology bacon."

"Thank you for breakfast. And I'm glad we cleared the air." He tucked his hands in his pockets, lifting a shoulder against the cold breeze. "You know, you should go to Kincaid's Pub sometime. I think you'd like it."

"I'd like to. I've heard a lot about it." She wasn't sure if he was hinting around that he'd like to meet her there for a drink or not, but she found herself hoping he was.

"Shoot me a text and I'll meet you there if I'm free."

And that answered that.

"Sounds good. See you around," she said, with a smile on her face, and then she turned and walked away before the disappointment could show through.

"What's up with you and that EMT?"

Gavin didn't answer for a few seconds, trying to decide how to play it. Grant had become his best friend, so he wanted to be honest with him, but if Gavin opened that door even a crack, Grant was going to barge right through it.

It was Friday, and he hadn't talked to Cait since Tuesday, but he'd sure thought about her a lot. And done a lot of kicking himself in the ass for not having a way to contact her.

He hadn't been able to judge whether she'd enjoyed the breakfast as much as he had. He thought she had, but there was a chance she'd see it merely as what she'd said it was—apology bacon. And because of that possibility, he hadn't come up with a smooth way to get her number. There were other ways he could get it, he was sure. They had some contacts in common. But that would make people ask questions, and it wouldn't be cool. If she wanted him to have her info, she'd give it to him herself.

In the meantime, he was left thinking about how badly he'd screwed up his shot.

"What makes you think anything's up?" he asked, since Grant was still waiting for an answer.

"I saw the way you two looked at each other the other day, when she was on standby." Grant snorted. "I was waiting for the flashover."

Gavin definitely didn't know what to say to that. He could barely admit to himself that the lingering eye contact with Cait had felt like imminent flashover—when a room got so hot everything burst into flames—so he didn't like knowing others could actually see the simmering chemistry between them.

"Just ask her out already," Grant pushed. "If there's something there, go with it. If not, as least I won't feel like I need to carry a fire extinguisher with me if I'm going to be around the two of you."

"I tried," he finally confessed. "I blew it."

"What? *You? You* never blow it."

"Bullshit. But I told her she should stop by the pub and text me so I could meet her there."

"Good plan. Kind of a date, but not so obvious it's awkward if she's not interested. Ball's in her court."

"Yeah. But what I actually said was I could meet her there *if I'm free.*"

Grant managed to make a face-palm into a huge dramatic production. "Women love when a guy wants to hook up if, you know, he's got nothing better to do."

"Trust me, I get it. I was trying to figure out how to make it sound casual while also reminding her my work shifts aren't like hers, and I opened my mouth before I nailed it down. By the time what I said really registered, she'd said goodbye and was walking away."

"It's not like you to choke like that. Makes me wonder if you're looking for your next hookup, or if you actually are really into her and your brain doesn't know how to handle that."

Gavin was pretty sure it went beyond wanting some action and Cait being hot. There was no shortage of attractive women in Boston. He wasn't hard on the eyes, either, and there were places he could go—especially in his BFD T-shirt—and not have any trouble finding company for a night or two.

There was just something about *Cait*.

But he wasn't ready to explore that possibility out loud with anybody just yet. Even his best friend. "I don't know, man."

"You need to go out and blow off some steam. Drink some beers. Maybe, if you're really lucky, you'll meet a woman who'll take your mind off whatever the hell's wrong with you. Take a wingman and go find some distraction."

There wasn't a woman alive who could distract him from Cait Tasker, but Gavin sure as hell wasn't going to admit *that* out loud. "What do you mean, take a wingman? You're my wingman, dumbass."

"I have a date," Grant said. "Maybe a girlfriend."

"No shit. How did I not know this? Who is she?"

"Her name's Wren. It'll be our third date…kind of. And I know it's too soon to tell, but you might need a new wingman, Gavin."

Gavin stared at the guy, trying to wrap his head

around it. How the hell had his best friend not only been dating a woman, but maybe *the* woman, and he hadn't heard about it? "Kind of your third date? What the hell does that even mean?"

"She's not… It's hard to explain. I think maybe she's been through some stuff so she's not looking for a relationship. But she likes me and we've had coffee a couple of times. Dinner's next." He shrugged. "I really like her, so I'm letting her set the pace, you know?"

"Like what kind of stuff?"

"I don't know. I mean, nothing horrible, I don't think. But sometimes when she laughs, her face and her eyes light up, and it makes me realize how often that light isn't there. Or it's, like, subdued or something."

That was deep, coming from Grant, but before he could ask more questions about the mystery woman, the tone sounded for an MVA with visible smoke and they were hauling ass.

The last thing Cait wanted to do after a busy Saturday shift was make her way to the North End, but a busy professional and personal life left her best friend very narrow windows of time for herself.

As it was, squeaking out enough time for tonight's dinner and wine at their favorite Italian restaurant had taken three weeks to nail down, so Cait didn't cancel. She sucked it up and showered and changed quickly before heading to the T. There was no way she was driving through the city when she didn't have to.

When she checked in at the hostess's podium, she was pointed in the direction of the table where they'd seated Monica. After a quick hug, Cait sat down across from her and took a sip of the white wine Monica must have ordered for her when she got her 5 mins away text.

"This is so good," she said, forcing herself to set it down. First she'd quench her immediate thirst with the glass of ice water and then she'd savor the wine. Being drunk on the T wasn't in Cait's future plans.

"I didn't think you'd mind if I picked the wine."

Cait laughed. She knew nothing about wines and the one time she'd tried to order for them, Monica had intervened before the server could walk away. "Did you order food, too?"

"Of course not. I know how you like to argue with yourself for at least ten minutes and then order something totally different when the server comes."

"You know me so well. I hope you haven't been here long."

Cait and Monica Price had only been friends for a couple of years, but they'd become almost as close as sisters since striking up a conversation in line at a coffee shop because they were both carrying the same book. Actually, as far as Cait was concerned, they were closer than sisters, since she and Michelle weren't exactly the best of friends.

Monica worked for an insurance company in one of the tall glass buildings in the Back Bay, using her impressive math skills and industry data to make educated guesses about when prospective insurees might die.

"I've only been here about ten minutes," Monica said. "The in-laws are visiting, so I left them to their thing and snuck out to get my nails done before dinner."

She flashed her hand, showing her perfect, long nails in a fresh coat of a shimmery cream color that looked amazing against Monica's dark skin, and Cait felt a pang of envy. "Gorgeous as always. I love the color."

"We should get a manicure together sometimes, although I'd pick a bright red or dark purple for you."

Cait laughed. "If I got that color you're wearing, I'd look like I had weird fingers with no nails, but I'm not really a red nails or lips kind of person."

"Only because you haven't tried it. I think dark purple, though. We should try to schedule it."

"You already know what I'm going to say."

Monica sighed. "Yeah, but I'm going to keep trying."

"Enough manicure talk." It wasn't going to happen. Cait kept her nails short and neat and clean, and that was enough for her. And it wasn't really the job. There were other EMTs with nails maybe not as long as Monica's but as beautifully manicured. She just didn't have the patience for the manicure process, or the process of chipping and peeling she inevitably had to deal with.

Monica picked up her phone and, with a few taps, pulled up the list of things she'd been making to talk about when they had the chance. Cait always laughed at her extreme organization skills, but Monica often had the last laugh when she'd get an *oh, shit, I forgot to tell you this* text message from Cait after they'd parted ways.

They gave work about thirty seconds. They were both still working and could afford dinner and wine, and that was that. Monica's husband was still being a great husband and dad while earning obscene amounts of money in real estate. They cooed over pics of Monica's one-year-old daughter, and then spent time talking about books and movies that it seemed like neither of them had time for. Most of that was covered on a regular basis during their many phone calls while one or both of them was sitting in traffic.

"Okay," Monica said, looking at her phone. "Next on the list is your sex life."

Cait rolled her eyes. "You can delete that one."

"Come on. Are you even trying?"

"Not really. Though there might be a glimmer of hope on that particular horizon."

That got Monica's attention. She leaned forward, setting her phone on the table. "Holy shit, girl. You've got a date?"

"I don't think so. No." She frowned. "Maybe?"

"Maybe?"

"Gavin said he'd meet me at the bar they go to *if he's free*. Not that he wants to take me there and buy me a drink or something."

The disappointment on Monica's face confirmed her take on it. "You are way too awesome to put up with that shit. If he wants you, he can come to you. But you do need to get out, Cait. You've put your life on hold for your family, which I admire, but it was supposed to be temporary."

"It won't be much longer." She hoped.

"You said that two months ago. You need to start taking care of you. Your mom will see that and figure out that, for you to live your life, she needs to take care of hers. And Carter."

"She wants to. She's trying."

"Was she like this when your dad died?"

Cait took a sip of her wine and shrugged. "I was only three, so I don't really remember. I know her sister was around a *lot*, but she's in Florida now and they're not as close as they used to be. Maybe having a teenager makes it harder than having little girls who don't really know what's going on, but at least have each other. And cancer killed my dad, so his death wasn't a total shock, like Duke's was."

"That's probably a lot of it. But, look, life goes on. She needs to accept that so you can get on with yours."

"I know," Cait said, because she did. But it wasn't that easy.

"I think you should go to that bar when you know Gavin's going to be there, and ignore him. Or be nice, but find some other guy to get busy with. That'll show him what he missed out on."

Cait grinned. "Maybe I should."

She wouldn't. Kincaid's Pub was, at its heart and soul, a firefighters' bar. While it got street traffic, Cait was sure that at any given time, most of the customers would have some connection to Gavin. If she "got busy" with a firefighter he knew, it would kill any chance she had of getting busy with *him*. And she wasn't sure yet if that was something she wanted to do.

But she was definitely leaning toward yes.

Chapter Six

A few days later, it was Karen, one of the ER nurses, who destroyed Cait's resolve to stay away from Kincaid's Pub. She wasn't about to hang around the place, hoping a man had nothing better to do than meet her there, nor did she think Monica's plan to make him jealous by way of another pub customer was a good idea. So she'd skip it.

"How's your mom?" Karen had asked when they crossed paths in the ER. They'd struck up a casual friendship during the short windows of standing around and grabbed coffee together a few times.

"A little better, I guess. But she's getting more dependent on me now, instead of herself, so I'm starting to think moving back home was a bad idea."

"There's no way to guess the right thing to do when it comes to family. How are *you* doing?"

Cait shrugged. "It's been six months and I'm starting to feel like this is my life now. Like, not my *temporary* life, you know?"

"You need to get out and have some fun. I'm picking up a shift for Lydia at the pub Saturday night. You should stop in and have a beer. And some nachos."

Cait knew Lydia Hunt was the owner's daughter. And she was married to Aidan Hunt and her brother was Scott Kincaid. Both guys were assigned to Engine 59, out of the same house as Gavin. Same tour schedule, even, since they'd been on the scene when she and Gavin delivered the baby in the hallway.

She'd forgotten that Karen sometimes worked the bar at the pub. She'd done it more often before she became a wife and mother, but a few times a month she liked giving dad and baby some bonding time and herself some adult interaction outside of the hospital.

"Come on," Karen pushed. "One night out. Your mom is a grown woman and your brother is a teenager."

"It's not them. It's me, really. I'm just tired and it seems like so much work to dress up a little and do more than put my hair in a ponytail."

"That's exactly why you need a night out. You're getting into a rut and, from the sound of it, a pretty deep one. I'll tell them to put extra cheese on your nachos."

And that's how she came to be walking into Kincaid's Pub alone on Saturday night.

Karen spotted her right away and waved her over to an empty seat on the back side of the massive bar. Two older men were sitting at the far end, and there were a few customers watching the big TV on the wall. There were a lot more customers than she'd expected sitting at the tables, too.

"I was starting to wonder if you were going to come."

"So was I, but Mom finally started the process of packing up some of Duke's things to donate and…it was an emotional day and I had to get out of there."

"What'll you have?"

"Whatever you recommend, and nachos." She grinned, already feeling lighter than she had in a long time. "With extra cheese, please."

While Karen poured her beer, Cait looked around the place. She saw a few faces she recognized enough so she could probably strike up a conversation if the mood to be sociable struck her.

At the far end, past the tables, was an alcove. A guy was standing in the opening, holding a pool cue and laughing at somebody in the room. When he turned his head, she recognized Rick Gullotti, Gavin's lieutenant. He must have recognized her, too, because he smiled and waved. She waved back as Karen set down her beer.

"It's pretty busy tonight," Karen said. "I'll be doing drive-by conversations, so I'm sorry in advance."

"No problem. It feels good just to be out of the house."

It was true. She didn't mind sitting alone, relaxing with a beer and the low chatter of people who weren't looking to her for anything they needed.

But she couldn't help but wonder if Gavin was in that back room. Maybe playing pool. Bent over the table, his jeans hugging his ass while he concentrated on lining up his shot.

Damn. Cait gulped her beer, hoping it would cool her off. That had certainly escalated quickly.

Earlier, she'd decided against texting him to let him know she'd be there. If he wanted to get together with her for a drink, he could make the time for her. But she regretted it now, because all she could think about was whether or not he was in that alcove, but she couldn't come up with a good excuse to look. She could say hello to Rick, she supposed, and if he was in there, some of the other firefighters probably were, too.

But the lightning rounds of conversation with Karen gave her an excuse not to work up the courage, and then she had nachos she didn't want getting cold.

She had a mouthful of extra cheesy goodness when the door opened and Gavin walked in. The way he turned toward the bar immediately and spotted her made her wonder if he'd known she was there. Managing not to choke, she chewed faster and was able to wash down the nachos with a swig of beer before he reached the empty stool next to her.

"Is this seat taken?"

"Help yourself." She played it cool—she hoped—because if he *had* come there to see her, she wasn't going to make it easy on him. "Nice place."

"The best. I'm glad you decided to check it out."

"I ran into Karen at the ER and she told me she was working tonight and invited me to stop by."

Something flickered in his expression and she knew he'd gotten her point. She was there because of Karen's invitation, not his.

His phone, which he'd set on the bar, buzzed. He picked it up and sent a quick text and, although he tilted the screen slightly away from her, she had excellent peripheral vision and was able to read an earlier text in the conversation.

Your EMT's sitting at the bar. Alone.

Averting her gaze as heat crept up her neck, Cait picked up a chip and dredged it through cheese sauce. Then she waited until he set his phone down to pop it in her mouth so, no matter what he said next, she'd have as much time to answer as it took her to chew and swallow. And she chewed slowly.

Somebody had sent him a text message letting him know she was there. Somebody in the pub right now. And that meant somebody knew he was interested in running into her again.

It was the opposite of telling her he'd join her *if he was free* and she had no idea what to make of it.

Your EMT...

"You okay?"

Once she'd swallowed and was sure she wouldn't say something stupid, like asking about the text message, she nodded. "Yeah, why?"

"I don't know. You seem quiet tonight. I mean, not that you've talked to me a lot, but... I don't know. You seem quiet. Rough day?"

"I've had worse." She sighed, giving in to the weariness instead of expending energy she didn't have on maintaining the illusion everything was awesome. "But I've had better, too."

"You want to talk about it?"

She didn't, really. It was nice that he recognized that she'd had a bad day—that he really *saw* her—and that he cared, but she didn't want to verbally wallow in it.

But Gavin may as well know right up front that she wasn't a fun party girl looking for a good time. She had responsibilities—hers *and* her mother's—and it would no doubt be a fast way to put an end to the confusing chemistry between them. So she gave him an abridged version of her current situation, starting with Duke's death and her moving home, and ending with her mother sitting in the middle of her bedroom, crying into a pile of Duke's shirts.

"Has she talked to a professional?" he asked when she was done.

"She saw a therapist twice, but then refused to go back. She said talking about Duke was too hard and no amount of discussing it would make it hurt less." She shrugged. "Honestly, I was surprised she went at all. I pushed the subject, but I can't make her do it."

"I'm sorry it's rough on you, but family means everything, so it's good that you're there for her. And good for your mom. Letting go has to be hard, but it'll probably help her move on."

Cait wasn't so sure, but she didn't want to spend the little time she had with Gavin talking about her family. Again. They'd pretty much taken over her life and become the only thing she had to talk about anymore.

And instead of looking at the time on his phone or giving some other sign he wanted to run for the hills, he actually turned toward her on the stool, leaning his elbow on the bar.

"You have to take care of yourself, though, too."

He actually sounded interested. And even a little concerned. "There's not a lot of time or energy left for me. Maybe *that's* why these taste like the best nachos I've ever had."

"What about some girlfriends? Maybe you could have one of those girls'-night-out things or whatever."

"We've talked about it. But, to be honest, I want to relax more than I want to go out and have fun." His brow furrowed, and she realized she was being a drag, but it felt so good to admit out loud how much of a drain it was. "I'm sorry. It's just…hard. I love my mother and my brother, but being back home is hard. There's only one bathroom. And only one television which, to be honest, might be even worse than only having one bathroom. And they filled my old room with so much crap, I feel like I'm sleeping in a storage unit."

"If you need a night away, just say the word. *Mi casa es su casa.*"

She appreciated the effort—whether it was a kindness or an attempt to get her alone at his place—but he didn't get it. A night out would be nice, but what she really wanted was space. Quiet. She wanted to be alone. "I'll keep it in mind."

"I'm serious. You can come over and I'll show you where everything is and how to use the remote control, and then I'll go crash at Grant's for the night. You can watch whatever you want. I've got menus for every delivery place in driving distance. And you can take a long bubble bath—uh, bring your own bubble stuff, though—or read or just sit on the couch and do nothing. It's a pretty decent couch."

Cait stilled, letting his words sink in. He *was* trying to get her alone. Literally. "I... Are you serious? You'll just let me have your apartment for a night?"

"Sure. It's not that big of a deal. Wouldn't be the first night I've spent on Grant's couch."

It was that big of a deal. Maybe not to him but, right now and in this place in her life, it was everything to Cait. The idea of a night all to herself almost made her cry, but there was no way she was shedding tears in front of Gavin. "You're not afraid I'll snoop around and find your secret porn stash?"

His eyes widened for a second, and then his expression settled into a look that Cait's grandmother would have called cheeky. "Are porn stashes supposed to be a secret? I can write the passcode for my laptop down on a sticky note for you before I go if you want."

He was joking, of course. And even if he wasn't, there was no way she could say that, yes, she'd like the passcode for his laptop. But damn, she was curious about what turned Gavin on. What images on that laptop screen would make his heart rate increase and his dick harden until he wrapped his fingers around it, stroking the hard length until he found release.

And, *shit*, just like that, she could feel the heat turning her neck and cheeks red, and she looked away. Taking a sip of her beer, she cursed silently at the predicament she'd gotten herself into.

Tony had been right. She *did* want Gavin Boudreau to rub her the right way.

With Cait's pale skin framed by her dark hair, Gavin couldn't miss her blush and his own blood heated in response. Of course, he was probably blushing a little himself, since he wasn't used to joking about porn collections with a woman.

He realized she'd had her hair up at the market the same as when she was working, so this was the first time he'd ever seen her like this, with her long hair down. It was thick and straight, and he was tempted to bury his hand in it to see if it was as heavy as it looked. He didn't, since they hadn't reached that point yet.

And he was still coming to grips with there even being a *yet*—that he really did want to get to know Cait that well.

He was sincere in his offer. He'd let her chill in his apartment for a night and he'd crash at Grant's. It was no big deal.

But he already knew he'd be lying awake tonight, imagining showing her around his apartment. Then, when it was time for him to go, she'd wrap her arms around his neck and whisper that maybe he should just stay instead. And he'd *finally* get to feel that soft mouth of hers under his.

"But seriously," he said, wanting to get the conversation back on track before he went too far and said something stupid. He didn't want to give her an excuse to leave. "If you need some peace and quiet, just let me know. I mean it."

"Thanks." She took a deep breath, the pink fading

from her skin. "Am I keeping you from playing pool with the guys or anything? I'm sure you came here to hang out with them."

He hadn't, actually. He'd practically sprinted there when he got a text telling him she was there. Alone. At the bar.

But if he told her that, he'd have to explain why the guys in the pool room would think he was interested in knowing Cait was there. And he still didn't know if she was aware of the Snapchat incident. She hadn't mentioned it at breakfast or tonight, but it would probably be as awkward for her to talk about as it was for him.

"I'd rather sit here with you, if it's all right."

She smiled, her eyes crinkling with warmth. "Of course it's all right. And we've talked about my family, but you haven't told me about yours yet."

"I live within walking distance of the house I grew up in and my parents still live there. My sister and her husband and their two kids live a couple of miles away. We're all close, so there's not much to say, I guess. There's enough distance so we're not in each other's business unless we want to be, but close enough so we can have a family dinner when the mood strikes us."

"And how often does the mood strike?"

"Whenever my mom says it does."

She laughed and he let himself drink in the sound. If he had his way, she'd laugh a lot more often.

In his peripheral vision, he saw two heads pop out of the pool alcove like nosy groundhogs. It looked like Aidan and Scott, but he didn't turn his head to get a better look. Cait didn't seem to notice them and, after a few seconds, they went back to whatever they were doing. Probably talking about him and Cait, and planning whatever harassment they were going to throw his way next tour.

He didn't care. Putting the guys out of his mind, he focused all of his attention on the beautiful woman sitting next to him.

They talked about music—country was her favorite, while he'd rather listen to nails screeching down a chalkboard. But she listened to a lot of different music and conceded his classic rock wasn't so bad. He liked horror movies. She liked comedies and disaster movies. They agreed action movies were a good compromise.

She loved books. He didn't, quite so much, maybe because he'd been better at math in school, while reading had been a struggle. But he liked finding odd and interesting articles online to read on his phone, and they shared some of the more bizarre things they'd read on the internet.

When the conversation slowed and her second mug of beer was almost gone, Gavin knew Cait would probably leave soon. And he didn't want to let her go without having some kind of a plan for seeing her again.

"I've been racking my brain since we had breakfast," he finally said, "and I can't come up with a good excuse for asking for your contact info other than I'd really like to be able to call you or shoot you a text."

Her mouth curled into a smile. "That's generally why most people ask for somebody's contact info."

"Yeah, but I don't have a valid reason for needing to call or text you, other than…you know." He didn't usually suck so hard at this. At least he didn't *think* he did.

"I'll give you mine if you give me yours," she said, and his brain had all kinds of fun with that one.

Luckily, nothing stupid or super cheesy came out of his mouth, and he unlocked his phone to pull up the contacts.

"It's *C-A-I-T*," she said, and he deleted the *K-A* to fix it. "Trust me, I get that a lot."

"I like it."

She shrugged. "My dad loved the name Kate, but my mom thought it was boring. That was the compromise, though I guess he kind of won, since it sounds the same."

"You are *not* boring. And neither is your name." He handed her the phone so she could put in her cell number, and took hers so he could do the same.

He was so focused on hoping none of the smart-asses in the pool room sent him a text while she had his phone, he almost screwed up his number, but they got it done and the phones switched back before they could accidentally embarrass him with shitty timing.

"It's getting late, so I'm going to head home," she said, and he felt a wave of disappointment. He could sit and talk to her for hours.

But, based on his last glance at the time, he already had. And she'd had an emotional day with her mom. "I could walk you home."

The two of them leaving together would not go unnoticed by the other guys, but he didn't really care. It was a way to spend a little more time with her. And, maybe, if he didn't screw it up, get a kiss goodnight on her doorstep.

"No, I'm good. You stay in here where it's warm and I'll see you around."

She stood up, but after a moment's hesitation, he decided not to. It would only make the saying goodbye more awkward. "Will you text me to let me know you got home okay?"

"Maybe." She picked up the coat she'd draped over the back of her stool. "If I'm free."

Ouch. He stood up after all, taking the coat and holding it so she could slide her arms in. "What I meant to say that day was that I'd like to meet you here, but I work twenty-four-hour shifts, so we'd have to figure out a time we both have off. It came out wrong."

She zipped her coat and turned to face him, tilting her head back. "A little bit."

"Totally wrong." They were so close, he could kiss her and screw what anybody in the bar thought.

Her lips parted slightly, and he stared at them for a few seconds. He didn't think she cared what anybody in the bar thought at that moment, either.

"Hey, Cait, you heading out?"

The moment was lost, and Gavin slid back onto his stool when Cait turned to face Karen, who had the world's worst timing.

"Yeah, it's getting late," she said. "For me, anyway. I'll probably stop by again, though. Everybody's right about this place."

"Yeah, don't be a stranger."

Cait said goodnight and then turned back to Gavin. "Goodnight."

"I'll talk to you soon," he said, and then forced himself to look at his beer rather than watch her walk away, considering how that had turned out last time.

He almost made it. She was almost to the door when he looked up, fighting the urge to run after her and get that goodnight kiss. Because he was looking, he saw her pause and look back at him. After another quick smile, she pushed open the door and left.

Two seconds later, his phone chimed with a text message from Scott, continuing the group chat. Gentlemen walk ladies home, dumbass.

A gentleman respects the lady's wishes, asshole.

Turned you down? Somebody get a hose because Boudreau's going down in flames.

He looked up to see if any of them had stepped out from the pool room so he could flip them off, but they were probably huddled around Scott's phone, laughing at him. Suck my hose, Kincaid.

They for sure laughed then, since everybody in the bar could hear it. Rather than join them, he signaled Karen for another beer and read the closed captioning of a guy on the TV screen dissecting the last Celtics game.

Finally, his phone chimed. I'm home.

Thank you. Goodnight. He added a smiley face emoji at the end.

She sent one back.

It wasn't as good as a kiss goodnight, but Gavin smiled as he pulled out his wallet to pay his tab. It was a start.

Chapter Seven

On Tuesday afternoon, Chris Eriksson bellowed to Gavin, who was three-quarters of the way through a magazine article, "Boudreau, you have a visitor."

Even though he didn't care about turkey hunting, he was annoyed at the interruption and wanted to finish, just because he'd started it. It was a slow day, with a light drizzle that wasn't quite cold enough to freeze over and cause problems so he'd been that bored. But his first thought was *Cait*, so he tossed the magazine on the table.

It wouldn't be her. She was probably working today since she had the weekend off. But that didn't stop him from double-timing it down the stairs to the apparatus bay.

It wasn't Cait. It was her younger brother. Or half brother, anyway, not that it mattered. Carter, of the Snapchat incident.

"Hey, Carter," he said, reaching out to shake the boy's hand.

"You remember me?"

Of course he did. They were still giving him shit about the picture Carter had taken and shared, even though it had disappeared. If they knew it had disappeared into his bag and then to his house, they'd really lay it on. But he let them assume it had gone out with the garbage.

"Yeah, you're Cait's brother. What's up?"

The kid shifted his weight, looking anxious. "I heard my sister talking to my mom about the fire. You know, the one with the truck that crashed into the house? They think I don't hear anything because of my earbuds, but it's not like they're noise-canceling or anything. They're just cheap ones because I shove the wires in my pocket all the time and they don't last very long."

Gavin just nodded, since he still wasn't sure what the kid wanted. And he had that same problem with earbud wires, too.

"Anyway, she said you were ordered out of the building and you wouldn't leave her, even when she told you to go."

"I shouldn't have disobeyed orders, because orders and rules help keep us safe," Gavin responded, because he really did believe that, regardless of his actions. "But there was no way I was leaving Cait in there alone. Or the little boy. And, to keep it real, they didn't really expect me to."

Carter shifted his weight from one foot to the other. "I just wanted to say thank you, I guess. In person. If something happened to Cait, my mom… I don't know. Without Cait, our lives would be total shit right now."

There was a lot of emotion and half-information in the kid's words, and Gavin really wanted the other half. But pumping Cait's brother for info about her personal life would be a douche move. "Just doing my job, kid."

"Except the part where your job was to evacuate the building like you were told."

"Well…yeah." The big, old-fashioned clock hanging on the back wall caught Gavin's eye. "How come you're not in school?"

"My last block's a study hall, so I signed out early."

"Your mom know you're here?"

Carter gave him a *seriously, dude?* look. "I'm six-teen."

"I'm pretty good at math, so that's still two years shy of not having to tell anybody where you are." Not that Gavin hadn't roamed far and wide as a teenager, but in today's weather, it seemed weird that Carter would just roam around the neighborhood.

Also, when had he turned into the old guy who has-sled teenagers?

"I just wanted to say thanks and it's on my way home," the kid mumbled. "That's all."

"I'm glad I was there with her. She wasn't going to leave the little boy, so all I had to do was keep an eye on her until they got us out."

"She's pretty awesome."

Gavin couldn't stop the corners of his mouth from turning up in a smile. "Yeah, she is."

The teen gave him a mildly questioning look, and then shrugged. "I gotta go. But thanks."

"No problem. You okay out in the weather?" A snort was the answer he got, along with a quick wave as Carter hit the sidewalk. "See you later."

Once he was gone, Gavin figured he could go back upstairs and finish the article he had no interest in. Or he could take advantage of having an excuse—no mat-ter how flimsy—to finally make use of Cait's number.

It wasn't much of a competition. He pulled out his phone, figuring if she was busy, she'd text him back when she got a chance. Hey, Carter just stopped by to say hi and talk about the fire for a sec.

He should be in school.

That was fast. Study hall.

It was a minute before her response came back. We're a couple blocks away and nothing's happening. Will stop by.

He hadn't expected that. And even as excitement at the thought of seeing her rose up, he worried she was pissed off. About what, he didn't know, since he hadn't done anything.

A few minutes later, the ambulance pulled up out front and Cait climbed down. Even in her uniform, which didn't fit her quite as well as old jeans and sweaters, she was gorgeous and he couldn't hold back the smile.

"Hi," he said, but then fell silent because she didn't smile back.

"Hi. Was Carter okay?"

"Sure. A little damp, which means he was probably cold, but he was okay."

"No, I mean…like, emotionally. Was he *okay?* It seems weird for him to come talk to you about the fire."

"He wanted to thank me for being there with you, and he said it's on the way home."

"Kind of, but not really." She frowned, then blew out a hard breath. "It seems weird."

"Teenage boys are weird. Maybe he was just curious about me since I was there with you." And because he'd been checking out her ass, to the amusement of Carter's Snapchat friends. "I wouldn't read too much into it, Cait."

"I can't help it. It's hard to tell what's normal teenage boy and what might be a sign he's struggling emotionally."

"Maybe he needs an outlet."

"I've tried to get him to talk to somebody. He blew smoke up the school psychologist's ass, so that went nowhere. And private therapy's expensive as hell."

He shook his head. "I'm not talking about therapy. I'm talking about a physical outlet. And some… I don't know. Some *guy* stuff."

"If *guy stuff* is some kind of euphemism for sex or getting him a hooker or something, I'm going to kick you in the balls."

"No, I'm not talking about hiring a prostitute for your sixteen-year-old brother. Jesus, Cait."

"Oh. So guy stuff means…what, exactly?"

"I don't know. He needs to shoot some hoops or hit the gym. Sweat. Talk some shit. Say some bad words. Work through his emotions and shit."

"I think talking to a professional is better for working through emotions than dropping the f-bomb during a basketball game."

"Okay. Tell me again how that worked out for him." She gave him quite a look and he immediately put up his hands. "Sorry. I'm sorry, Cait. I didn't mean for that to come out the way it did."

"I'm doing the best I can. I just… I don't know how to help him."

"You're doing amazing, Cait. They're lucky to have you, and I mean that. But he's a teenage boy. It's hard to blow off steam when you live with your mom and your big sister, you know? Does he go out much?"

She shook her head. "Not really. Most of his interactions with his friends seem to be on his phone or on the headset he uses for his video game. Sometimes I make up chores I need done just so he gets up and moves around and doesn't become one with the couch."

"I play basketball on Saturday mornings sometimes. Just a casual pickup game we've been doing for years at a gym within walking distance. It only has a half-court, but it works for us. He could go with me. See if he likes it."

"I don't know how good he is. He used to shoot hoops in the driveway with some neighborhood kids, but I don't know if he's ever played a real game. And I haven't even seen him touch a basketball at all since I moved back in."

"He'll be fine."

"I don't want him to drag down your game."

He laughed. "It's pickup ball, not the NBA. We're there to have some fun and blow off some steam."

"If you're sure you don't mind. But I don't know if he'd even want to go, honestly. He'd have to put his phone down for five minutes."

"Ask him tonight and if he's interested, give him my number and we'll figure it out. You can call me and let me know how it goes." If she called instead of texting, he'd get to hear her voice. Normally he didn't like talking when texting would suffice, but for her, it was different.

Her partner honked the horn and, when she turned, gave her a *come on* wave. "Gotta go. I'll let you know."

"Be safe."

She nodded. "You, too, Gavin."

He watched them pull away, and he was still basking in the afterglow of seeing Cait when Danny Walsh spoke behind him. "Getting involved with her family might not be a great idea at this point."

Gavin had no idea how long Engine 59's LT had been in the bay, but he'd obviously heard some of the conversation. "It's pickup basketball. And the kid stopped by, so what was I supposed to do?"

"If you start hanging out with the kid and his big sister doesn't let you in her pants, you still going to play pickup ball with him?"

"Wow. You really think I'm an asshole?"

Walsh shook his head. "I don't think you're an asshole. But family members add layers and complications, so if you're looking for a quick hookup, don't get too involved with her brother is all I'm saying."

"I like her."

That's all he said, but it was enough to make the other guy nod. "Good. I don't know her all that well, but I hope it works out for you."

Gavin wasn't sure what *works out* meant to the LT, but if it meant getting to see Cait off-hours again—getting to talk to her and hear her laugh—then he definitely hoped so, too.

Her mom was having a rough day. Cait had known from the minute she walked into the house and smelled the pot roast in the slow cooker that there would be tears.

Pot roast with potatoes and carrots and her mom's gravy had been Duke's favorite meal, and she hadn't made it since he died. But it was also Carter's favorite and he'd been after her for a few weeks to make it, as she often did during the cold months.

And now it was going to be a shit show because her mom was emotional. And Carter would feel guilty that he'd asked for the pot roast, while no doubt also feeling resentment that he couldn't have his favorite meal because his dad had died.

She wasn't wrong. Most of the dinner went in the garbage because watching their mother move food around on her plate while sniffling had killed Cait and Carter's appetites. And her brother had disappeared as soon as he was given the okay—not just to the living room, but to his bedroom, where he slammed the door with enough force so Cait winced.

Yeah, fun times at the Hill house.

Sometimes her mother wanted to talk about her feelings, but tonight was one of her silent moods. With tears shimmering in her eyes and her lips pinched tightly, she just wanted to clean things and be left alone.

Cait was okay with that. But before she could go hide in her room, she decided to check on Carter. When she knocked on his door, she got no answer and sighed. Taking out her phone, she sent him a text.

Take out your earbuds so you can hear me knock. Or just open the door.

He opened the door a few seconds later and then flung himself on his bed, the earbuds strung around his neck still blaring some music that made Cait's teeth ache.

"You didn't eat much."

"Neither did you."

"Busted." She leaned against the doorjamb. "It'll get easier, Carter. Things come up that Mom has to work through, so it feels like it's not, but it *is* getting better."

"Whatever."

"No, not whatever. You're allowed to love pot roast. And when she gets like that, maybe it's even more important that you let her see that you still love pot roast. She'll be stronger for you, but you walk away and she doesn't see it."

"She used to laugh all the time."

Cait's heart squeezed for him. "She will again. I promise. And sometimes, maybe if you laugh, she'll laugh with you."

For a long moment, she didn't think he was listening, but then he nodded slowly. "I'm just sick of being sad and she makes me sad so I don't want to be around it. You know?"

Yes, she definitely knew. "All I can do is tell you that

it's okay for *you* to be happy, and that Mom will figure out how to be happy again, too."

"There was a movie on the other night and I was going to ask her if she wanted to watch it because we all laughed our asses off at it, but I knew she'd remember how much Dad loved it and cry through the whole thing."

"Then *you* watch it and you laugh and you remember how much you loved watching it with your dad. Your feelings are your own, Carter."

She heard a movement and looked down the hall to see her mom standing there. There were tears running down her cheeks and Cait had to assume she'd heard most of that. She braced herself for a meltdown, but her mom just gave her a sad smile and crept back down the stairs.

Cait turned her attention back to her brother. "I heard you stopped by Gavin's firehouse today."

"So?"

She blinked at this tone. "It wasn't an accusation, Carter. Just making conversation about your day."

"I was going by and wanted to meet him. And say thank you for being there with you, I guess. Are you mad?"

"Of course not. I just want to make sure you're okay about what happened. Stuff like that hardly ever happens to me, you know." She was in more danger on a daily basis from drug users, angry drunks and domestic calls, but she didn't think it was a good time to mention that.

"I know. I was just… He likes you, you know."

"What?" That was one hell of a conversational curve-ball.

"That firefighter. Gavin. He likes you."

She hoped so, though she wasn't sure she needed her teenage brother up in her business. But she couldn't help herself. "What makes you think that?"

"He said you're awesome. And, like I said, he was checking out your a—uh, butt, at the market."

"No, he wasn't."

"I tried to show you this then, but you took my phone away." He unlocked his phone and for a few seconds, she thought he was just ending their conversation. But then he held it up so she could see the screen. It was a picture of Gavin, most definitely checking out her butt. And it was captioned.

"Uh, Carter. That's a Snapchat caption. Did you send this to anybody?"

He shrugged. "Just a few friends. It wasn't like public or anything."

"Isn't one of your friends a firefighter's daughter?" How many people had actually seen it?

"Yeah, but she just said *LOL*. It's not like anybody really cares the guy was checking you out."

But the caption made it clear the guy was a firefighter, so maybe the girl had shared it with her dad for laughs. And Cait didn't know who her dad was, but she knew it was a small community and it wouldn't take long before Gavin knew about it. Or saw it himself.

"Men are always checking out women's butts," she said. "It means nothing. And don't share pictures like that online. Privacy, dude."

"Whatever."

"Anyway, Gavin asked me if you'd want to play some pickup basketball with him on Saturday mornings. To get out of the house."

"The guy's game is so weak he has to be nice to me to get at you?"

"No. It's not like that." At least she didn't think it was. Gavin's offer had seemed sincere. And they'd already spent some time together. He had no reason to think he needed that kind of tactic to get to know her better. "He knows you're stuck in the house with your mom and sister all the time and thought you might like to hang out with some guys. That's all. Here's his number if you want to text him."

He took the scrap of paper she handed him. "Maybe. Thanks."

She started to leave, but then stopped and turned back to him. "If you do text him, keep it on topic. Do *not* violate my privacy or comment on my personal life, even to be funny, okay?"

"I won't."

He looked like he meant it, so all she could do was hope giving him Gavin's cell number wouldn't come back to bite her in the ass.

Which led her right back to that Snapchat photo. As if there wasn't enough on her plate, she had to wonder if Gavin had seen that somehow. Or worse, if the guys on his crew had seen it. He hadn't mentioned it, but he probably wouldn't, since how would that come up in conversation?

Hey, have you seen that embarrassing picture your little brother took of me checking out your butt in the market and sent to his friends?

That would be awkward.

Cait went into her bedroom-slash-storage-room and sat on the edge of her bed. She just didn't have the energy left at the moment to go downstairs and hang out with her mom. Overhearing Cait's conversation with Carter might lead her mom to some introspection and she did *not* want to interfere with any emotional lightbulb moments she might have.

She pulled out her cell phone and called her sister,

instead. It had been a while since they'd talked, and she missed having Michelle close.

"Hey, Cait. Everything okay?"

"Yeah." It seemed like an odd way to answer the phone, as if she wouldn't just call her sister to chat. "You busy?"

"Always, but I have a couple of minutes. How are Mom and Carter?"

Cait decided not to tell her she would know how they were if she ever called or messaged them. "They're doing okay. Good days and bad. Christmas was tough, but we're past that now."

"I wish I could have come home for the holidays, but you know how it is."

"Sure." She didn't know what it was likeback seatbe there for family that needed her, actually.

"Is Mom any better?"

Cait caught her up on the last few weeks—how they were starting to donate Duke's things and Carter's grades slowly coming back up and today's pot roast. It felt good to talk to her sister about it—to share the emotional load with another family member.

"What do you want me to do, Cait? I'm in Texas, for chrissake."

She actually recoiled from the phone in her hand for a second. "I'm not asking you to *do* anything."

"You're telling me all these problems, which I don't even have time for, so what is it you expect me to do?"

Listen. "Nothing. I just needed somebody to talk to for a few minutes."

"And now we both feel like crap, but there isn't even anything I can do about it because I'm halfway across the country. How does that help?"

Michelle was right. It wasn't helping anybody. Especially Cait, since she was not only aggravated with her mother and her brother, but now she could add her sister to the list. "I guess you're right. Let's talk about Noah instead. How's he doing?"

Her sister might not have had time to hear about their mom and brother, but she had a good twenty minutes to spare talking about her son. Cait didn't mind. She welcomed it, actually, since it seemed like Noah was the only member of the combined Tasker-Hill family who was totally happy at the moment.

And this was temporary. Her mom was going to get her feet under her and Cait would be able to move on with her life. And when that time came, she wanted to still be on good terms with her sister. Maybe Michelle wasn't able to be there for her now, but if Cait pushed, she wouldn't be there for her at all.

That had always been one of the biggest differences between them. When something was a problem, Cait rolled up her sleeves and faced it head-on. Michelle put it in a box and slid it under the bed to deal with later. Or maybe never.

"Give my love to Mom and Carter," Michelle told her as they closed out the conversation.

"Sure. Tell Paul I said hi, and kiss Noah for me."

After they disconnected, Cait lay back on her bed and stared up the ceiling. She needed to get out of the house. It was time—well past time, actually—for her to have some Cait time.

Before she could talk herself out of it, she pulled up Gavin's name in her contact list and hit the button to send a text message.

Were you serious about letting me use your apartment?

Chapter Eight

"What if she goes through your drawers?"

Gavin snorted. "Then she'll see my clothes."

He had about an hour left before Cait showed up at his apartment, and he really didn't need Grant filling his head with a bunch of stupid crap. Cait wasn't going to rummage through his drawers and his cabinets. And if she did, she was going to get bored pretty quickly and find something else to do.

Most of his life was in his computer. His personal documents were in a fireproof safe in the closet because his mother had given it to him for his birthday and insisted he use it. Other than figuring out he liked boxer briefs, crew socks and cheese-flavored snacks, there wasn't much to be gained from snooping in his apartment.

But he did have one concern about handing the place over to Cait, and it made him scrub the kitchen table a little harder than was necessary. "What if she has a guy over?"

Grant snorted. "Why would she bring a guy home to your place? That would be weird."

"Because I told her to treat it like it's her own place for the night. And maybe having sex with a guy is something she'd do in her own place. Don't forget she's been living with her mother and kid brother for a while."

"Just tell her straight out," Grant said. "It's your apartment. Your rules."

"There's no way I can tell her that. 'Hey, Cait, make yourself at home, but please don't bring a guy back to my place to bang because I kinda want to bang you myself.'"

"You don't kinda want to bang her. You *really* want to bang her."

"I sure as shit ain't telling her *that*."

"Then it's on you if you come home and find some strange guy's skivvies under your bed."

"Jesus, Cutter. What the hell is wrong with you? Who even says skivvies anymore?"

"My grandpa calls them skivvies."

"Okay, when you're the same age as your grandpa is now, you can call them skivvies, too. I think it's because you're from New Hampshire. You people are backward as shit."

"Kiss my ass, flatlander."

Gavin threw the wet sponge at him, but he ducked and it hit the wall. "Why are you even here?"

"I was bored."

"Shouldn't you be getting ready for your date?"

"Okay, so when I say bored, what I really mean is that I was driving myself crazy thinking about tonight and I needed a distraction."

Gavin grabbed a soda out of the fridge and offered it to Grant, who shook his head. He shrugged and popped the tab. "Why are you overthinking tonight? I've never seen you drive yourself crazy before a date."

"It's our first *real* date, I guess you could say. Like, I'm not her coffee buddy or a friend, but a guy she wants to see romantically, so I'm picking her up at her place and taking her out to dinner."

"If she's looking for romance, it might be—" Gavin

cut off the *your last date, too* when he saw Grant's expression. Damn, the guy was seriously into this Wren woman, but being romantic wasn't his strong suit. "A good idea to get her flowers or something."

"Like a dozen roses?"

That seemed excessive. "Probably not a dozen. Do you think she likes roses?"

Grant picked up the sponge and tossed it into the sink before leaning back against the counter and crossing his arms. "No. No, Wren wouldn't like a dozen roses. Something small and delicate, maybe. Purple. She likes purple."

"My mom has a friend who owns a flower shop. She could totally hook you up." He sent a text to his mom asking for the name of the place and got the information back a couple of minutes later. After jotting it down on the back of an empty envelope, he handed it to Grant.

"Thanks." He looked at his watch. "I should head there now, in case they're busy or close early or whatever. You have your key to my place, right?"

"Yeah. I might stop by my parents' first, but I'll be there before you get home." He chuckled. "Do me a favor. Don't forget I'm crashing at your place and bring your date back."

"I think it'll be a while before I have to worry about that. We're taking it slow."

Gavin snorted. "What's that like?"

"Since your girl's staying at your apartment tonight alone, while you're sleeping on my couch, you tell me."

They laughed together, and then Grant left. Gavin had never seen his friend like that. They both dated. They'd had some girlfriends that came close to being actual relationships. But he'd never seen Grant nervous about a girl before.

He was a little nervous himself, he thought as he did a last sweep of his apartment. The toilet was clean and the seat was down. Fresh towels. Fresh sheets, which he was trying like hell not to think about.

It wasn't working, and he suspected it would be a lot worse when he was stretched out on Grant's couch, imagining Cait sliding between his sheets and resting her head on his pillows. He'd *really* like to know what she wore to bed.

When the buzzer sounded, he almost jumped. But he got ahold of himself and hit the button to open the glass door downstairs. He was on the third floor—by choice because he couldn't stand people above him—so he had a couple minutes before she knocked on his door.

"Hi," he said, standing back to let her in.

"Hi."

She was wearing black yoga pants with a long red sweatshirt over them, and her hair was up in a messy knot on top of her head. With no makeup on and an overnight bag slung over her shoulder, she looked like she was on her way to the gym.

And it turned him on. At this point, he wasn't sure she had a look that *wouldn't* turn him on. All she had to do was look at him.

"I feel weird about this," she said, standing just far enough into his kitchen so he could close the door.

"You won't once I'm gone. Think of it like a hotel room, only I won't charge you for opening the fridge."

She laughed and it seemed to ease her tension a little. "Nice hotel room, I must say."

Gavin looked around the apartment, trying to guess what she might think of it. It was probably cleaner than she anticipated, since most women assumed bachelors lived like frat boys their first year away from their mommies. It was open-concept, which was a nice way of saying it was all one living space. They were in the kitchen, which had an island separating it from the dining area. He had a table with chairs there, and it had a double closet where he hung coats and kicked his shoes. That space was open to the living room, which had a small alcove for a desk, on which his computer sat. There were two doors in the back wall. One went to the bedroom and the other to the bathroom, which also had a door into the bedroom.

There were only windows down one wall in the living room—behind the couch—and two walls in the bedroom because it was the corner of the building, but they were big and let in a lot of natural light. He had light drapes, so they gave him privacy while letting the sun shine through. The sofa and recliner were brown leather, and the bedding was tan. He wasn't much in the decorating department, but he also didn't lose sleep over it.

It wasn't big, by any means, but it was a fairly recent rehab of an old industrial building, so he was the first and only tenant in this unit so far.

"It's really nice," she said.

"Put your bag down and I'll show you around." When she did, he grinned and held out his hand. "So this is my apartment."

Maybe it was cheesy and said for the easy laugh, but he liked her laugh and he wasn't about to pass up any opportunity to hear it.

"There's a bunch of stuff in the fridge. There's a Keurig, but I'm pretty boring with the flavor choices. There's just coffee flavor."

"As it happens, I'm a fan of coffee-flavored coffee."

"You're in luck, then. I should probably be embarrassed by how many frozen pizzas are in the freezer, but you won't starve. If you don't like meals out of the microwave, I put the delivery menus on the counter."

"Okay." She laughed and put her hand on his upper arm. "I'm pretty sure I'll survive twelve hours alone in your apartment."

He knew she was right and he was being ridiculous. But he didn't open his mouth to agree with her because he couldn't focus on words while she was touching him. The heat of her hand burned through his T-shirt, and he wanted to shift sideways until her hand slid down far enough to cover his bare skin.

But he didn't want to give the impression he was pulling away from her, so he stood still. Maybe it was wishful thinking on his part, but the touch seemed to linger and her fingertips trailed over the thin fabric to the bottom of his sleeve as she moved away.

Gavin had to concentrate on keeping his voice and body language relaxed as he led her toward the bedroom. "I put clean sheets on the bed, and the towels in the bathroom are fresh."

He'd stepped across the threshold into his bedroom already before he realized Cait wasn't with him. She'd stopped halfway across the living room.

"I figured I'd just sleep on the couch," she said when he turned around. "I think it would be super strange to sleep in your bed."

"Well, there's something I've never heard before."

That made her laugh again, and he wanted nothing more than to sit on his couch with her and say funny shit for the entire night.

"You know what I mean," she said.

"I told you, think of it like a hotel room."

He knew she'd relax once he was gone. If she felt the sexual tension crackling between them as strongly as he did, she knew the two of them being within falling distance of his bed at the same time could derail their plans.

Or her plans, anyway. His only plan for the night was to hang out at Grant's and think about Cait sleeping in his bed. Maybe after she soaked in his tub, full of hot water and good-smelling bubbles.

And things might have gotten even more tense if she hadn't walked over to the TV at that moment. It gave him a second to give the front of his jeans a quick adjustment, while trying to think unsexy things.

Then she bent over to look at the front of the TV—the sweatshirt riding up to show off her ass in that stretchy fabric—and he knew the only way he was going to cool off was to literally stick his head in the freezer. And even that wouldn't do much for below the waist.

"Do you want me to show you how to work that?" he asked, hoping to distract himself with a task. Any task, even if it was explaining his remote control.

"Nope. It's the same model my mom has. I'm just going to plug my iPad into the HDMI port and catch up on my Netflix queue."

So much for tasks. He was going to ask what she had lined up to watch, but he really needed to get out of there. Promising her she could have alone time and then putting the moves on her when she took him up on his offer would be a douche move.

"You can always text me if you have any questions or can't find something." He'd already put his duffel bag in his Jeep, so he grabbed his coat out of the closet and slid it on. Then he retrieved his keys from the end of the counter. "There's a spare key here so you can get back in if you decide to go out somewhere. The plastic card's for the main door, then the key opens this one."

"Got it."

"I guess that's it, then."

Then she moved close, coming in for a hug, and Gavin braced himself. *Just a hug.* Her arms slid around him, just above his waist, and he wrapped his arms around her shoulders. Breathing in the scent of her hair, he tightened his hold just for a few seconds.

Her hands were pressed against his coat, and he cursed himself for not anticipating the hug—for missing the opportunity to feel her embrace through the thin fabric of his shirt instead of the bulky coat.

"Thank you for this," she said, pulling back as he reluctantly let her go.

She was still close enough for him to kiss. He wouldn't have to take but one step and her mouth could be his. But if he kissed her once, he was going to try to stay, so he gave her a smile. "No problem. Enjoy your night."

Then he turned around and walked out the door before he—or she—could change his mind.

She should have asked him to stay. The words were simple. *You don't have to go.* But she couldn't bring herself to say them.

Gavin had been a perfect gentleman, although she'd been aware of the heat simmering between them. It would have been impossible to miss the way he got perfectly still when she touched his arm, or the way he was trying too hard to be casual when he was leading her toward his bedroom.

She wished she'd hugged him *before* he put his coat on, though. The bulky fabric had blocked the warmth of his body and the feel of his back under her palms. The temptation had been strong to slide her hands up under the jacket so only the T-shirt separated them from his skin, but she hadn't worked up the nerve before she had to pull away or make it awkward.

Now that she was alone, though, in a silent apartment with zero people looking to her for help or support, she knew letting him go without exploring whatever was going on between them was the right thing to do.

Once enough time had passed so she knew he was on the road and not running back upstairs for something he'd forgotten, she went into his bedroom. She'd made up her mind she was going to crash on the couch, but as soon as she saw the king-size bed with its black wooden sleigh-bed-style headboard and footboard, she wavered. It was wide and covered in simple, crisp tan bedding with a few jumbo pillows.

He *had* told her to treat it like a hotel room, and it seemed like such a shame to let a bed like that go to waste.

Before she could dwell on what she'd rather be doing in that bed, and with whom, she went through the door into the bathroom. This, she thought, is where she would be spending most of the evening.

There was no cheap, combination bath-and-shower unit from the 1980s in this bathroom. The shower was wide and deep, with two glass walls and dual shower heads. But the tub...

The tub was made for soaking in, with a glass of wine and a good book, held high so the fragrant bubbles didn't touch it. She would have guessed Gavin was a quick in-and-out-of-the-shower kind of guy, but the jar and the bottle of body wash on the rack near the tub said different. Leaning closer, she could see the label on the old-fashioned mason jar said *Epsom salts*, which made sense. There were probably days Gavin needed to soak away the aches and pains and tension that came with a physically demanding job.

Two would fit in that tub.

And on that note, she went back to the living room and plugged her iPad into the television. She figured she'd watch an episode or two from the series she was behind on while she ate a microwaved pizza, and then take the iPad into the bathroom. A movie while she soaked in that tub sounded like heaven.

A few hours of blissful peace later, Cait stood next to Gavin's bed and made her decision. The couch plan had gone out the window hours ago, but she still had to work up the nerve to pull back his covers and slide between his sheets. They were crisp and clean, and surprisingly soft. She was wearing panties and an oversize tee, unable to bring herself to sleep naked in his bed. She wore sleep pants with the tee at home because she could run into her brother during middle-of-the-night bathroom runs, but now she ran her freshly shaved legs over his sheets as if they were made of satin.

While she appreciated the effort he'd gone to to make her comfortable, a part of her wished he hadn't put freshly laundered sheets on his bed. They smelled like fabric softener instead of Gavin, and she could picture herself pressing her face into his pillow and inhaling the scent of him.

Instead, she had to smell the fresh breeze or whatever it was and try to put him out of her mind so she could sleep. A hotel room, she told herself.

They both had iPhones, so she hadn't taken her charger out of her bag. She plugged her phone into his charger and set it on his nightstand. Her hand hovered there for a few seconds, *so* tempted to open the drawer and peek inside. But she didn't. He'd trusted her with his apartment and she had to respect that, even if she wanted to snoop in the worst way.

But as she reached for the lamp switch to turn it off, she noticed the bookshelf on the far wall. It didn't hold many books, which didn't surprise her. It looked like mostly safety manuals and job-related books, but what caught her eye was the frame sitting on the top shelf.

She got out of the bed to take a better look, then covered her mouth with her hand because she had no idea what to make of the fact Gavin had a framed photo of him checking out her ass in his bedroom.

Stalker. She forced herself to give the word consideration before discarding that theory. While they may have gone from verbal sparring on the job to her being alone in his apartment fairly quickly, he didn't exhibit any red-flag behavior. And if he had an unhealthy obsession with her, he probably would have framed a photo in which he could actually see her face. Not that she didn't have a good ass, but this was the only picture. And it was one that would have come to him by way of other firefighters, so it was probably a joke. Why he'd put it in his bedroom was a mystery, though.

She liked Gavin and he seemed like a great guy. And if he was a creep, gossip about him would have spread through the first responders' grapevine by now. They didn't all know each other, but some things got talked about. But, on the other hand, she was about to sleep in the man's bed.

After unplugging her phone, she snapped a picture of the bookshelf and sent it to him. She was expecting a text message back, so it startled her when it rang.

"Hello," was all she said, giving him nothing of her frame of mind.

"Okay, that looks weird, but I can totally explain."

His words were rushed, as if he thought she might hang up or not give him time to talk. "I meant to take it with me and then forgot."

"That explains why it's here now, but not why it was here in the first place."

"Right. So it's from your brother's Snapchat and—"

"I know the source of the picture."

"You knew about it?"

"Yeah. I wasn't sure if *you* knew about it, but obviously you do."

"Okay, so Carter and Jeff's daughter go to school together. They're not close friends, but he included her because he knows her dad's a firefighter and she showed it to Jeff. Carter didn't know that her dad and I are on the same crew. Anyway, I showed up for tour one morning and the guys had printed it out and framed it. It was sitting on the TV stand."

Cait had to bite back a chuckle. She wasn't quite ready to let him off the hook, even though he was confirming her theory the other guys in the house had used the picture to give him a bunch of shit about her.

"I didn't want to throw it away," he continued. "I don't know why, but I wasn't tossing it in the garbage, so I stuck it in my bag. And then, when I got home, I still didn't want to throw it away. But the guys stop by my place a lot, so I…I put it in my bedroom. And this morning, when I was making the bed, I saw it and was going to throw it in my bag, but obviously I forgot."

She climbed back into his bed and turned off the lamp. It was warm, so she left the covers back, but she rested her head on his pillow. "I think it's cute you didn't want to throw it away."

"Cute is better than stalker."

"That was my first thought."

"Ouch."

"But only for a few seconds. I figured out it was a firehouse gag."

"So you're not going to run screaming into the night, then?"

She laughed. "I'm not the screaming type, and I'd have to put on clothes before I could leave. It seemed easier to ask you about it first."

There was a long moment of silence and then she heard him clear his throat. "So if you saw the picture, you're sleeping in my bed?"

"It's a nice bed."

"And you're not wearing any clothes?"

No, I'm not and you should get in that Jeep and see how fast you can get back here.

"Goodnight, Gavin." She smiled and hit the disconnect button.

A few seconds later, her phone chimed. Sweet dreams, Cait.

Chapter Nine

Cait woke the next morning to her phone chiming. As she reached for it, she wondered if it was even still morning. It felt like it had to be at least noon, and she hoped the text was from Gavin letting her know he was outside with coffee and a box of doughnuts.

It was only nine thirty and the text was from Carter. Where's the cleaning stuff?

She'd told him she wanted the bathroom clean before she got home and that she'd probably be home by ten or eleven. He was cutting it close. Under the sink where most people keep cleaning stuff.

Whatever.

She tossed the phone back onto the nightstand and stretched, surprised by how well rested she felt. Despite fearing she'd spend hours tossing and turning thanks to the memory of Gavin's voice on the phone and his parting text. But she'd been so relaxed after an evening of doing nothing that she must have drifted off.

Despite having soaked so long in his tub last night that she was probably still waterlogged, Cait treated herself to a quick shower, just to see what it felt like. The steaming hot water pulsing over her skin was even more amazing than the bubble bath had been, and she stayed in there until she realized she didn't know exactly when

Gavin was coming home. Maybe not until she told him she was gone, but she couldn't be sure.

She was getting dressed, debating whether or not she should strip the sheets off the bed—she didn't know where he kept clean ones, or if he just washed this set and put them back on—when her phone chimed again.

This time it was Gavin. You awake?

Depends. Are you outside with coffee and doughnuts?

I will be in 30 mins.

Twenty-five minutes later, there was a knock on the door. She liked that he didn't just use his key, she thought as she opened the door to let him in. And, as promised, he had a cardboard holder with two large coffees in it and a box of doughnuts.

"Hey, Sleeping Beauty," he said as he kicked the door closed behind him and walked to the table to set down their breakfast. "You look like you slept well."

"I did. How did you sleep?"

"As well as can be expected for a guy trying to sleep on a couch with a raging hard-on." He turned to face her, the corners of his mouth turned up. "That was mean."

It was out there now. She'd known things would be different between them after last night's conversation, but seeing the heat in his eyes right now left no doubt. He wanted her. She wanted him. At some point in the very near future she was going to end up back in that big bed of his, and she wouldn't be alone.

"You had it coming for making my ass a firehouse joke."

"Trust me, *I* was the firehouse joke. Your ass is no joke."

She rolled her eyes, but took a seat at the table and pulled one of the coffees out of the holder. "Cream and sugar?"

"Yeah. I realized after I should have gotten it black and let you add whatever you wanted here, but it was too late."

"Milk is never as good as that really fattening cream all the coffee shops use."

After hanging up his coat, he joined her at the table. "I bought that stuff one time, but you have a little more guilt when you have to look at the label every time you add it to your coffee."

Popping open the doughnut box, she perused the selection. "Two of each kind?"

"That way we won't have to engage in mortal combat if we like the same kind."

"What if I want both jelly doughnuts?"

His eyes narrowed for a minute and then his mouth curved into a smile that promised nothing but mischief. "Then we'll have to negotiate my surrender, if I agree to your terms."

It was utterly ridiculous that a conversation about jelly doughnuts should be such a turn-on, but Cait was hard-pressed not to squirm in her chair. Then he took a big bite out of a chocolate glazed and she laughed at the chocolate stuck to his mouth.

They talked about nothing much while they ate two doughnuts each and drank their coffee. The movie she'd watched in the tub—the mention of which had put that hot, hungry look in his eyes—and the miracle of plumbing that were his dual shower heads.

She ate the second doughnut more slowly, trying to stretch out the time they had left together. Once breakfast was over, there was really no reason for her to stay, but she didn't want to go without…something. At the very least a plan to get together again.

Once her coffee was gone, Cait reluctantly got up. She threw away the cup and napkin, then rinsed her hands at the sink. When she turned, Gavin was standing close, his hip resting against the counter. He wasn't close enough to crowd her, but closer than a casual acquaintance.

"I'm glad you enjoyed your night here," he said softly.

"I did. Thank you." There were other things she'd enjoy doing here, too.

"You should come back anytime. I mean that. Just pop in."

He was nervous. She could tell by the tightness in his jaw and the way his pinkie was tapping against his jeans.

Screw this. She was tired of dancing around it.

Reaching out, she snagged the front of his T-shirt and hauled him close, rising up on her toes to press her lips to his.

That was all the invitation he seemed to need. There was no hesitation or feeling each other out. His mouth claimed hers with a hunger that matched her own. He had one hand on her hip and one in her hair, and she ran her hands up his back.

His kiss was hot and intense, and she dug her fingertips into the muscles of his back. His hand tightened in her hair in response. He moved closer, pinning her body between his and the counter as one of his knees slid between her legs.

Yes and *finally* were the only two words Cait had left in her vocabulary as his tongue skimmed over hers.

When she caught his lip with her teeth, Gavin moaned and his thigh pressed harder between her legs.

She wanted him naked. Now would be good, although she'd be happy to go first if he wanted her to.

He broke off the kiss, lifting his head and dropping his hand from her hair to her shoulder. She wanted to say something, but her brain was fuzzy with desire and she was a little out of breath.

He ran his thumb over her lower lip. "I've been thinking about kissing you for quite a while, and it was still better than I imagined it would be."

"You don't have to stop." And he didn't need to stop with her mouth, either.

He made a sound that was part sigh and part low growl. "What time do you have to be home?"

"I don't have a curfew, seeing as how I'm a grown woman and so is my mother."

"So here's the deal." He paused for a second, as if he wasn't sure what he wanted to say. "I promised myself I wouldn't hit on you while you were here, until you'd left and I found a different reason to get you back here."

"You asked if I was naked in your bed and told me you had a raging hard-on. And we were just kissing."

He actually blushed, which she found adorable. "Okay, I promised myself I wouldn't *touch* you, then. And you kissed me first, so I'm not counting that. But the longer we're here, the harder it gets."

"Literally?" she asked, and then she slapped her hand over mouth when he laughed. "Sorry."

"Yes, literally, smart-ass."

"Leaving the apartment is kind of a technicality, don't you think? I had my sleepover and now it's over."

"I…want to say yes, but I had some strong feelings about what a douche move it would be for me to take advantage of you having some time to yourself, so it's going to be a thing for me."

Watching him struggle with his sense of honor—as overrated as she thought this particular battle was—gave her a warm, fuzzy feeling. He was trying so hard to be a gentleman. "What if I go drive around the block and come back?"

He laughed, but shook his head. "You want to grab a pizza?"

Pizza. She wasn't sure if somebody had told him pizza was her dietary Achilles' heel or if it was a lucky guess, but it was a sure thing, as distractions went.

Hell, yes. She very much wanted to grab a pizza, but she'd already had so many cheat days that month, she wasn't sure she could really call them cheat days anymore. They didn't always eat well on shift—fast and easy rarely equaled healthy—so she tried to make halfway decent choices on her own time. And there were the doughnuts she'd already eaten to consider.

"You know you want to," he said when she didn't respond right away. "I can see it on your face."

"It's not even noon. And we just had doughnuts."

"It'll be lunchtime by the time we get there."

She frowned. "Where, exactly, are you planning to get pizza?"

"Brockton."

"You're taking me to Brockton for our first date?"

He broke out the charming smile. "So it *is* a date, then?"

"Yeah, I'll have pizza with you. And it's a date." When he scowled slightly, she cocked her head. "What's wrong?"

"I'm trying to figure out if there's any way I can make it the second or third date."

"Nope." She shook her head firmly. "Veggie omelets together wasn't a date. That was an apology. And beer at Kincaid's could have been our first date, but you blew that. And being here now isn't a date. So pizza in Brockton will be our first date."

She really hoped Gavin didn't have a *thing* about putting out on the first date because she had plans for him later. And if he was still trying to be a gentleman, then… well, they'd just have to negotiate terms for his surrender.

Cait wasn't sure what was so special about the place Gavin brought her, but she'd enjoyed the drive. They took his truck and, after skipping over the country stations as quickly as possible, he found a radio station with songs she didn't hate. He kept the music low, anyway, while they talked—mostly funny stories from their childhoods. They both had very bossy older sisters, so they bonded over that.

He held her hand, their arms resting on the center console, and every once in a while, he would run the tip of his thumb in circles against her palm.

It wasn't a bad way to spend almost forty minutes on the road. And he'd been right. She was hungry for actual food by the time they pulled into the parking lot.

She didn't even think to wait for him to walk around and open her door for him, but he met her in front of the truck and held out his hand. When she threaded her fingers through his, she felt a fleeting sense of panic.

It hadn't been so long ago that the mere sight of him was enough to annoy her. And yet here they were, holding hands like they were a couple. Were they a couple? Or was this just an extension of the very mini vacation from her life he'd offered her with his apartment?

She didn't know, but it felt right and she was enjoying herself, so she was going to go with it.

"So what kind of pizza do you like?" he asked, once they'd been seated at a fairly private table and given menus. They were seated across from one another, and his leg rested lightly against hers.

She shrugged, because she wasn't really picky. "I like most toppings that aren't vegetables. Except mushrooms, I guess. They aren't my favorite, but I can live with mushrooms in a combo with something else. My mom loves them, so I've had to develop coping skills over the years."

"How about buffalo macaroni and cheese?"

"I like…" She stopped, frowning. "Wait. Do you mean on a pizza?"

"Yeah. Baked macaroni and cheese with buffalo chicken. And, bonus, it doesn't have any vegetables."

"When I said I like most toppings, I meant normal ones. Pepperoni. Sausage. Maybe some bacon. I'll even have a slice of Hawaiian in a pinch, though I personally think pineapple on a pizza is a little sketchy."

He raised one eyebrow, and then his mouth curved into a smile. "Do you trust me?"

"No."

Gavin's eyes widened. "Seriously?"

"Pizza's serious business. It takes time to build that kind of trust."

"I can't earn your trust if you don't let me try."

She considered that, and he was right. "Okay, I'll try it. But just know I can hold a grudge for a long time."

He winked at her as the server approached. "I won't let you down."

They both ordered sodas and he took care of ordering the pizza. Cait shook her head at the offer of bread, because of the doughnuts, and because putting baked macaroni and cheese and buffalo chicken on a pizza probably didn't do much for its calorie count.

When they were alone again, he reached across the table and took her hand in his. It seemed as though he was a very touchy-feely person, which was sweet. Cait wasn't, really, and her mom and Duke hadn't been much for touching in public. But she liked the contact, and the fact he wanted it.

But when he ran his thumb over her nail, she wanted to curl her fingers and hide her hands from him. "I'm not really good at the whole long-fingernail thing, I guess. Or nail polish."

"So? Some women paint their nails and some don't. Some guys have beards and some don't." He chuckled. "I tried once, before I joined the fire department. I don't grow a cool, hipster beard. Mine's more like somebody glued dust bunnies to my face. Fuzzy and splotchy and… not a good look."

That made her laugh. "I got a manicure once, with my mom. She got a gift certificate from my stepdad and brother for Mother's Day a few years ago and made me go with her. It took forever and the nail polish lasted maybe two days."

The corner of his mouth lifted. "Interesting word choice, *made*. Most of the women I know love to go to the salon or the spa or whatever the hell you call it."

She pulled her hand free and curled it into a fist, to hide her nails. "I guess I'm not like most of the women you know."

"No, you're not." He pried gently until she uncurled her fingers, and then he ran his thumb over her palm. Cait wondered if he could see the shiver that ran down her spine. "So you don't paint your nails or grow them long. So what? You take care of your family with these hands. You save lives. You flip off firefighters. I like your hands."

She wasn't sure if she wanted to cry or climb over the

table, straddle his lap and kiss him until they both forgot what they'd been talking about.

"Tell me the Joe Grassano story."

She was confused for a few seconds by the abrupt subject change, though the name seemed familiar. "Who?"

"The firefighter you pushed down the stairs."

"That was an accident!"

He laughed, because he obviously knew that. "As *I* heard the story, you and Tony were going down the stairs and Joe got in the way. You bumped into him and then you yelled something, stuck your arm out and he fell down the stairs."

"That is *not* what happened," she said, but after a few seconds of thought, she frowned. "Okay, that is what happened. But it's all in how you say it, I guess."

"How would *you* say it?"

If it was just a random firefighter asking her that, she'd probably get defensive. But she knew Gavin didn't believe she'd deliberately pushed Joe Grassano down the stairs. "We were carrying the stretcher down the stairs, and…let's just say the guy could have used a calorie tracker. I bumped into Joe, which jostled my patient. And, yeah, I think I yelled something at him because what moron stops on the stairs in front of two EMTs carrying a stretcher? But I saw the *oh, shit* expression on his face and realized he was off balance, and I was reaching to grab his turnout coat—with my back jammed up against the stretcher to help stabilize it, I might add—when he fell. My fingertips did brush the coat, but I didn't push him."

He grinned, leaning back in his chair. "I didn't think you did."

"If I thought you believed I pushed the man on purpose, I wouldn't still be sitting here."

"For the record, Joe knows you didn't push him."

"I know. We had ice cream the next day and laughed about it. But I know how you guys like a story."

"How come Tony was at the back, though? It seems like he should have gone first since the stretcher being at an angle puts more weight on the person in front."

That got her back up a little, even though she supposed it was a valid question. "I went first because that's where I was. You think I should have stepped aside and let the man handle it?"

His eyes widened and she saw the instant he realized his misstep. "Whoa. That's not where I was going with that. Jamie would kick my ass."

The name was vaguely familiar. "Jamie?"

"Jamie Rutherford...Kincaid, I guess. Scott's wife. She's LT at Ladder 41, but she filled in at E-59 when Walsh got hurt. She's a great firefighter—one of the best—and she would kick my ass if she thought I implied a woman couldn't do the job. Or your job."

"As she should."

"But when you're a team, you've got people with different strengths and weaknesses—uh, not that carrying victims would be a weakness for you... I'm going to shut up now."

She laughed, letting him off the hook. "Tony was at the back, but he also had all the gear slung over his shoulder and I had none. And yes, going down multiple flights of stairs makes it more difficult, but being at the front enables me to set the pace, and Tony has the strength to hold his end not only up, but back if necessary, so it isn't pushing *me* down the stairs."

"You guys have worked together awhile?"

"Four years. We don't even really need verbal communication at this point. We're a good pair, I think."

He nodded, his face serious. "Do you guys spend time together off the job?"

Cait felt her eyebrows shoot up, and she cocked her head a little. The day was going so well, so she really hoped he wasn't going there. "What exactly are you asking me, Gavin?"

Gavin kept his mouth shut for a few seconds, until he could work through what had just happened. He was having one of the best days he'd had in a long time, but right now he felt like he was leaning out over a cliff and Cait was deciding whether she'd reach out a hand to pull him back in or not.

"I was just asking if you guys hang out when you're not working. Like, Grant was at my place yesterday before you got there. And I had dinner with Rick and his wife, Jess, a few weeks ago because I helped him do her closet shelving stuff. We all hang out at Kincaid's and shoot pool. Like, are you friends in addition to being partners?"

Her face relaxed and he hoped that was a sign he'd given the right answer. "Okay, I'm sorry. You'd be surprised how often people say shitty things to one of us, with the whole *wink wink nudge* thing. I can get a little cranky about things."

"No, you don't say," he said, laughing and squeezing her hand so she'd know he was messing with her.

"I was going to say I can be a little touchy, but I know you'd turn that into an invitation."

He grinned. "Absolutely."

"*Anyway.* Tony is married, and he and his husband have two kids who call me Auntie Cait. We're friends, and I go to the kids' birthday parties and their barbecues and stuff, but he and I don't generally hang out apart from his family just because we work together all day. There are more of you, so you can switch up who you're drinking and playing pool with, you know?"

"That makes sense. The important thing is that you have such a strong working relationship. Makes the job easier, for sure."

Somehow they were leaning toward work talk, and he didn't really want to do that. They were both first responders so they had that in common, but it also meant work talk could become all they talked about. He'd dated a dispatcher for the PD once and the relationship conversation had gotten stale very quickly.

But he didn't really want to talk about their families, either, because he didn't want her thinking about her mom and brother right now. She'd had a relaxing night and a fun day, so far, and he'd seen the emotional toll worrying about them took on her.

He wanted her to keep enjoying herself because he was *really* hoping she'd go back upstairs with him when they got back to his place, rather than getting in her car and going home.

"I can't believe you've never been here," he said, for lack of anything else he considered a safe subject.

"I guess I've probably heard the name, but I don't come down this way a lot and when there's good pizza less than two blocks over, you don't feel a need to broaden your pizza horizons."

"I really hope today doesn't ruin your usual pizza place for you forever."

She laughed. "There you go, being cocky again."

"Confident," he corrected.

When the pizza arrived, she looked at it and groaned. "I might actually have to go for a run to work off those calories and I really hate running."

"I hate to tell you this, but there's no way you're going for a run after you eat this pizza. We'll probably have to sit here a few minutes before we can even walk to my truck."

"Look at this thing. I have to do *something* to offset these calories."

Even though he could think of a lot of ways they could burn a few calories together, Gavin kept his mouth shut. But the struggle must have shown on his face because she looked at him and rolled her eyes.

"You'd have to be really good to work off a slice of this."

"Go ahead and have two slices," he said with a grin.

She arched an eyebrow at him. "Is that confidence again?"

"No, that's cocky."

He knew as soon she took her first bite and made a low sound of appreciation that his spur-of-the-moment idea to bring her here had been the right decision. Just getting to spend the extra time with her in the truck had been enough, but the jolt of pleasure he got at seeing her enjoyment was a sweet bonus.

"Good, isn't it?" he asked when she'd practically inhaled a few bites.

"It's okay." Her eyes crinkled with amusement, though, because she knew it was a hell of a lot better than okay.

They each had two slices, and Gavin was tempted to go for a third, but then he'd be uncomfortably full and he really hoped he had plans for the evening.

"I invited you," he pointed out when she reached for the check. "So it's my treat, if that's okay with you."

After a few seconds, she pulled her hand back. "Thank you. It was delicious."

"You can take the leftovers home to your family, if you're not afraid they'll turn their noses up at your regular pizza from now on."

She laughed as they pushed back their chairs. "I don't know if it was *that* good, but I feel like we should do some laps around the parking lot because I'm so full."

It felt natural to take her hand when they got outside, and she laced her fingers through his. They didn't do any laps, but they did take their time walking back to his truck. It wasn't a warm day, by any means, but it wasn't bitterly cold. Or maybe it was just the heat of hopeful anticipation keeping him warm.

And the closer they got to his apartment—and her car—the more intense that hopeful anticipation got, until he would have been drumming his fingers on the wheel if he wasn't holding her hand.

Once he'd found a place to park and killed the engine, he tried to come up with something smooth to say. The truck was parked between his building and her vehicle, so he'd either be walking her to her car or walking with her to his front door. He knew which direction he wanted to go, but he was inexplicably nervous and his brain couldn't come up with anything that sounded charming or casual.

"You want to come up for a while?" *Please say yes. Please say yes.*

She said yes.

Chapter Ten

Cait had no idea why she was nervous all of a sudden. She wanted Gavin and he wanted her. And while she sometimes wished she could lose a few pounds without making much of an effort—especially after stuffing her face with pizza—she wasn't particularly self-conscious about being naked.

But for some reason, the thought of being naked with Gavin made her feel jittery and anxious, and she told him she was going to use his bathroom while he put the leftover pizza in his fridge.

After using his bathroom and stealing some of his mouthwash, Cait rested her hands on his vanity and looked at herself in the mirror. She looked so serious, and she didn't want to be. She was going to be fun and free and enjoy the hell out of this night.

When she walked out of the bathroom, Gavin was leaning against his kitchen counter, drinking from a bottle of water. He set it down when he saw her and smiled. "You're not going to eat the leftover pizza while I'm in the bathroom, are you?"

"Maybe," she said, even though she couldn't eat another bite, and then she tilted her head and gave him a suggestive smile. "I guess you better be quick."

He was only gone a few minutes, but it was plenty of

time for the anticipation to start dancing in her stomach again. It had been a while since she'd spent any time in a man's bed and the last one hadn't affected her nearly as strongly as Gavin did.

When he walked out of the bathroom, he took his sweet time until he got about halfway to her and then seemed to hesitate. "So, do you want to hang out and watch TV or have a beer or…"

"I'll take whatever comes after the *or*," she said when his sentence trailed off.

He started moving again, at the same lazy pace. "Just to be clear, what came after the *or* involved you naked in my bed."

"Does it also involve *you* naked in your bed at the same time?"

"Absolutely."

She put her hands up as he reached her, running her hands over his chest. The muscles were firm under her palms, and she was looking forward to not having his shirt between them. "Then, yes, we're clear on that being why I'm here."

Gavin moved quickly then, his mouth covering hers. She moaned when his hand fisted in her hair and pulled her head back to give him more access. Her lips parted and his tongue slid over hers.

His other hand tugged at the hem of her shirt until he could slide it up under the fabric. The first touch of his fingers against her skin was a shock and she sucked in a breath.

Gavin chuckled against her lips. "Ticklish?"

"Not really, but a little bit in a couple of places."

He pulled back to look at her while his fingertips skimmed up over her rib cage. "What places might those be?"

"I'll never tell."

"I bet I can find them." He pressed his mouth to her jawline, then began kissing his way down her neck.

She tilted her head, sighing as the fingers still buried in her hair massaged the back of her skull, working their way toward the base. When Gavin's mouth reached the collar of her shirt, he made a low, growling sound of frustration.

"How about we fast-forward through this part," she suggested.

"You got somewhere else to be?" he asked, letting go of her hair so he could have both hands up her shirt.

"Yeah, like naked in your bed as soon as possible."

He grinned. "I'm all for skipping to that part."

They left a trail of clothes on the way to his bedroom, which amused Cait because it was such a romantic movie thing to do, but once they reached the bed and he looked at her with hunger hot in his eyes, the amusement faded.

After flipping back the covers, she stretched out on the bed and gave him a *come hither* look. She expected him to go straight for putting a condom on and getting down to business, but he slid onto the bed beside her.

He kissed her, a deep and intense kiss that curled her toes. Or maybe that was his hand cupping her breast and the jolt of pleasure as he rolled her nipple between his fingers.

Then he stopped, just looking down at her face while he combed his fingers through her hair, spreading it across his pillow.

"Last night," he said, "when you were in my bed, what were you really wearing?"

"I had a T-shirt on," she admitted. "I wanted to be naked, but I was afraid being naked without you here being naked with me would just keep me from sleeping."

"I didn't think I'd ever fall asleep." He paused to close his mouth over her nipple, his tongue making circles until he sucked hard enough to make her gasp. "I kept picturing you naked in my bed with your hair loose on my pillow and I swear you could have cut glass with my dick."

Cait reached down and closed her hand over the dick in question. "And what did you do about it?"

An image of Gavin in a shower, water streaming over his naked body as he stroked himself made her skin tingle and Cait knew she'd be savoring that one for a while. Maybe bookmarking it for a future date.

"I suffered," he said, and then he chuckled at her look of disbelief. "I thought if I fell asleep totally sexually frustrated, maybe I'd dream about having sex with you."

That was sweet and she rewarded him by running her hand up the length of his erection, squeezing just enough before skimming the tip with her thumb.

He groaned and grabbed her wrist. "Maybe you missed the part about how I went to sleep totally sexually frustrated. There aren't enough box scores or algebra problems to recite in my head if you keep doing that."

It was tempting to see just how far she could push him, but the possibility *she* could end up being the one totally sexually frustrated was enough to make her release him.

He kissed her again before making his way down her neck and to her breasts. Taking his time, he teased her nipples with his tongue and teeth until she was digging her nails into his back.

One of his hands slid between her legs and she moaned when he simply brushed over her clit with the heel of his hand and kept going. His fingertips bit into her thigh as he sucked one nipple deep into his mouth, but that wasn't cutting it anymore. She spread her legs more, rolling her hips slightly off the bed as a frustrated sound growled deep in her throat.

Gavin just chuckled and for a few seconds she thought she was going to have to give the man directions, but then his fingers were back, stroking her slick flesh. She moaned and ran her hands up his back.

"You didn't think I'd skip one of the best parts, did you?" he asked, and she could hear the humor in his voice. He was teasing her, and she would have slapped his ass in punishment, but she couldn't reach it anymore since he was kissing his way down her stomach. "Don't you trust me, Cait?"

"Getting there," she said through gritted teeth as the heel of his hand pressed against her clit.

Her pulse quickened as he slipped a finger inside of her, and then his mouth was there and, *holy crap*, he was not a man who needed instructions. He licked and sucked her clit as he worked another finger in, and his other hand gripped her hip to hold her still when she lifted them off the bed.

She thought it would be a courtesy—a quick check to make sure she was ready before getting down to the real business at hand—but Gavin didn't stop. When she groaned, grasping his hair where the cowlick stood up, he moaned against her and sucked harder.

Even when the orgasm hit, he didn't relent until it was over and her body relaxed on the bed. He kissed the inside of her thigh and then lifted himself enough to grin at her.

"Damn," she whispered, trying to get her breath back.

"I told you we'd work off two slices of pizza," he reminded her, his eyes dancing with heat and mischief. "One down."

When he trailed his fingers lightly down the back of

her leg, Cait tried to brace herself, but when his touch hit that tender spot behind her knee she made a squeaking sound and tried to pull her leg free.

Gavin's victory shout made her laugh, even though he wouldn't let go of her. Holding her down with one hand on her hip, he gripped her calf with his other hand and lifted her leg until he could press his lips to that spot. When she squealed again, he laughed and then ran his tongue over the ticklish spot.

Cait squirmed, but between her laughter, her postorgasm weakness and the fact he was maxing out her flexibility, she couldn't get away from him. She had to settle for pounding her fist on his shoulder, trying to make him stop.

"I told you I'd find your ticklish spot," he said when he'd had enough of torturing her.

"That was mean." But she couldn't stop herself from smiling.

When he tucked his hand under her thigh and danced his fingers south a couple of inches, as if he was going for that spot again, she laughed and scrambled away. In the ensuing wrestling match, he ended up on his back with her straddling him. Judging by the smug look on his face, that was right where he wanted her.

He reached over to the side table and grabbed the condom he'd taken out of the drawer while she was stripping off her jeans, and she tried to be patient while he put it on. But she was so ready for this.

Gavin did the guiding as she slowly lowered herself over him. It was exquisite, the sensation of being filled, and she savored it, taking her time. She watched his jaw tighten and heard the slight hitch in his breath as she rocked, taking him a little deeper with each stroke.

"Fuck," he said in a hoarse whisper, as if the word was torn from his throat.

His fingers dug into her hips as she rocked, and he lifted himself enough to nip at her breast before dropping back. They both moaned when she ground hard against him, and then he grinned up at her.

Cait grasped his face, her fingertips making indents in his jaw as she tipped his head back. "See? I told you that you never take anything seriously."

"Because I'm smiling?" He released her hips and slid his hands around to cup her ass. "I'm smiling because I'm the happiest fucking guy in Boston right now."

She leaned down to kiss him and he took advantage of the moment to roll her onto her back.

Cait wrapped her legs around him and kissed him again until he thrust hard into her and she gasped. She closed her eyes for a few seconds, but he was looking down at her and she wanted the eye contact.

Each stroke came deeper and faster, until he reached over her head and grasped one of the slats of his headboard. Pulling himself with that arm, he drove into her until her back arched off the bed. She pressed her face against his neck, muffling her cry.

A few more hard thrusts and then he released the headboard to grip her hair as his own orgasm hit him. She cupped his ass, holding him close until the tremors passed and his breath came hot and ragged against her cheek.

He shivered when she trailed her fingers over his back until she could wrap her arms around his shoulders. With the hand holding her hair, he nudged her cheek until she turned to face him so he could kiss her.

Then his head flopped onto her shoulder and they did

nothing but breathe and savor the aftermath for a couple of minutes.

She closed her eyes when he reached down to hold the condom as he withdrew from her with a reluctant sigh.

"Don't move." He was only gone for a minute, and then she felt the mattress dip as he climbed back into bed. Once she was snuggled up against him, with her head nestled in against his shoulder, he kissed her hair. "That was the best thing to happen to me in a long time."

"Mmm." She had to agree with that. "I probably could have had a third slice of that pizza."

"Way better than going to the gym," he said, starting to sound drowsy. "I only found one of your ticklish spots, though, so you're going to have to go out with me again."

"I'll give you another shot at it, but no hints. You're mean when you tickle."

He chuckled, the sound vibrating through his chest, and then held her tighter while he shifted to get more comfortable.

After a few moments, Gavin's breathing slowed and, though he wasn't quite snoring, she could tell he was falling asleep. She should go now, before he was really asleep and her getting up disturbed him.

But she was so comfortable and her body so relaxed that she couldn't force herself to move. Just a few more minutes, she told herself. Then she'd go.

Despite her resolve to get up and get dressed, Cait was almost asleep in Gavin's arms when her phone chimed. She couldn't stop the heavy sigh that escaped her as his arm loosened to let her up.

"Who's that?"

"It has to be my mom."

"It's not like you're a teenager with a curfew. You can stay if you want to."

She wanted to. But she knew that text chime was her clock striking midnight. The ball was over and it was time to go back to her life. Hopefully with both shoes, though.

After fumbling on the nightstand, she retrieved her phone and read the screen. "My mom's worried about Carter and just leaving him alone isn't something she's good at."

"Speaking of Carter, he hasn't reached out about basketball."

"I'll give him a nudge." Sighing, she threw back the covers and put her feet on the floor.

Before she could stand, though, Gavin's arm snaked around her waist. He kissed the base of her spine and she shivered.

"Text Carter and see if he's okay. Then tell your mom to go to bed," he murmured against her skin. "And you can stay in *my* bed."

She didn't want to explain to him that her mom wouldn't have bothered her at all if she wasn't really upset. And Carter's moods being what they were, things between the two of them could blow up into an emotional shit storm with just a word or a look. It was easier to mediate between them now than to let it get worse and have to cope with the fallout of that. But she didn't want to go into all of that while in Gavin's bed.

"I have to go" was all she said. She heard him sigh, but he kissed her back again before withdrawing his arm.

He not only got out of bed and threw sweatpants on, but he pulled on a hoodie and shoved his feet into sneakers to walk her out to her car.

"You don't have to do this, you know," she said when he pushed open the building's main door and the cold hit them.

"I want to."

Cait had to admit it was pretty sweet, and she tried not to be too angry with her family for dragging her out of this man's bed.

Once she was in her car and the engine was running, he leaned in through the open door to kiss her goodbye. "Call me tomorrow, if you get a chance."

"If I'm free."

He laughed. "I'm never going to live that down, am I?"

"Nope." She tugged on the front of his sweatshirt to get one last kiss and then pushed him back. "Go inside where it's warm now."

She watched him in her rearview mirror until he was out of sight and then tried to refocus her attention on the family drama waiting for her at home. But she was *definitely* going to call Gavin tomorrow.

She wanted more of him.

The calm before the storm—literally—really sucked, Gavin thought as they moved around the big double bay, doing final checks on their gear and the apparatus. It felt as if they'd already checked and rechecked everything a dozen times, but that was the job. When lives depended on the equipment, you didn't let things slide or assume, because you hadn't used something in a while, it was still in working order.

According to the forecast, freezing rain was going to hit the city just before lunch, and the long and boring morning was going to become a grind of MVA responses. And EMS would have their hands full with the accidents, along with falls and pedestrians hit in crosswalks by cars that couldn't stop.

And thinking of EMS brought him right back to Cait.

He shouldn't have been surprised. It had been at least six minutes since he'd thought about her, so he was overdue.

He was trying his hardest not to be annoyed by her mother interrupting what had been an amazing night and making Cait leave. Family was everything and he could never see falling for a woman who didn't share that value. When his own family needed him, he was there.

But his family didn't need him *all the damn time*.

It was one thing when Mom's car didn't start or Jill had the flu and needed her kid picked up from school. Family did things for each other. But Cait's mom and brother seemed to need Cait to fulfill that maternal role for them. He knew dating a woman with kids was tough. Dating a woman whose "kids" were her own mother and a teenage brother might be worse, because he wouldn't have a lot of patience with a grown woman interrupting their time together because her teenager had a shitty attitude.

"You look pissed," Grant said, interrupting that unhappy train of thought. They'd run out of things to do and were currently polishing the chrome on the trucks, which was the default busy work.

"No, just lost in thought."

"So catch me up. Did the EMT toss your apartment, or what?"

"Her name is Cait, which you know. And no, dumbass, she didn't toss my apartment." She'd left his sheets smelling like her body lotion. Berries, maybe. Something sweet that made his mouth water.

"You left my place in a hurry so I thought you might be worried about it."

"I left your place in a hurry because she asked if I had doughnuts and coffee, so I wanted to get her doughnuts and coffee before she left. And then we had pizza."

Grant grimaced. "You had doughnuts and pizza? I'm confused."

"We went to Brockton."

"No shit. So you guys spent the day together, then?" Gavin nodded, but didn't say anything else, which he could see was killing the other guy. "And..."

"It was a good day."

"Gav, I'm not asking for locker-room shit here. You're my friend and I don't know what's up with this woman. I mean, you guys didn't get along and now you're having post-doughnut pizza, of all things. Are you friends now? Hooking up? Dating? Am I getting a save-the-date card?"

Gavin laughed and chucked the balled-up rag at his head. "You're such an asshole."

"That doesn't answer the question."

"Let's just say she would have spent the night—with me actually there—if she hadn't gotten a text from home and had to leave."

"Okay. One more question."

"Don't make me hit you, Cutter."

"Not that kind of question," he said, holding up both hands. "Was she going to spend the night because you couldn't find a smooth way to send her on her way, or because you wanted her to?"

"After she got the text from her mom, I tried to talk her into staying."

Grant gave a long, low whistle and Gavin shrugged. "So it's like that, huh?"

"I don't know yet, but it's not *not* like that."

Scott, who'd been walking by with a compressor, stopped. "Do I want to know what you two are talking about?"

"Nothing," Gavin said, at the same time Grant said, "His EMT."

"I swear I'm going to hit you," Gavin warned.

"Don't," Scott warned. "Trust me, Cobb hates that shit."

Gavin remembered when Scott and Aidan had been called onto Chief's carpet for throwing punches at each other at the ice rink. Scott found out Aidan had been seeing his sister behind his back and—since they were not only on the same crew, but had been best friends for years—he didn't take it well.

Cobb definitely hated that shit.

"The rain's starting to freeze on contact," Scott told them, "so we're about to get busy."

"Knew it was coming," Grant said. "We're ready to roll."

"Waiting sucks." Scott shook his head. "I don't mind a little down time, though. I'm still trying to figure out how to do the whole Valentine's Day thing when my wife will be on the job for the entire twenty-four hours."

"Oh, shit," Grant said, mirroring Gavin's thoughts. "When is that?"

"Next Wednesday, dumbass." Scott shook his head. "The date never changes. And obviously this is why I have an awesome, gorgeous wife and you two idiots don't."

"You're right," Gavin said. "Women totally think it's hot when guys panic and try to throw together romantic gestures at the last minute."

"Next Tuesday would be last-minute, shithead." Scott leaned against the truck and crossed his arms. "So what do you have planned with your EMT?"

"Her name's Cait," Grant muttered.

Gavin hadn't even given it a thought. In the past, if he happened to be seeing somebody when the day rolled around, dinner and a box of chocolates generally sufficed. Generic Valentine's Day stuff. But he didn't want to give Cait generic anything. "I don't know yet."

"Neither do I. Maybe a gift certificate to a spa or a nail place or something?"

Imagining Cait's reaction to him giving her a manicure for Valentine's Day made Gavin laugh, and the other guys looked at him, clearly waiting for an explanation. "Sorry. I was thinking about something else. Does Wren like having her nails done?"

"I... Maybe? Her nails always look nice and when she paints them red? Dude."

"Not to rain on the parade of brilliance happening here," Scott interrupted, "but gift cards are boring and not romantic. Especially when they're for something she'll do alone, later, when you're not with her."

Gavin tuned out the ensuing back-and-forth between the other two guys and thought about Cait. Did she have any Valentine's Day expectations? She hadn't said anything. A lot of women started dropping hints as soon as the calendar flipped to February, making it known they expected the day to be special.

It wasn't going to be easy to plan what—or even if—he should do without some kind of definition to their relationship. They'd joked about the trip to Brockton being their first date, but they were closer than one date implied. Or at least he thought they were. If, in her mind, they were friends and the date was just a means to a casual hookup, then a big romantic gesture from him would be awkward.

And there was her family to consider. Maybe he didn't want to move too fast until he got a better handle on how they would affect his relationship with Cait.

But she deserved something special, and he *wanted* to make the day special for her. He just needed to figure out a way to balance doing something special with not even knowing if they were at that point yet.

How the hell had his life gotten so complicated in three and a half weeks?

When the tones sounded, he shoved Valentine's Day to the back of his mind. He was ready to go, so he climbed into the truck and started gearing up as the other guys hit the bay.

MVA with entrapment. Confirmed injuries. Multiple victims.

The storm had begun.

"I need coffee." Cait tried not to cry or press her face to the glass as Tony drove by a coffee shop.

He shook his head. "If you have coffee, you'll have to pee and we ain't got time for that today."

"Boston's been a city for almost four hundred years. I shouldn't have to go without coffee because people haven't figured out the pavement gets slippery when the rain freezes on it."

"You are in a *mood* today, and I don't think it has anything to do with not having coffee."

"If you stop so I can get a coffee, I'll smile for the rest of the shift."

He snorted. "No, we'll get a call and your coffee will get cold while we pick somebody up off the sidewalk and dust them off, and then you'll bitch even more."

"I'll get an iced coffee. Problem solved."

Before he could agree to her brilliant compromise, dispatch broke into the conversation. Surprise, it was a slip-and-fall on the ice, and Cait tried to resign herself to the fact she wasn't getting caffeine until they were back in the garage, handing the truck over to the next lucky EMTs.

Between the constant calls, the lack of caffeine and the sound of the chain system that kept them from sliding into all of the other vehicles sliding around, she was starting to get a headache.

"Out with it, Cait. We're about three minutes out, so talk fast."

"I slept with Gavin."

"Okay, that was concise." He laughed. "In the two minutes and fifty seconds we have left, tell me why that's a problem. Was it disappointing?"

She imagined she could hear Gavin's affronted *hey* in her mind, and she laughed. "No, it wasn't disappointing. Far from it. But having to get up and leave after because my mother needed me was *very* disappointing."

"You already know how I feel about your mother leaning on you as much as she does," Tony said, and she did. When you spent five or six days a week in a vehicle together, you talked a lot. About everything. "But tell me, if she hadn't reached out, would you have spent the entire night?"

"Yeah."

"Because you didn't want to make your way home in the dark or for snuggling."

She smiled. "For snuggling."

"It's about damn time," Tony said.

The dispatcher's voice came through the radio. "Victim is an eighty-two-year-old female, confirmed head injury with possible hip fracture."

"Shit," Cait said as Tony gave it a little more gas.

She had her gloves on and was ready when Tony pulled the ambulance up to the curve. A woman was kneeling on the ground next to the victim, and a couple of men had taken their coats off to hold them above the women in an effort to keep the cold rain at bay.

"I was holding her hand, but when she fell, we both went down," the younger woman—maybe a granddaughter, judging by the ages—told her as she knelt on the other side.

"Hi," Cait said when the older woman looked at her with clear eyes. "I'm Cait."

"She's my gram. Her name's Barbara."

"Hi, Barbara," Cait said to the grandmother. "Did you lose consciousness?"

"I don't think so."

When Cait looked at her granddaughter, she shook her head. "She didn't lose consciousness. She wanted to get up, but her hip hurt and I thought maybe I shouldn't move her."

Tony unclipped his pen light from his pocket and checked Barbara's pupils and asked some questions of her while Cait took some notes. Each time she answered, he glanced at her granddaughter, who would nod confirmation her answers were correct.

"We need to check your hip now," Tony said. "Cait's going to touch you, but if it hurts, you let me know and I'll pinch her for you, okay?"

Barbara chuckled a little, and Cait saw Tony's big hand close around hers before turning her attention to the hip the woman had landed on. Luckily, she didn't think there was a break. Her head injury didn't seem severe, either.

"Okay, Barbara, what do you say we get you into the ambulance where it's warm?" Cait said. "I don't think you broke your hip and I know you didn't lose consciousness, but you should see a doctor. Maybe get an X-ray to make sure you don't have a minor fracture that can cause problems if it's not treated."

"I'll go with you, Gram. I can go with her, right?" Tony nodded. "I'll call Dad once we get there. I didn't want to call him until I calmed down because the roads are icy and I didn't want him rushing."

"Barbara, that's a smart granddaughter you have there," Tony said while they positioned the board. "We're going to lift you onto the stretcher now, okay?"

Once the women were in the ambulance and the good Samaritans were thanked and back in their wet coats, Cait was hatching a plan to grab a coffee in the emergency department. But EMS was at zero citywide availability with pending calls, so they had to hand Barbara over and head right back out for an MVA with multiple injuries.

As they pulled up to the scene, seeing Ladder 37 gave her pulse a little kick, but then she saw the two mangled cars and the thought of seeing Gavin again became secondary.

But the driver of one car and the passengers of the other had already been handed over to the first EMS crews on scene, so Cait and Tony got their equipment and stretcher ready and then they had to wait for the firefighters to finish extracting the remaining driver.

Her gaze was drawn to Gavin, who was waiting to help fold back the roof after they were done cutting the frame supports. He was totally focused on the car, and the intense focus on his face triggered memories of the last time she'd seen it, when they were alone in a collapsing house with an injured boy. She still felt a pang of guilt every time she recalled the way she'd accused him of not taking his job seriously.

In less than a minute and a half, they had a collar on the unconscious driver and were ready to extract him from the wreck. Cait's body tensed, ready for the signal for them to come in while cursing the lack of paramedic availability. The middle-aged man looked to be in rough shape.

The firefighters lifted him from the car onto their stretcher and Cait and Tony did a fast examination while packaging him for transport. The best thing they could do for him was get him to the hospital as soon as possible.

As she picked up her gear, she made eye contact with Gavin and he gave her a quick wink before slinging her bag over her shoulder.

Then they were loading the victim and all of her attention was on her patient. She could feel the speed of the ambulance as Tony pushed as fast as he could without endangering them or people stupid enough to still be out on the streets. She communicated the visible injuries to his head and chest to the ER as they went, and they were ready when they rushed him through the doors.

Cait could have cried when, while waiting for the stretcher, a nurse shoved a paper cup of coffee with a lid on it into her hand. "I love you, Jan. Until the day I die."

"It's black," she warned over her shoulder. "No time for cream or sugar."

"I love you," Cait yelled again.

Dispatch wanted an ETA on their arrival to the pending call, so she risked burning her mouth with the strong, bitter coffee while they walked back to the truck.

Tony gave her a stern look as she buckled her seat belt one-handed in order to keep sipping. "Don't blame me when you're peeing in a hazmat bag going down the road."

Chapter Eleven

The next day, Gavin sent a text message asking Cait if she'd be interested in getting a bite to eat after her shift and was pleasantly surprised when she said yes. Based on what she'd said about her mom, he'd half-expected her to tell him she couldn't get away and needed to have dinner with her family.

Instead, she gave him a time she'd meet him at his place, which his mind kept turning over and over, like it was a puzzle.

Either she wanted to meet him there so they could have some alone time after dinner, or she didn't want him picking her up at her mom's house. If that was the case, it could simply be a safety measure that was common in new relationships or it could mean she didn't want him to meet her mom.

But when he saw her walking up the sidewalk toward him, he didn't care. All that mattered was that she was there and she was smiling.

"Waiting for me on the sidewalk? You must be hungry."

"I'm starving, actually. This is a little later than I usually eat." And he was afraid if she'd gone upstairs, he wouldn't be able to keep his hands off her. Not that there was anything wrong with that, but he needed food first.

They'd made it to the end of the block when his phone chimed. It was the chirpy bird sound he'd assigned to his sister, so he pulled out of traffic and looked at the screen.

The upstairs toilet won't flush and if my kids and my husband have to share the downstairs bathroom I'm going to run away from home.

"Do you mind if we stop by my sister's house so I can figure out why her toilet won't flush? It should only take a few minutes, but if you don't want to, I can put it off. They have a half-bath downstairs, so they won't suffer too much."

"I don't mind."

"Thanks." He told his sister he was on his way and pulled back out onto the street.

"Didn't you tell me she's married?"

Gavin chuckled. "Yeah, she is. Henry's a great guy, but he's… Let's just say he's not all that handy around the house. He'll do anything for anybody, but if it involves tools in any way, you're better off doing it yourself. So I get the maintenance calls and, in exchange, I can mooch meals off them on a regular basis without feeling like a jerk."

"Huh." The way she said it made him glance over, but she was looking out her side window, so he couldn't really see her face.

"Huh?"

"So when your family calls, you help them out."

"Well, yeah. They're my family." He knew what she was getting at. "And when I call my family, they help *me* out."

"My mom has always been my rock," she said quietly. "Life kicked her pretty freakin' hard—for a second time—and she just needs a little time."

"A second time?"

"My dad died of cancer when I was three. I don't re- member much of that time, but I do know she thought losing him was her tragic backstory and she would live happily ever after with my stepdad."

"I'm sorry, Cait. I didn't know."

"Oh, I know," she said, and she sounded more like herself again. "It's just that for people who don't know my mom, it's hard to understand that this really is tem- porary. She's strong enough to get through this, but she had the wind knocked out of her."

Part of him thought that, after six months, her mom should be coping a little better, but he'd never suffered that kind of loss, so he kept his mouth shut. Cait was right. Not only did he not know her mother, but he hadn't been in Cait's life long enough to get a true picture of their family dynamic.

But they were pulling up to his sister's duplex, so he let it go. And at this point in their hopefully-a-relationship, it was still really none of his business. After pulling in behind Jill's SUV, he parked the truck and killed the engine.

"I promise this will only take a few minutes."

"Is that your way of asking me to stay in the truck?"

"Of course not." He knew if he did, Jill wouldn't hesi- tate to walk outside and introduce herself, anyway.

The entire family was in the living room when he gave a quick knock and then let himself in and he felt weirdly nervous as Cait moved to stand next to him.

"This is my sister, Jill. Her husband, Henry, and their rugrats, Bella and Matt. Everybody, this is Cait."

Cait smiled at them. His sister looked a lot like him,

with dark hair and eyes. Henry was tall and thin, with blond hair and glasses. Bella looked like Henry and Matt like his mom. "Nice to meet you all."

"Nice to meet you, Cait," Jill said. "I've heard so much about you."

Cait looked at Gavin. "Oh."

"Okay, not a lot," she confessed. "Just that he has a girlfriend."

Gavin's ears got hot and he cleared his throat. "We've got plans, so I'm going to take a look at that toilet."

Belatedly, he realized he had two options. He could ask Cait if she wanted to go upstairs and hang out in the bathroom with him while he diagnosed his sister's toilet, or he could leave her downstairs. With his nosy older sister.

He hadn't really thought this through very well.

"Can I get you something to drink, Cait?" His sister gave him an innocent smile. "It never takes Gavin long to fix things."

It sure as hell wouldn't tonight, he thought as he practically ran up her stairs. Not even five minutes later, he'd reattached the lift chain and went downstairs to find Henry and the kids in front of the TV and Jill and Cait nowhere to be seen.

They'd be in the kitchen, he thought. His mom and sister always retreated to the kitchen to drink coffee or wine disguised in coffee cups, which fooled nobody. He would have been tempted to linger outside the arched doorway to the kitchen and eavesdrop, but Bella was watching him. If he stood there doing nothing, she'd start asking him questions and he'd be caught, so he forced himself to move.

"That was *really* fast," Jill said, and then she pressed her lips together to keep from laughing. He could see in her eyes that she knew he'd been nervous about leaving the two of them alone.

"If the whole firefighting thing doesn't work out for you," Cait said, "you could be a plumber. Maybe don't charge by the hour, though."

"You guys are funny. All fixed, so you ready to go, Cait?"

Cait knew, too, and he had no doubt she would give him a bunch of shit when they got back to his truck.

"I can heat you up some leftover chili if you want to stay," Jill said.

"Thanks, but we have plans. Oh, and your lift chain came unattached and I can't even guess how."

His sister smiled. "All I heard was *blah blah call me if it happens again blah blah*, but thanks for fixing it."

He walked over and kissed her on the cheek, and then gave Cait an expectant look. She smiled and then set her half-empty glass of water on the counter.

"It was nice to meet you, Jill."

"You, too. I'll be in touch about that thing we talked about."

Gavin frowned, but Cait just smiled and preceded him into the living room. After saying goodbye to Henry and the kids, they walked in silence back to his truck.

He made it maybe an eighth of a mile before he cracked. "What *thing* did you and Jill talk about?"

She burst out laughing and it was a few seconds before she could answer. "There's no thing, Gavin. God, you're easy."

"You have a mean streak."

"It wasn't me. It was your sister. I just went along with it."

"What did you guys talk about?" He tried to ask the

question casually, but he was pretty sure she wouldn't be fooled.

"You."

He snorted. "Obviously. But what?"

"You were barely gone long enough for her to get me a glass of water. I only drank half of it." When he glanced over at her, she shrugged. "She asked me if I was the woman in the Snapchat picture."

"*She's* seen it?" It had to be Grant. He was the only one of the guys who'd spent enough time with his family to send them things like that.

"I told her no and pretended to be pissed off."

He whipped his head around to look at her and almost side-swiped a parked car. "Jesus, Cait, why would you do that?"

But she was laughing again, and he was tempted to downgrade their dinner plans to a fast food drive-through. "You really are easy to wind up. And you say it's easy to push *my* buttons."

"So she hasn't seen the picture?" Maybe he wouldn't have to kick his best friend's ass, after all.

"Oh, she's seen it. But when she asked if it was me, I said yes. Then she called you a creeper." She gave him an angelic smile that he knew was totally fake. "I didn't tell her you have the picture framed in your bedroom."

Despite her twisted sense of humor being a pain in his ass, he took her to his favorite wings place. It was a little loud, but the food was good and he was a regular.

He'd made the mistake before of trying to impress women. Putting on button shirts and taking them to nice restaurants. Washing his truck. But he couldn't sustain that standard long and it was better to let a woman know what she was getting right from the beginning.

The server gave them menus and Cait ordered a beer.

He ordered an ice water for now and a beer to arrive with his food, since he'd only have one.

"Do they have boneless wings?" Cait asked when they were alone, scanning the long, busy menu.

He scowled at her over the top of his. "Boneless wings aren't wings."

"But you can eat them without looking like a toddler who stuck his face and hands in a bucket of sauce."

"It's popcorn chicken tossed in sauce."

"You have strong feelings about wings."

"I do, yes."

He could tell by her expression that she was trying not to laugh at him. "Am I allowed to sit with you if I get boneless wings? Or is there a roped-off section for people who don't like cleaning wing sauce out from under their fingernails for hours?"

"I could lick the sauce off your fingers for you."

She laughed, but it faded into a *no* look. "I can't decide if that's sexy or not. I'm leaning toward no."

"Too far," he admitted with a grin. "I told you I do that. But I'll try to behave while you're eating sauced-up popcorn chicken with a knife and fork."

"I might eat my fries with a fork, too, just to embarrass you."

They both laughed and when their eyes met over their menus—her eyes sparkling with humor—he felt a little kick to the chest.

He *really* liked this woman.

After great wings—even if they were boneless—a couple of beers, and with a stomachache from laughing so much, Cait couldn't remember the last time she'd had such a fun night out.

She'd probably be sorry when her alarm went off at an

obscenely early hour tomorrow, but when Gavin asked her if she wanted to go upstairs, she said yes.

And when they'd gotten their coats off and kicked off their shoes, and he pulled her hard up against his body, Cait stopped caring about early alarms and ran her hands down his back to cup his ass. With a groan, he gripped the back of her neck and kissed her hard.

She surrendered to his mouth, flicking her tongue over his as he pressed her hips against the cabinet. All night, she'd been wanting this—wanting *him*—and even as he kissed her, she was pulling up the hem of her shirt. She wanted his hands on her, and she wanted him naked.

He broke off the kiss and helped her pull the shirt over her head. But one of his fingertips skimmed the back of her arm, from her elbow up. She yelped and jerked her arm down.

Gavin's eyes widened in confusion for a few seconds, and then a slow smile curved his lips. "Found it."

"Did not."

"I found your other ticklish spot. I told you I would."

"You found it accidentally." Hoping to distract him, she pulled the shirt off and tossed it away. Then she tossed the bra after it and reached for the button of her jeans.

"I still found it," he said, though he didn't look as smug now that he was following the progress her fingers made with her zipper. He only looked away long enough to strip off his sweater. He dropped it on the floor and reached for her.

Cait shoved her jeans down, taking her panties with them, and kicked them away. He kissed her hard, his hands cupping her breasts. She moaned and undid his jeans, hoping he'd get the hint.

But he took his sweet time kissing her before moving his lips to her breast. He sucked one nipple—gently at first, but then hard enough to make her gasp—while running his thumb over the other.

She braced her hands on the end of the counter as need pulsed through her. "If I'm naked, you should be naked, too."

"Yes, ma'am," he said, and she chuckled at his response. Funny how it didn't bother her at all in this context.

He didn't notice her amusement, though, as he was in the process of ditching his clothes. Then he was back, his mouth on hers and his erection grinding against her. She moaned, so ready for him…and he danced his finger up the back of her arm again.

She couldn't get away from him, since she was sandwiched between his body and the cabinets, but she tried. And in the ensuing tussle, they ended up on the floor. He was laughing, but when he rolled to his back and she straddled him, there was no doubt his amusement had zero impact on his desire.

"If you tickle me again, I'm going home," she warned, even though it was an empty threat.

With his hands pressing down on her thighs, he rolled his hips so the length of his erection slid over her slick flesh. "You don't want to go home."

Cait reached down and closed her fingers around the base of his cock and he sucked in a breath. She squeezed, stroking the length of him in her fist. "You don't want me to go home, either, so no more tickling."

He arched his back as she stroked him again, and he reached out to grab his jeans. After pulling a condom from the pocket—and she wondered if that was cockiness or confidence on his part—he tore open the package.

"You need to stop," he said, his jaw clenching. "I've

been thinking about this all night—shit, since the last time—and I can't wait."

"I'm done waiting." She shifted to give him space to roll on the condom and then lowered herself onto him.

She rocked her hips slowly, easing down the length of his cock as he lifted his hips. His thumb brushed over her clit and she moaned, taking him all in. He reached one hand to her breast, pinching her nipple between his thumb and finger, while his other grasped her hip.

"God, you're beautiful," he said, his voice raspy.

She looked down at him, her hair falling forward, and the look on his face made her believe him. And when he let go of her breast to press the back of his knuckle against her clit, she moaned and quickened her pace. His knuckle kneaded against her, a hard pressure that stole her breath and sent jolts of sensation through her body.

The orgasm was intense and she cried out. Gavin grasped her hips in both hands, his fingertips digging into her flesh as he raised her and then pulled her down harder and faster until he came with a guttural groan.

Then he reached up and threaded his fingers through her hair, pulling her down so he could kiss her. She moaned against his mouth and then collapsed on top of him. She could feel his heart beating, his pulse as quick as her own, and she savored the feeling as she tried to catch her breath.

"I'm so freakin' sorry," Gavin whispered a moment later.

It took a few seconds for his words to penetrate the pleasurable fog her mind was lost in. "Sorry for what?"

"When we were coming upstairs, I planned to put on some music. Be romantic and seduce you into my bed." He blew out a breath, making her hair tickle her neck. "The kitchen floor's not very romantic."

"You took the bottom. That was kind of romantic."
Then she laughed and kissed him. "Trust me, I'm not complaining."

"I could have at least gotten you as far as the couch, though."

The fact he'd wanted her so badly he couldn't wait to cross the room more than made up for the hard surface, as far as she was concerned. "Next time."

The *mmm* sound he made vibrated through her. "Definitely next time."

With a reluctant groan, she pushed herself up. The floor might not be romantic, but it would make the going-home part easier. Getting out of his bed had been hard. Now she slipped back into her clothes as she gathered them and several minutes and a quick trip to the bathroom for him later, they were both fully clothed again.

"I guess there's no sense in telling you that you don't have to walk me to my car?"

He shook his head. "If you won't stay, I'll walk you out."

"I can't." She grabbed her phone. "What if we video chat while I walk? You can see me, but you don't have to go out in the cold."

"Not going to happen. I was raised better than that."

"I know. That's why you called me *ma'am* the day we met." When he frowned, she laughed. "You did. I was trying to work up the courage to ask if you'd want to get a drink sometime and I don't even remember what we were talking about, but you called me *ma'am*."

"No shit? You were going to ask me out?"

"I was."

"It's just a habit."

She rose up on her toes to kiss him. "I know that now,

but at the time I didn't think it was the kind of thing a man called a woman he might want to have drinks with."

"I can't believe I missed out on you this whole time because of that. Next time, I'll definitely make sure we get at least as far as the couch."

By lunchtime on Friday, Gavin was seriously dragging ass. He'd gone to bed mostly on time because they really had to be careful about Cait's sleep schedule since nobody wanted treatment from a sleep-deprived EMT.

But getting out of bed to walk her to her car each night tended to wake him up enough so he had trouble falling asleep. Last night she'd fallen asleep in his bed and this morning had been chaos as she raced to leave his place and get home to change, while he tried to get ready for his shift. Throw in the fact that a higher volume than usual of idiots who totally forgot how to drive in Boston in the winter were starting to add up and he'd like nothing more than to go upstairs and crash in his bunk for an hour or six.

Unfortunately, they were doing visual inspections of the lines, which were stretched down the length of the bays and onto the sidewalk, and nobody got excused from that.

When his phone vibrated in his pocket, he stood and pulled it out, hoping it was Cait. These days, that was always his response to his phone going off. *I hope it's Cait.*

And he wasn't disappointed. Are you busy?

He was, but he was tired and a few seconds wouldn't make a difference. Yeah, but I have a sec.

Carter's been talking about playing basketball, but I think he's feeling awkward about sending you a text message.

Gavin wanted to make a comment along the lines of how, if you wanted to run with the big dogs, you had to be able to send a text and not have your older sister do it. But he was the one who'd brought up basketball in the first place, so he took the high road.

Can he walk to the firehouse? It was between his place and Cait's mom's house.

Yes.

Tell him to meet me there at 8am if he wants to play ball tomorrow. If something changes and I can't go, I'll try to text.

After a few seconds, he got a reply. He'll be there. Thank you, Gavin.

Do you want to play, too? If there was one unwritten rule of their Saturday morning games, it was no women. But Scott had brought Jamie a couple of times, so he was willing to risk it.

I want to play, but not basketball.

Damn. Twenty-four-hour shifts were really a pain in the ass sometimes. Best of seven series?

LOL. We'll start with a best of three series and see how it goes.

He laughed, and then remembered where he was. Sure enough, the guys had all stopped what they were doing to look at him.

"Something you'd like to share with the entire class, Boudreau?" Rick asked.

"No way in hell, LT."

"Tell her goodbye and let's go."

Gotta go back to work. Talk soon.

Be safe.

He slid his phone back in his pocket and gave his full attention back to the job at hand. They had to tell dispatch they were temporarily off-line when they checked the lines, so the faster they were done, the sooner they were back on the job.

"Cait's brother's going to play ball with us tomorrow morning."

"Uh-oh. Getting in with the family now. Shit's getting serious."

"I invited him to play before Cait and I… Before she even borrowed my apartment. What about you and Wren? You guys get to the meeting-the-family point yet?"

Grant shook his head, frowning at the line stretched out in front of him. "Not yet. Meeting my family means going to New Hampshire and I think she's still not ready for a road trip together. And she doesn't really talk about her family, I guess."

"Lucky you," Gavin said, maybe more wryly than he should have.

"Nothing changed on that front?" He shook his head. "Now that I think about it, it's kind of strange how little I know about Wren's family. She's pretty good at changing the subject, I guess."

"You said you thought she'd been through some stuff. Maybe it has to do with them. I wouldn't poke too much. If there's something to tell, she'll tell you when she's ready."

"Yeah. And in the meantime, we'll shoot some hoops with your girlfriend's little brother."

The way he said it made Gavin nervous. "Okay, but that whole thing where we talk about shit while we play ball? Like women and stuff? That can't happen."

"You mean talking about sex? That's the only reason I show up."

"We're not talking about *my* sex life in front of the woman's little brother."

"Of course we're not. Jesus, I was kidding." Grant threw up his hands. "Seriously, do you think I was raised by wolves or something?"

"Hell if I know. You were raised in New Hampshire, so who knows? I've heard stories."

"You are such an asshole."

"You're both assholes," Scott said. "Quit running your mouths and get back to work."

The next morning, Gavin, Grant and Aidan hung back when the tour ended since it didn't make sense for them all to go home and then meet again at the gym. Especially Aidan, since he and Lydia had bought a house in the suburbs. She didn't like getting up early after closing the bar, so Aidan was a regular at the Saturday morning games.

When it was time, Gavin walked down the stairs and outside to find a sleepy-looking teenager standing on the sidewalk, trying not to shiver because he was too cool to wear a coat. "Hey, Carter."

"It is so early, dude."

"Best time to shoot hoops. You get a little exercise in the morning and have energy to get a bunch of shit done during the day." He nodded for the kid to follow him and headed for the lot where he parked his truck. "Plus, if we went home and made plans to play later in the day, none of us would show up. Going straight from work is the only way it happens."

The other guys greeted them with a general *hey* when they arrived, though he did introduce Carter to Aidan and Grant, since they worked with him.

They played for almost two hours, which was longer than usual for them, but Carter seemed to be having a good time. He relaxed pretty quickly and even laughed a few times, and he got more aggressive with the ball as he got to know the other guys.

But once they had to hand the gym over to the next group, the others left pretty quickly. As they walked back to his truck, Carter relived some of the highlights of the game, and Gavin laughed at a few of them.

It had been a good morning, and he was glad he'd invited him. Not just for Cait's sake, but because he liked the kid. They didn't have a lot in common, but he was smart and funny, like his sister.

"So I guess you and my sister are hooking up?" Carter asked once they were on the road, killing the good mood.

Gavin tamped down the verbal cuff upside the head he wanted to give the kid for being disrespectful and counted to ten. Maybe that was what his generation called dating nowadays, for all Gavin knew.

"Cait and I are seeing each other," he corrected.

"Cool."

Gavin waited, but that seemed to be all Carter had to say on the matter. "She's a pretty awesome lady."

"She's not bad," Carter said, his mouth quirking up in a rare show of humor. "We'd be pretty fucked without her."

He knew he had to tread carefully here, because putting his finger in Cait's family business behind her back wouldn't go over well with her. On the other hand, she had to know when she agreed Carter could use some guy time, that he might vent.

"I think you'd do okay," he said. "I know losing your dad was a hard blow, but your mom has raised three kids. She can handle things if Cait finds her own place."

Or moves in with me, he thought, and then he had to clench his jaw to keep from cursing out loud. Apparently his brain was on fast-forward, because they were nowhere near that yet. If they got there at all.

But, man, it would be sweet to have Cait waiting for him at home. Or to be waiting there for her when her shift was done.

Carter shrugged, picking imaginary lint or bugs or something off the truck door. "I know Cait will move back out someday, but I hope it's not for a long time."

That was the opposite of what Gavin hoped, though he wouldn't say so. "It would be an adjustment, but you'd be okay. And it's not like she'd move to Wisconsin or anything. She'd stay close by."

"Do you know why Cait moved back into the house?"

"To help you and your mom out. Managing everything yourself can be overwhelming if you're used to having a partner to help out."

"She moved back in the day I came home from being out with my friends and found my mom crying on the kitchen floor and she wouldn't get up. She just kept saying she wished she had died, too."

"And Cait was afraid your mom would try to hurt herself?"

"We both were."

Gavin rubbed a hand over his jaw, trying to figure out what to say, while also trying to process the new information. Cait hadn't moved home just because her mother couldn't figure out how to pay the bills or unclog a sink.

She'd been afraid for her and maybe she was afraid of what could happen if she left too soon.

As tempting as it was to find a place to park so he could really focus, he also knew from experience that kind of focus could make a young man clam up. Sometimes it was easier to talk while there was something else to focus on.

"I think she's better now," Carter continued. "I don't know if she really wanted to hurt herself then, either. I think she just wasn't eating or sleeping and she was trying to pretend to me that everything was okay, and she just had some kind of a breakdown. But Cait said we couldn't take a chance like that."

"She's right." Gavin took a right turn, buying them a few more minutes in the truck. He wasn't sure if Carter noticed or not. "Maybe it's like a well. Your mom fell all the way to the bottom and she's been climbing out. And maybe Cait's pulling on the rope a bit and keeping her from falling back down, but your mom still has to climb. And she *will* get out of that well."

"I know." Through the corner of his eye, Gavin saw the boy nod and it seemed as if his back was a little straighter. Then he looked over at him. "Do you have an Xbox?"

"Nah. I never really got into it, but my buddy Grant has a PlayStation and sometimes he kicks my ass at Madden NFL."

Carter talked about video games until they got near his house, and then he gave directions. He had Gavin pull over in front of a small blue cape and unbuckled his seat belt. "Do you want to come in and meet my mom?"

"I would, but since Cait and I are dating, I should probably wait until *she* invites me over to meet your mother."

"Yeah, probably. Cait's working today. She wasn't supposed to, but she picks up extra shifts on the weekends sometimes because it's good money." He hopped out, but hesitated a second before closing the door. "Thanks for letting me shoot hoops with you guys today."

"Anytime, Carter."

As he drove away, Gavin drummed his fingers on the steering wheel. The information Carter had shared added new layers to Cait's life that he had no business picking at. And being another layer of her life wouldn't be easy for him.

But, blowing out a breath, he made the only decision he could make. He'd be patient and see where things went because it was still early, but he was pretty sure Cait was worth it.

Chapter Twelve

Because she'd picked up what turned out to be an outrageously busy Saturday shift that wiped her out so much she didn't have the energy to do more than talk to Gavin on the phone for a few minutes, Cait slept in on Sunday morning.

She probably would have slept in even later, but she thought she could smell bacon. Bacon was worth getting out of bed for. And if her mom was getting back into the routine of making Sunday breakfast, Cait would show up for it.

When she finally made her way down the stairs, she was pleasantly surprised to find her mom and Carter in the kitchen together. She was laughing and scrambling eggs while he buttered toast.

For a few seconds, she was tempted to sneak back up to her room because this kind of moment—her mom and brother learning to laugh and enjoy each other's company again—was what she'd been waiting for for months.

But her brother spotted her and gave her a smile. "Hey, I was wondering if you'd get up today."

"I smelled bacon."

She was stealing sips of her coffee while setting the table when her phone chimed. *Gavin.*

But it was Monica, and she tried not to show her disappointment when she realized her mom and Carter were looking at her. "It's Monica."

They both went back to what they were doing, and she shook her head before opening the message.

Have to meet sister-in-law for a dress fitting for her wedding and I'll be going near your area. Meet for coffee at 2? It'll be a quick one.

Usually she would jump at the chance for in-person time with Monica, but because she'd worked yesterday, Cait hadn't done the big shopping trip and she'd planned on doing that today.

"Everything okay, honey?"

Cait looked at her mom. "Yeah. Monica's going through this afternoon and wants to meet for coffee."

"That sounds like fun."

"We have to go shopping."

Her mom smiled and shrugged. "I can do that. You go and see Monica."

Cait's first instinct was to ask if she was sure or to postpone coffee, but she squashed it. There was no uncertainty in her mom's expression and, once again, this is what she'd been hoping for. "Thanks, Mom."

She responded with the address of a coffee shop that would be easy for Monica to get to and then sat down to breakfast. While they ate, Carter talked more about how much fun he'd had playing basketball with the guys. He'd told her about it last night, as had Gavin on the telephone, but Cait didn't mind hearing it again because it was so good to have her happy, chatty brother back for a little while.

Since she'd missed out on the cooking part of breakfast, Cait washed the dishes and cleaned the kitchen.

She took her time, keeping an eye on her mother as she prepared for her shopping trip. After double-checking the fridge and pantry, comparing the contents to the big list, she kissed Cait's cheek.

"You have fun with Monica. Don't rush home."

Carter even looked up from his phone long enough to give his mom a goodbye smile, and Cait felt something loosen in her chest. They were going to be okay. It had been a long road and they weren't there yet, but there was light at the end of the tunnel.

Because it sounded like Monica wouldn't have much time, Cait made sure she was at the coffee shop ten minutes early. After ordering two coffees, she was reaching for her phone when it chimed, and this time it was Gavin.

She really needed to pick a text tone just for him, she thought, so her heart wouldn't do that hopeful leap every time. She'd know.

You working tomorrow?

She wasn't working tomorrow. And her mother would be at work and her brother at school. Her entire day was her own, and damn the chores and errands she'd planned to do.

Nope. You going to fill me full of more junk food?

Whatever you want to do. I'm all yours.

Cait read the words a few times, her heart hammering in her chest. Her cheeks were warm and she felt ridiculous, but she couldn't help wondering if she was reading too much into a casual turn of phrase.

Was he all hers?

Text me when you get up and I'll come over. She smiled to herself. I'm sure we can figure out something to do.

Yeah, we can. What are you doing now?

As much as she loved seeing her friend, she wished she could say *nothing* and maybe they'd get together now. Meeting a friend for coffee, but it won't take long.

I promised a friend of my dad I'd help fix his deck this afternoon and his wife will want to feed me dinner. Dad will be there, so they'll talk forever.

So later was out. I'll see you tomorrow, then.

Definitely. Have fun with your friend.

Monica rushed in, so Cait fired off a quick emoji and tucked her phone back in her pocket. She was only a few minutes late, but Monica looked flustered as she sat down and took a sip of the blueberry coffee Cait had ordered for her, even though she personally couldn't stand the smell of it.

"I have thirty minutes *max*," Monica said. "Give me the highlights."

"We could have rescheduled."

"No way. I feel like I'm always rescheduling you and you are not only getting laid, but you're *dating* somebody. As in multiple dates? I want to hear more details and text messages aren't cutting it. So spill all of it, but quickly, so I have time to comment."

Cait laughed and considered where to begin. Then she started with the day she—with Gavin's help, of course—delivered the baby in the hallway and went straight through to the present. Luckily, she talked fast and there was still plenty of time for comments from Monica. Or maybe not luckily, depending on her opinion.

"He took you to a plumbing emergency? It's been a while since I was out there dating, but it seems like the bar used to be higher."

Cait laughed, because Monica had a point. "It wasn't really like that. I mean, sure, it's a thing that happened over the course of our date, but it wasn't *part* of the date."

"He should have told her he was busy and to call a plumber. Or brought you back to his place to wait so you weren't on a plumbing call."

It probably would have been the gentlemanly thing to do, but then Cait would have lost out on the extra time with Gavin. She liked riding shotgun with him, actually. He was a relaxed and confident driver, and he liked talking while he drove. Or sometimes singing along with the radio, which was fun because he was probably one of the worst singers she'd ever heard. He knew and didn't care. He just sang, anyway.

"Or," Monica continued, "maybe it was a sneaky way of introducing you to his sister without the pressure of an official meeting. It was all very casual, but now you've met her."

"We're nowhere near the meeting-the-family phase, if we're even heading in that direction," she responded, but Monica's words had already started the mental wheels turning.

She could be right. Gavin was obviously close with his family, which was one of the things she liked about him.

"You said Carter played basketball with him yesterday, so there has been meeting of the family," Monica pointed out.

"Yeah, but he'd already met Carter. Remember the Snapchat photo?" She paused while Monica laughed, remembering the string of text messages they'd exchanged about that one. "But he hasn't come to the house and been introduced to my mother. And I haven't met his parents."

"Introducing a girl to your older sister is probably almost as daunting as introducing her to your mother."

Cait smiled, remembering the look on his face when Jill told her she'd be in touch about the *thing*. She hadn't gotten to talk to his sister for very long, thanks to his anxiety about what she might tell Cait, but she liked her.

"Look at you," Monica said, leaning back in her chair. "You practically glow when you think about him."

"Maybe I'm thinking about how good the pie in that case looks." But she knew Monica wouldn't buy that. "Yeah, I like him. A lot. Which still seems bizarre to me because he's the *last* person I ever thought I'd date because…well, I told you about how he called me *ma'am*. I guess he was just being a gentleman."

"Those are the ones you've gotta watch out for. When are you seeing him again?"

"Tomorrow. We both have it off, so it'll be like a Saturday on a Monday, I guess."

Monica shook her head. "I don't think I could survive weird schedules. I like my nine-to-five just fine."

Cait kind of liked it. Sometimes it was hard to mesh their schedules—especially hers, since it tended to change a lot—but having a weekday off together felt almost like stolen time just for them while everybody else was stuck in their usual routine.

"What's your schedule look like for the end of the month?" Monica asked, pulling up the calendar on her phone. "We have to schedule drinks or a coffee or something so I can get an update."

"I don't even know." But she pulled out her phone and unlocked the screen, which was still in the texting app. "Oh…shit."

"What? Are you that busy?"

Cait turned the phone so she could see the screen. "I meant to send him the thumbs-up emoji and I must have missed and sent him the heart. I use it to end conversations with my mom, mostly, so they're next to each other."

"Girl." Monica inhaled slowly, and then let it out with a breathy chuckle. "I guess that sends a message."

"Maybe he'll think it's just a girl thing. He's probably used to women signing off with hearts."

"Maybe. How long have you guys been texting back and forth?"

"A couple of weeks, I guess." Cait sighed. "And no, I haven't signed off with a heart before."

But she had now, and she had no idea what Gavin would make of it.

Gavin was up and showered by the time Cait sent him a text the next morning. And as soon as he opened the conversation to respond, he saw the heart again.

He'd spent quite a bit of time yesterday pondering what that meant. He'd even managed to hit his thumb with a hammer in front of his dad and his friend, which had been embarrassing as hell. But his mind wouldn't leave it alone.

It was just an emoji, he kept telling himself. But Cait always ended their conversations with words or with the thumbs-up, so the heart was definitely a new development.

It had to be a mistake, he thought. Or maybe the heart was meant as a thank-you because he'd told her to enjoy her time with her friend. Cait wasn't the kind of woman who'd rush into things and throw the *L*-word around too soon.

Love.

He sucked in a breath and forced himself to focus on the text at hand. It was definitely too soon for the *L*-word, even if the thought of a just-right moment being in their future made his pulse pick up speed.

Are you awake yet?

He tried not to look at the heart while he typed. Hopefully it would scroll up and out of sight soon. I'm awake. Are you here yet?

On my way.

By the time she buzzed at the door, Gavin had gotten his mind straight. It had to have been a mistake or a thank-you, and if she didn't bring it up, neither would he. If the heart popped up again in future conversations, he'd know it wasn't a mistake.

When he opened the door and Cait pressed her body against his for a hello kiss, he stopped caring about emojis entirely. "Good morning."

"Good morning," she said, holding up a bag. "I grabbed some muffins on my way because I walked by the bakery and the smell was too good to resist."

"Healthy muffins or good muffins?"

She laughed and walked past him to set the bag on the table. Then she slipped off her coat and went to hang it in the closet. "Are healthy muffins even a thing?"

"I don't know. My mom said something to my dad about bran muffins, but I tuned it out."

"These muffins are not the healthy kind, I don't think. Although, someday we're going to have to start eating better or I'm going to have to order new uniforms in a bigger size. Trust me, no woman likes doing that."

"But we burned a lot of calories last week, even if I didn't get to see you over the weekend," he pointed out while he peeked into the bag. "Oh, I think we'll have to burn a little extra today."

They ate the apple cinnamon muffins drizzled with a sugary white glaze and drank coffee, debating on what to do for the day. In the end, they came up with a crazy plan to bundle up and find a beach to explore on the South Shore. They both loved the ocean in winter and there probably wouldn't be a crowd.

Despite a frigid winter wind blowing off the water, it was damn close to a perfect day for Gavin. They found a little mom-and-pop-type diner for lunch and then walked the beach for as long as they could stand the cold. Every so often she'd turn her face up to his for a kiss or burrow her face against his neck to warm it up.

With his arms around her and her breath against his skin, he couldn't believe what a lucky bastard he was.

And it was time to maybe step up his game a little. They weren't just *dating* anymore. They were a couple—she was his—and he hoped it was going to stay that way for a long damn time.

They thawed out in his truck and stopped on the road for a quick bite to eat. And once they were on the highway, heading back into the city, he decided it was time to broach the subject that had been in the back of his mind all day. Or for days, really.

"So… Wednesday is Valentine's Day."

"I've heard the rumors."

That didn't give him much to go on, as far as her expectations. "I, uh… Maybe we could go out for a dinner. Someplace that has food you eat with a knife and fork instead of your fingers?"

She widened her eyes in exaggerated shock. "No paper-lined baskets?"

He squeezed her hand, which, as always, was laced with his between them. "I haven't heard you complain, smart-ass."

"Just so you know, I'm not big into Valentine's Day. I mean, dinner sounds great. I just don't want you to feel any pressure to make it a big deal."

"I'm a little more into it this year than usual," he admitted, earning him a warm smile that encouraged him to take the plunge. "Actually, I've been thinking all the hearts and romance stuff might be hard on your mom, so maybe I could take all three of you out."

She got very still and that made him nervous. And then she sighed, which made it worse. He knew meeting her mom should have been her idea, but he was hoping including her would make the date more special for Cait.

"That's really sweet, but you don't have to do that."

"I wouldn't have offered if I didn't want to, Cait."

"I don't know how it's going to affect her. She hasn't said anything, but I know Duke used to always get her a little something. So she might be good company or she might sit and be miserable the entire time. Or burst into tears."

"I understand that. Why don't you ask her? And if she's up for it, we'll go. And if it proves too hard for her, we'll leave." He squeezed her hand. "Or if *you* feel like it's too much, then forget I said anything. We can do whatever you want to do."

"I'd like to invite her and Carter, if you're sure." He nodded. "I've been thinking about inviting you over for dinner, anyway. The whole meet-the-mom thing, since I met your sister."

"And my mom's been up my ass about meeting you, so expect that to happen soon. Hopefully it won't be when she shows up on your doorstep because it didn't happen fast enough for her."

Cait laughed. "If she's anything like your sister, I can actually imagine her doing that."

"Trust me, she's not shy."

"Let's get through you meeting *my* mom first and then—Gavin!"

He barely had a second to glance in his mirror before jerking his wheel to the left and hitting the brakes as the tire blew on the car in front of them. The driver overreacted and hit the guardrail. It started to spin and the tires caught and it flipped, rolling totally before landing with a thud on its wheels across two lanes.

Gavin skidded to a stop, barely avoiding contact with the wrecked car, and hit the button for the four-way flashers. Then he took a few precious seconds to back up and position the truck to block the highway and hopefully offer some protection for all of them until a state trooper or the local first responders arrived.

"Bag?" Cait barked as she unbuckled her seat belt.

"Floor, behind your seat. Gloves in the front pocket."

She was already giving the 911 operator their location as he put the truck in park. They hit the ground at the same time, but she had to grab his bag, so he got to the cars first.

A quick visual sweep told him the victims' injuries

posed more of a threat than fire or debris, so he turned as
Cait reached him. She'd already put on a pair of gloves,
and she handed him a pair.

"I'll take the phone. You check them," he said as
he pulled them on, and she tossed him her phone and
dropped the bag. By the time he identified himself to
the 911 operator, Cait had her head through the window
of the car.

He heard the squeal as another vehicle came to an
abrupt stop, but he didn't hear an impact. After a few
seconds, a guy ran around his truck. "Are you guys okay?
Can I do anything?"

"We're first responders. Stay in your car with your
seat belt on, sir."

"I need you to be still," he heard Cait say before she
called Gavin's name. "Gauze, and I need you here."

He opened a package of gauze and moved in beside
her. The airbag had deployed, but the driver still had a
badly busted-up face. Maybe he'd hit it on the window
or the passenger's shoulder or head as they rolled.

"Hold his head to the back of the seat to keep him still
and try to staunch the bleeding as best you can. Listen
to his breathing."

Without waiting for an answer, she grabbed the bag
and went around to the passenger side. "Ma'am, can you
hear me?"

There was a low moan and Gavin watched as Cait
did a quick assessment. The car was a newer model with
multiple airbags, and they'd both been wearing their seat
belts, but it still been a hell of a ride.

"My head," the woman moaned. "My neck hurts."

"There's a foam collar in the bag," Gavin said. "It's
not much."

"It's better than nothing." Holding the patient's head

against the seat with one hand, Cait reached in the bag and found the collar. After fastening it around the woman's neck, she spoke again in a calm voice. "I need to look at your leg and it might hurt, but I need you to be very still and not move your head."

That's when Gavin saw the shard of glass in the woman's thigh. There was a lot of blood.

"I'm okay," the driver said, he voice rough and slightly muffled by the gauze. "I can hold this and I won't move my head."

Gavin looked to Cait and when she gave a sharp nod, he transferred the man's hand to the gauze and went around the car. The door wouldn't open, but he had to stay out of Cait's way, so he crawled through the broken window into the back seat. The roof was slightly caved, so it was a tight fit, but he was able to reach from behind and hold the woman's head against the seat.

"Got her."

He could hear sirens, but cars had been jamming up on the other side of his truck so, depending on which direction they were coming from, it could be a few minutes.

Cait worked with quick, efficient movements, cutting away the fabric so she could see the wound. Then after a quick examination, she delicately packed gauze around it. Then she ran tape over it to keep the glass from moving.

"Get it out," the woman pleaded, her voice weak.

"That could make it worse," Cait explained in a calm, firm voice. "The ambulance is almost here and I'd rather wait until we can get you out of the car and get a better look at it, okay?"

Unless it was a paramedic unit responding, they'd probably wait until they got her to the hospital, Gavin thought.

"How are you doing, sir?" she asked the driver.

"I'm okay," he said again. "Just take care of my wife."

"Your wife is—don't move your head, sir. Your wife is going to be fine. The fire department and the ambulance are pulling up now."

The first face Gavin saw through the busted window was Jamie Kincaid's. Scott's wife leaned over to look in as an EMT took over for Cait. He was putting a proper collar on the passenger, but Gavin waited until he was given the signal before letting go of her head.

"Hey, Gavin. You want to climb out before we break out the hydraulics?"

"I'm not sure I can."

But he made it through and stood back as Jamie's crew moved in to cut open the car. Cait was talking to EMS and he was glad to see one of the guys was a paramedic because that thigh wound didn't look good.

Then he saw the guy he'd told to go sit in his car. He'd gone back behind the truck, but he was standing on the other side of the bed, cell phone in hand and obviously taking a video.

Great. As tempting as it was to say something to the idiot, Gavin just turned his back on him. The last few years, bystanders filming accident and fire scenes had become par for the course and most of the guys ignored them. There had been one video they all watched, though, because the bystander had run it on fast-forward to funny cartoon music and they'd gotten a laugh out of it.

While Gavin was more than happy for them to hand responsibility of the scene over to the folks officially on the clock, it felt like forever before they were allowed to leave. There were reports to fill out and paperwork to do and explanations to give.

But finally, they were back in his truck and on their way back to his place. It was a quiet ride, with their hands clasped on the center console. The music was turned up and Cait sang along quietly. It was decompressing time and he was content to let her be.

"I should head home," she said when he parked— miraculously within sight of her car. "But I don't want to."

"I want you to stay." He always wanted her to stay.

"You have to work tomorrow and it's already late."

"It's going to take me a while to fall asleep after what happened," he said, squeezing her hand. "I'd rather spend the time with you."

It was too late for a soak in the tub, but they stripped down and stepped into the shower, running the water as hot as he could stand it, which was how she liked it. Some of the tension eased from his muscles as the water beat against his body, and he smiled at the way Cait closed her eyes and turned her face into the spray.

"I'm sorry my shampoo doesn't smell very pretty," he said as he squeezed some into his palm. Then he started working it through her thick hair, kneading her scalp with the tips of his fingers.

She groaned and tilted her head back against his touch. "I don't care what it smells like when you're doing that."

"If you tell me what you like, I can get a bottle." He managed to say it matter-of-factly, as if offering up space in his shower wasn't a huge step for him. One he'd never taken with a woman, actually. The only girlfriend he'd gotten close to that serious with had her own apartment and preferred they spend their time there.

"I have an extra bottle," she said. "I'll try to remember to put it in my car next time I come over."

He kissed her shoulder, avoiding the shampoo running down her back. "Step back and I'll rinse your hair."

They didn't linger long in the shower. It was late and he wanted her in his bed. He wanted his arms around her and his mouth on hers. It had been a rough ending to their date and he wanted to push those memories away.

He was wrapping a towel around her when she started to tremble slightly. "Cait? What's wrong?"

"That was scary." He watched her blink back tears, her breath a shuddering sight. "I thought we were going to hit that car. And I thought somebody would have to call…"

The words trailed off, but he watched her throat work at swallowing and knew where her mind had gone. She was imagining what would happen if her mother got a phone call that something had happened to her daughter.

He pulled her close, her hair damp under his chin. "We didn't hit them. We're okay and they're going to be okay."

"I know. I'm sorry. I just… It was scary."

"Hell yeah, it was." He didn't even want to think about it, honestly. "But we handled it."

She pulled her head back so she could look up at him. "We did. We're a good team."

He grinned and was relieved when she smiled back. "We're a *damn* good team."

They finished drying off and he shut off the lights while Cait climbed into her side of the bed, telling him to hurry up because the sheets were cold.

He liked that she had a side of the bed.

When he slid in beside her, he pulled her into his arms. He didn't push further, not sure if she was still feeling a little shaky. Holding her was enough. But then her hand slid over his chest and she kissed him, nipping at his bottom lip.

Gavin lost himself in her, making love to her until they were both breathless and sated. He loved exploring her body, finding the spots that made her sigh and squirm. And he loved the sight and taste of her, and the way she sprawled over him—her breath hot and quick against his skin—when it was over.

She fell asleep quickly, but he lay awake for a few minutes, savoring the feel of her in his arms.

As the events of the night passed through his mind again, he couldn't help but smile at the memory of how well they'd handled the emergency together. And how right it felt to have her in his bed with him.

They were definitely one hell of a good team.

When the alarm went off and it was still dark, Cait groaned and pulled the blanket up over her head. She didn't have to work today, but Gavin did. He was the kind of morning person who slept until the last possible second and then sprinted through the shower and the kitchen on his way out the door, so he was ready to kiss her goodbye by the time she stumbled into the kitchen.

She didn't even want to imagine what her hair looked like, after making love and falling asleep with it still damp from the shower.

"I'll call you later," he said, and then he risked her morning breath for a second kiss. "Let me know what your mom says about dinner tomorrow, okay?"

"Be safe," she told him as he walked out the door.

She thought about brewing herself a mug of coffee, but decided instead to throw her clothes back on and head home. It was a pain in the ass not having a fresh set of clothes or her own toothpaste—she hated Gavin's brand of gel—and there was no sense in starting her day twice. At least this time, she wouldn't be rushing to get home and get ready for work before her shift.

But he'd offered to buy her shampoo. It was the first step in having some of her things at his place, and her stomach knotted. It was a big step—and a scary one, considering how things were at home—and had surprised her.

Gavin had also surprised her yesterday—on a couple of levels—Cait thought as she drove back to her mom's house. First was extending the Valentine's Day dinner invitation to include her mom and Carter. That was sweet and unexpected, and it said a lot about how seriously he was taking their relationship.

But he'd also surprised her at the accident scene. After taking a minute to make sure the car was safe, he had been quick to hand the scene over to her. There had been no doubt she was in charge and he hadn't even blinked. She'd been in the first-responder business long enough to know there were a lot of men who took over just because they were men, and Gavin wasn't one of them.

He rocked her world, made her laugh *and* respected her professionally. It was like winning the lottery and butterflies danced in her stomach when she allowed herself to imagine a possible future with him. And she was imagining it a lot lately.

When she let herself into the house, she was surprised the living room light was on. And seeing her mom sitting on the couch, sideways so her head rested against the back, set off alarm bells in her head. The TV was on, too, though the volume was turned down low.

"Mom, it's early. What are you doing up?" She tossed her keys on the side table and sat down on the other end of the couch, curling her legs under her. "Is something wrong?"

"Nothing's wrong. I just couldn't sleep so I decided to watch TV for a while." She was trying too hard to sound cheerful, and Cait's stomach sank.

"Why couldn't you sleep?"

"I don't know. Just restless, I guess. It's so quiet at night without Duke's snoring, so I can't go to sleep. Then I can't *stay* asleep. I thought if I came downstairs and turned the TV on, maybe I'd fall asleep on the couch for a little while."

That was a recurring theme. Most women complained about their husbands' snoring, but her mom had found it comforting and it was one of the things that hit her every night when she went to bed. Cait had bought her a white noise machine, but it wasn't the same. And there was nothing she could do to help.

"I saw you on the news this morning," her mom continued. "At that accident."

Okay, so maybe this was residual anxiety from the emotional meltdown her mom had after Cait was trapped in the house with Gavin and the little boy. She could deal with that. "The accident was in front of us, but the car made it look worse than it was. The people are fine. I guess everybody will be talking about it at work."

"I don't understand why you *wouldn't* want people to know. You're both single. He's very attractive. So what if they talk."

"It's not that I don't want anybody to know. To be honest, most of the people in our lives already know. But being on the news will make everybody want to talk to me about him and I don't like talking about my personal life at work. Other than with Tony, I mean."

"You hardly talk to *me* about him, so I don't imagine you want other people in your business."

Cait heard the little bit of hurt in her tone and sighed. "We're still getting to know each other, so I guess I just don't want it to be a thing in case it doesn't work out and then everybody knows."

"Are you afraid to share being happy with a new love with me because I'm still struggling with losing Duke?"

Cait squirmed, not really wanting to answer that. It had been important to her from the beginning that her mom not feel bad or shamed about her grief, but she also couldn't deny that it might play a part in how little she'd shared about seeing Gavin.

"I want you to be happy, Cait. I want you to fall madly in love and make a home and a family. I lost your dad and I lost Duke, but I wouldn't trade the years I had with them for anything. I want you to…" The words trailed off into a sob, but instead of coming undone, she took a deep breath and continued. "Will I get to meet him soon?"

"Actually, he wants to take all three of us out to dinner tomorrow for Valentine's Day."

"Was that his idea or yours?"

"It was his. He wants to meet you and it'll make the day more special."

Tears shimmered in her mom's eyes, but they didn't fall. "That's so sweet. But I don't want to intrude on your date. It's a day for romance."

"I want you to go out with us, Mom. And so does he."

She smiled. "I guess you can always have dessert privately after dinner."

"Mom!" Cait laughed. "That might be part of the plan, yes."

"I love how happy you look lately, so I definitely want to meet this young man. And it'll be nice to have an occasion to dress up a little."

Cait grimaced, which made her mom laugh. She hadn't considered the dressing-up part. She and Gavin were perfectly happy going through life in jeans and sweatshirts or sweaters, but her mom was right. Valentine's Day dinner out was an occasion for a little bit of glamour.

She just hoped she had something in her closet that didn't look like she was going to a funeral or holding a bride's flowers.

Chapter Thirteen

Jeff barely let Gavin get in the door before he brought up the accident. "Hey, Boudreau, I saw you on the news last night."

He'd been expecting that. Even if not a single guy on either crew had watched the news, Scott's wife had responded to the scene, so he knew. And what he knew, *everybody* knew.

"It could have been a lot worse," he said. It was a pretty standard response for anybody talking about an accident with no fatalities, but the sentiment behind it had cost him some sleep last night.

It could have been worse. He could have been unable to stop and plowed into the rolling car. Cait could have been the one in the neck brace with a shard of glass in her thigh.

His stomach rolled and he tried to shake off the what-ifs. He was usually good at that, since it was a useful skill in his line of work, but too many scenarios had tormented him as he lay in his bed in the dark.

"Jamie said he was playing the EMT's assistant when she got there," Scott said, obviously trying to get a reaction out of him.

"She had it all under control," was all he said, refusing to rise to the bait.

He had to retell the story several times as they did their equipment and apparatus checks before moving on to some housekeeping chores. He'd just finished stowing the vacuum when Rick Gullotti reached past him into the storage closet for the broom and dustpan.

"So you and Cait are a pretty steady thing now, huh?"

"We seem to be, I guess."

"I've gotta be honest with you. I did *not* see that coming."

Gavin laughed. "Trust me, neither did I."

"Got plans for the big day tomorrow?"

"Yeah, I'm taking her and her mom and brother out to dinner."

Rick's eyebrows shot up. "So you've already met the family and you're doing family dinners?"

"Not exactly. I met her brother when he played basketball with us recently, but I'll be meeting her mom tomorrow night when I pick them up."

"Sounds like you guys are a more steady thing than I thought."

"She's… I don't know." He was still having a hard time admitting to himself how important Cait was to him already, so he certainly wasn't ready to talk about it with somebody else. "I really like her. We have fun and enjoy each other's company and stuff and she's got…a *lot*. Her family's pretty needy sometimes. It's hard to explain."

"It's not hard to explain at all," Rick argued. "She's a woman with adult responsibilities and you don't want to help carry anybody's baggage."

Gavin frowned because the LT's tone made it clear he was criticizing, not empathizing. "That's bullshit."

"You like her, but her family needing her might be too much for you to put up with?"

He gave himself a few seconds to get his temper under

control before responding. While they might just be having a casual conversation, if push literally came to shove, Rick was his superior. "I don't want to start helping her carry her baggage and then decide it's too heavy for me and drop it on her."

Rick looked at him for a long moment before nodding. "You really do care about her, then?"

"I do. I know it hasn't been a long time, but I have a hard time picturing my days without at least talking to her on the phone anymore. And I don't want to picture it."

"Sounds serious. I haven't seen her at Kincaid's with you, though."

Gavin was aware of that, since he'd been thinking about that very thing lately. He liked Cait being part of his life, but right now she only got some of it. The guys he worked with were family to him, and the more time he spent with Cait, the less time he spent with them. Not that he expected her to hang around the bar all the time, but it was time to merge his life together.

And it was time for the other guys to know Cait was important to him and for them to get to know her beyond EMT Tasker.

He'd never brought a woman he was dating to Kincaid's to hang with the guys before and while she wouldn't be aware of that, the guys would and they'd know.

"I'll ask her if she wants to hang out there Saturday night," he said, knowing if he said it out loud, he'd have to do it.

"Maybe I'll stop by," Rick said. "And it wouldn't be cool to hit Kincaid's without letting the other guys know I'm looking to shoot pool."

Gavin groaned. "I don't think everybody needs to be there the first time."

Rick just smiled and walked away, leaving Gavin shaking his head. Taking Cait to Kincaid's knowing everybody would be there shouldn't be a big deal, but it was. It was a big step for him, and he had no idea how she'd take any ribbing they decided to hand out.

But first they had to make it through dinner tomorrow night, with her mother and brother. He believed himself capable of handling things if it went to shit, but he'd done a lot of worrying since Cait told him they were all in. Worrying about her mom breaking down. Worrying about Cait not enjoying herself. Worrying about saying or doing the wrong thing and setting it all off.

Usually he didn't sweat meeting anybody. He was personable and polite and people responded to his smile. Carter had taken to him pretty well. But if their mother didn't like him, he wasn't sure what Cait would do, and that had him losing sleep.

It needed to be perfect.

Hey, who died? was not the response Cait wanted to hear from her Valentine's Day date, she thought as she looked in the full-length mirror in her mother's room. But, despite her best efforts, she looked as if she was getting ready for a funeral.

"What is it the kids say nowadays?" her mom asked as she stepped into the room and their eyes met in the reflection of the mirror. "Oh, honey, no?"

"This is stupid. We don't even know where we're going, and Gavin likes me just fine in jeans and a sweater." She turned away from the mirror. "Why am I so nervous? It doesn't make any sense."

"You're introducing your boyfriend to me, so it makes perfect sense to be nervous. But just imagine how nervous *he* is."

As twisted as it was, it did make her feel better to know he was probably just as nervous as she was. If not more, since he'd be having dinner with a woman he didn't know and a kid he'd only met a couple of times. At least Cait would know everybody at the table.

"You should wear my red dress."

"No." Cait shook her head. The black sweater and long black pencil skirt with the tall black boots that enabled her to hide black tights so she wouldn't freeze her ass off were at least more her style, if slightly funereal.

"Just try it on. For me."

Cait rolled her eyes, but peeled off the sweater and unzipped the skirt. "I'm wearing the tights."

"They look nice with the bra," her mom said, giving her a pointed look before going to the closet.

And that was the Valentine's Day splurge. Black and lacy, it brought a lot more sexy than it did support, but it got the job done. Gavin had never complained about the plain but comfortable underwear she usually wore—in the mere moments between the clothes coming off and being naked—but she thought she'd spice it up a little.

The red dress was simple and the kind of dress that was never cutting-edge stylish, but was never really out of style, either. It had slim three-quarter sleeves and a V-neck that dipped toward the waist. Then it flared out over her hips and fell almost to mid-shin.

Cait had to admit it looked good on her, even if she wished the vee weren't quite so deep. And it was longer than the tops of the boots, so she didn't have to lose the tights.

"You're wearing that," her mom said, and it wasn't a question.

"Yes. Thanks, Mom." She looked at the outfit her mother had chosen. A sheath dress with a matching jacket in a pale blue, which matched her mother's eyes. They had the same hair coloring and skin tone, but Cait had gotten her dad's dark eyes. "You look beautiful, by the way. Very elegant."

"Let's go see if Carter managed to tuck his shirt in."

They found him in the living room, fussing with the buttons on his sleeves. He was wearing khaki pants and a blue button shirt that complemented their mother's dress. The top two buttons were left undone, but he'd tucked it in and was wearing a belt, so Cait considered it a win.

The sound of a vehicle pulling into the drive caught Cait's attention and she frowned as she walked to the window. It didn't sound like Gavin's truck.

It wasn't. She watched Gavin get out of the driver's seat of a freshly washed red four-door sedan and went to open the door for him.

"Happy Valen—" The words stopped coming out of his mouth as his jaw dropped. His gaze followed the vee of the dress, skimming all the way down her body before returning to her face. "Wow. You look stunning."

"Thank you." His expression made the awkwardness she felt wearing the dress totally worth it.

He had flowers in his hand and he separated a small bouquet of wildflowers from the roses and held them out to her. "These are for you. As I was saying before I got waylaid by what a lucky bastard I am, happy Valentine's Day."

She took the flowers and pulled him close for a kiss. "Thank you. And you look pretty hot yourself."

He was wearing khaki pants, too, but with a black button shirt and a leather jacket. They suited him and she realized that, like her, outside of his formal uniform, his suit was probably fit for funerals, too.

"Where's your truck?"

"I swapped with my brother-in-law for the night. The truck has the back seat, but it's pretty full and I thought it would be awkward for two women dressed up for a night out." He shrugged. "And I don't have to worry about my truck because my brother-in-law can't back it up for shit and just takes my sister's car if he has to go anywhere."

Cait laughed and then stepped back inside. "Come in and meet my mom."

It felt as if butterflies were having a rave in her stomach as she led him into the living room, where her mom and Carter were waiting. They stood when he walked in, and her mom smiled.

"Mom, this is Gavin," she said. "And this is my mom, Diane Hill. You know Carter, of course."

Gavin walked to her mom and shook her hand before handing her the roses. "It's nice to meet you, Mrs. Hill. Happy Valentine's Day."

For a second, her mom's eyes got shimmery and Cait tensed, but then she smiled. "Thank you. It's nice to finally meet you, too, and you can call me Diane."

"Yes, ma'am."

Cait laughed when her mom shook her head. "He can't help it. He *ma'ams* everybody."

Once the flowers had been put in vases and they'd inhaled the scent of the luscious roses, her mom poked her in the side with her elbow and whispered, "He's very handsome."

"Yes, he is."

"And it was nice of him to bring me roses. Obviously he was brought up well."

Cait smiled and nodded, glancing over at Gavin who was deep in conversation with Carter, before leaning in to smell her flowers. They weren't as fragrant as her mother's roses, but they were pretty and far more her style.

When they were ready to leave, she wasn't surprised when Gavin offered his arm to her mom. Or that he led her to the front passenger side before opening the door for her. Her mom was definitely right about his upbringing, she thought as he closed that door and then opened the back door for her. She climbed into the back seat with Carter, wondering if she'd like Gavin's mom or if she'd be too nervous about her own manners.

Gavin had chosen a small Italian restaurant that was nice enough so they didn't stick out in their dresses, but not so fancy or popular that there was a Valentine's Day crowd at the door. Once they were seated, and after consulting with her mom, Gavin ordered a bottle of wine and a soda for Carter.

"I can already tell I'm going to eat a week's worth of calories tonight," her mom said, looking over the menu.

Gavin grinned at her. "It's Valentine's Day. I've heard rumors that calories don't count on holidays."

Her mom laughed and Cait felt herself relaxing. She knew her mom's laughs and that one had been warm and genuine. She liked Gavin and she was having a good time. That meant Cait and Carter could have a good time, too.

And they did. Throughout dinner there was small talk and a few funny firefighting stories from Gavin, which her mom found fascinating. The food was incredibly good, and so was the wine.

But as they were nearing the end of the meal, Cait noticed her mom's gaze being drawn repeatedly to a couple at a nearby table. The man didn't bear a strong resemblance to Duke, but they were about her mom and Duke's age, and they were clearly having a romantic dinner for two. There was a lot of touching across the table and soft laughter and meaningful looks.

And it would have been them if Duke hadn't died.

"Do we want to see the dessert menu?" Gavin asked.

Carter groaned, putting his hand on his stomach because he'd just demolished the biggest, thickest slab of lasagna they'd ever seen. "I would literally explode."

Cait watched her mom fiddle with her napkin, her hands trembling. She didn't look up, but when she spoke, Cait could hear the slight tremor in her voice. "I'm so full. I don't think I could eat another bite."

Gavin didn't miss the signs, Cait noticed. His expression turned to one of concern before clearing again. After a quick glance at Cait, he signaled for the check. "That was quite a meal. I think a rich dessert would be too much."

When they got back to the car, her mom shook her head when Gavin opened the front door for her. "Cait can ride up front with you on the way back, and I'll sit with my son."

Ever gracious, Gavin opened the back door for her and closed it gently once she was inside. Before Cait got in the front seat, their eyes met and she could see that he knew where this was going. Her mom was on the verge of tears and it was hard to tell if she'd be able to hold it together long enough to get home.

She did, but barely. When Gavin walked them to the door and Carter had gone inside, she turned back to face him with almost dry eyes. "Thank you for taking us to dinner with you. The food was amazing and so was the company."

"I'm glad I got to meet you, and I hope you had a nice Valentine's Day," Gavin said.

Her mom tried to smile, but her face was crumpling and she nodded before turning away. Cait heard her footsteps practically running up the stairs and closed her eyes for a few seconds.

The feel of Gavin's finger touching her lip made her open them again. "I'm sorry, Cait. I shouldn't have mentioned the holiday when she was…having a rough time."

"It wasn't you, I promise. She was watching another couple at the restaurant and…anyway. She really *did* enjoy dinner, though. Up until the very end, all three of us had a wonderful night."

His eyes crinkled as he smiled. "So did I."

"I should probably go be with my mom."

The smile faded as he gave a sharp nod. "I guess. Although she might just need to cry it out. I have a mom and a sister and, well, sometimes women need to cry."

And they don't need supervision was the part he didn't say, but Cait could see the thought in his tense jawline. "It still makes Carter anxious when she cries too much and that makes it worse. I have to stay, Gavin. I don't want to, but I have to."

"I know you do." He hooked a finger inside the neck of her dress, sliding it down until it revealed a peek at the black lace bra. Then he inhaled deeply and let the breath out very slowly. "You'll wear this again soon?"

"Yes."

"Very soon?"

She smiled, but she knew it was a little shaky since she was trying not to cry. "I promise."

He kissed her, a sweet kiss that made the urge to cry even stronger. "Goodnight."

"Gavin," she called after him when he was halfway to the car. He turned back. "I'm sorry."

He looked at her for a few seconds, and then he gave her that charming grin of his. "We had a really nice dinner, Cait. I enjoyed it and so did you. I'll call you to-morrow."

After she closed the door, she leaned her head against it for a moment, trying to get her emotions under control. Gavin was being gracious, of course. They'd both had much different plans for after dinner than him dropping her off at home with her family. And she not only felt bad that he was going home alone, but she was angry about it, too. She didn't care if it made her selfish. She wanted to go home with Gavin tonight.

She did her best to swallow that anger and accept that they'd both known this could happen because the last thing she needed was for the sobbing woman upstairs to feel even worse.

After unzipping the black boots and pulling them off, she looked at Carter, who'd taken up a position on the couch with his earbuds in, and got a sad smile. She gave him what she hoped was a reassuring smile in response and, after taking a deep breath, walked slowly up the stairs.

Chapter Fourteen

"Gavin Patrick Boudreau, how many times have I told you not to take a bite of a chocolate and put it back in the box?"

He yanked his hand back before his mom could rap the back of his knuckles with the slotted spoon she had in her hand. Moms always seemed to have kitchen weapons when they needed them. "I don't like the coconut ones."

"Look at the diagram and only take the ones you like."

"I looked at the diagram." He showed her the drawing on the underside of the box lid and then tried to match it to the contents of the box. Even turning the lid a hundred and eighty degrees didn't make it look like the chocolates.

After a few moments of analysis, he picked up another chocolate and nibbled at the corner. "This one's coconut, too."

He was about to set it back in its slot, but his mom cleared her throat and he set it on the counter instead.

His dad wandered in and opened the fridge to grab the pitcher of lemonade he drank year-round. "Stop eating your mother's Valentine's Day chocolates."

"Did you buy these half-off at a gas station or what? The diagram is messed up."

His dad walked to the box and picked one at random.

After biting off a corner, he held it up. "This one's an orange."

"My favorite." Gavin reached for it, but his dad popped it into his mouth. "I'm going to remember that the next time your snowblower won't start and your back suddenly hurts too much to shovel."

"Hey, I have a bad back."

"And so will I if I keep shoveling your snow because you're too cheap to buy a new snowblower."

"Enough," his mom said, putting an end to the light-hearted banter. "I want to hear how your dinner went."

"South," he muttered without thinking and his mom's brow furrowed. "No, it was a nice dinner. And Diane is a super lady, which isn't a surprise considering how awesome her daughter is."

"So what happened?" his dad asked.

He filled them in on how the night had ended. He'd talked to them a little about Cait's family dynamic over the last couple of weeks, mostly because they were good listeners and also didn't hesitate to let him know if he had his head up his ass.

"I knew going in there was a chance it would be too hard for Diane, so I'm glad that we were able to have a good night together," he said. "But it's frustrating because Cait... It's not like her not coming back to my place was a big deal, even though it would have been nice. There will be other nights."

"You want a sign that Cait's going to be able to move on with her own life soon," his mom said quietly.

He nodded, because that was exactly right. "But I feel like an a—like a jerk, because that's selfish of me. If you needed me, I wouldn't leave you for anything or anybody."

She reached out and squeezed his hand. "You don't

have a selfish bone in your body. And of course you expect her to be there for her family, just like you would be."

"The problem," his dad said, "is that you and Cait have different ideas on whether or not her mom actually needs her as much as Cait thinks she does."

Gavin watched as his dad picked a chocolate out of the box and split the bottom just enough to see the inside before setting it back in its spot. Then he did another and another, until he found one with orange filling. He handed it to Gavin.

He popped the candy in his mouth, using the chewing time to process what his parents had said. Then he swallowed and asked the question he'd been asking himself since he walked away from Cait's door last night. "What do I do about it?"

"Are you willing to break off your relationship with Cait?" his mom asked.

"No." He said it without thinking, but he wasn't sure his answer would be any different if he had. And no matter how frustrated he'd been since dropping her off, it had never really crossed his mind.

The quickness of his response made his mom smile, but it was his dad who answered. "Then you're going to have to be patient, son. If you put Cait in a situation where she thinks she has to choose between you and her mother, you will lose."

"Even if you don't think it's a choice," his mom added. "Even if you think her mom's fine, if Cait doesn't, she'll push back against you. And I know right now you're thinking you won't let her, but no matter how much you love somebody, you can only be pushed away so many times before you don't come back."

He let the *L*-word slide, since he thought she was using

it in a general sense and not with regard to him and Cait specifically. Still, it rattled around in his brain for a few seconds, refusing to be ignored.

He judged relationships against others in his life—like his parents' and his sister's—and he didn't believe love was something that hit you like a wrecking ball. It was built over time, through good times and bad, and so far he and Cait had had a lot of good times.

And if he wanted to find out if what they had was love, he'd have to stick through the bad times, too.

He looked at his mom. "But she's lived there for months. Don't you think there's a possibility that having Cait there is keeping Diane from having to manage her grief? Or that Diane is manipulating her to keep her around?"

"That's not for you to judge, son," his dad said firmly.

"I know, but…it can be frustrating. That's all."

"You said that it was okay that Cait didn't go home with you because you spend a lot of time together. That's what you need to focus on," his mom said. "Sometimes we need you or the guys you work with need you and you're there. You'd expect her to understand. Like when you were leaving for a date but had to fix your sister's toilet first."

Gavin braced himself for what was coming next and sure enough…

"And don't think I'm not aware that Jill has met Cait and I haven't."

"I know. You will soon. I'm hoping she'll go to Kincaid's with me Saturday night and I'll bring it up."

"You're bringing her to meet your firefighter buddies before your own mother?"

Cornered, Gavin gave his mother his best grin as he

picked up the box of mauled chocolates and held them out to her. "Soon. I promise."

It wasn't until Friday's shift, when Rick gave him a questioning look he couldn't miss—and included a shooting-pool motion that looked obscene out of context—that Gavin made his decision. Before he could second-guess himself—or however many guesses it would be after days of overthinking it—he pulled out his phone and shot Cait a text.

The guys are planning to hang at Kincaid's tomorrow night. Wanna go shoot some pool with me?

It was almost an hour before he got a response, which was normal for the two of them. Sometimes it was immediate and sometimes it was hours, depending on what was happening. He liked that, because he'd dated some women who expected him to respond right away and couldn't seem to grasp that if he was at a scene, whether it was a fire or an MVA or a false alarm, he couldn't call a time-out to talk to his girlfriend.

Time to introduce me to the other guys?

He should have guessed she'd see the invite for what it was. She was too smart not to and, even though he hadn't been gifted with the heart emoji again, she had to be as aware as he was that they had turned the corner into a real, presumably long-term relationship.

Yeah. Also, I'd like to see more of that black lace bra.

It has matching panties, too.

Gavin actually groaned out loud. We'll have one beer and leave.

That would be rude.

So would banging you in the storage room.

She sent back a laughing emoji and then a final text. I'll see you tomorrow.

"You can't see through my shirt, Gavin, no matter how much you stare at my boobs."

"I have a vivid imagination."

"Your truck's going to run out of gas if we sit here much longer." She knew him—and herself—well enough to know if she'd gone upstairs to his apartment, they'd never make it to Kincaid's Pub.

Being introduced to the guys as his girlfriend was a big deal and she didn't intend to miss it. She knew some of them in passing and knew *of* most of them, but this was different.

So she'd sent him a text message that she was on her way and he should meet her outside. He'd tried to get her upstairs, but she'd been firm about it. And when he walked out the door and his gaze went immediately to her chest, as though he could see through her coat and shirt to the black lace below, she knew she'd been right.

He'd kept glancing over as they walked to his truck and now they'd been sitting in the idling vehicle for almost two minutes.

"She's got three quarters of a tank," he pointed out. "And she gets pretty good gas mileage. Plenty of time."

"I'm not having sex with you in a truck parked on the street. There is zero chance of that, so let's go to the bar and have a good time." She turned her head to give him a suggestive smile. "And *then* we'll come back and have a better time."

That got him moving. He had to park a little farther from the bar than she would have liked, considering how cold it was, but once her gloved hand was in his and his body was helping block the wind, she didn't mind the walk so much.

As they reached the door, he slowed their pace slightly. "So, listen. They all think they're comedians, so they'll probably give me a bunch of shit. And probably you, too. But it's all in fun, so just try to think of them as really annoying brothers."

"I doubt they'll give me any shit." Through the corner of her eye, she saw him wince. "What?"

"You're the EMT who pushed the firefighter down the stairs."

"Seriously? I'll just tell them the truth like I told you."

"They know the truth, Cait, but the truth isn't as fun. Annoying, wannabe comedian brothers, remember?" He bumped her shoulder with his. "I know you can handle them, but I figured I'd give you a heads-up."

It seemed like they were all there, and the introductions were a whirl of faces and names. They weren't technically introductions since she knew most of them in passing and they all recognized her, but she thought maybe it was more symbolic for Gavin. She wasn't being introduced to them professionally, but as his girlfriend.

"So," Scott said once they'd done the rounds and she had a beer in her hand, "tell us why you pushed a firefighter down the stairs."

She was never going to live that down, she thought with a laugh. "Joe got in the way. Then he wasn't in my way anymore."

Scott's eyes widened while the other guys laughed, which meant Gavin had been right. Scott Kincaid knew the real story of what had happened with Joe Grassano, but it wasn't a fun story. So she'd give him one.

"He's a big guy," she continued. "It wasn't easy."

After blinking at her a couple of times, Scott joined in the others' laughter. "My wife would like you. I don't want you in the same room because God only knows what evil you could get up to, but she'd like you."

They all milled around the alcove chatting and laughing, sometimes spilling into the bar area to make room for the guys shooting pool. At some point, a second mug of beer replaced the empty first and she made a mental note to keep track of how much she was drinking. She was a sleepy drunk and she had plans for later.

"Hey, do you know Derek?" Gavin pointed to a dark blond guy who'd come in later. He was in a BFD T-shirt like most of them, and Cait recognized the scar on his face. It made him look a little sinister, though she knew that was far from the truth. "He's Engine 59, but he works Wednesdays and Saturdays. Usually, anyway. I'm surprised to see him here tonight."

"We've met a few times."

Derek spotted them looking at him and made his way over. "Hey, Boudreau. Hi, Cait. How you been?"

"Good. You?"

"Same shit, different day. I had to switch shifts because my kids had a thing today, but it's their weekend with their mom so rather than go home alone, I thought I'd come hang out and shoot some pool."

She'd heard about his divorce through the grapevine, and rumor had it everything had been amicable. "How are the kids?"

He smiled, and it totally softened his face. "They're

good. It's tough during the school year because I have the Saturday tour and they don't have much free time during the week, but we make it work."

They chatted for a few minutes, and then somebody called his name, so off he went. The entire night was a rotating conversation, but she didn't mind. Gavin was clearly enjoying himself, too, and even though he was surrounded by guys who were like brothers to him, he was never far from her.

Cait got a little nervous when Rick Gullotti approached her. Not only was he Gavin's LT, but she knew he had a huge amount of respect for the man and his opinion of Cait could actually matter. Not that she thought he'd dislike her, but she couldn't help being aware of his importance in Gavin's life.

"You having a good time?"

"I am, actually. And that's not just the beer talking."

He laughed and lifted his own mug. "Doesn't hurt, though. Especially with this crowd."

"I was expecting a little more in the way of giving him a hard time, though. They're all being pretty nice."

"Give them time." He shrugged as he scanned the room. "But, yeah, they're going easy on the kid. It's the first time he's ever brought a girlfriend here."

"Really?" She filed that away to obsess over later—what did it mean—and limited herself to a mental *woohoo!*

"Yup. And I think I've met your sister, actually. Michelle, right?"

"Yeah. She married a military guy so she's out in Texas right now."

"It was a friend-of-a-mutual-friend thing, so I didn't know her well, but I remembered the last name."

She watched Gavin extricate himself from a group

of guys and head toward her. He nodded to Rick as he slid his arm around her waist. "What are you guys talking about?"

"Rick was just telling me he's met my sister Michelle before. It's a small world, I guess."

A few minutes later, it was Rick's turn to shoot pool and they were left alone in the back corner of the alcove. They watched people in companionable silence for a little while, until Gavin leaned close so she could hear him over the crowd noise.

"You know, I haven't really heard you talk about your sister much."

Cait shrugged, not really wanting to talk about her now, either. "I'm frustrated that she can't be here to help, and she's frustrated she can't help from there, and our phone conversations don't go well."

"I'm sorry to hear that. I would hate to have friction with Jill, so I can't imagine how difficult that is on top of everything you have to deal with."

"I do video chats with my nephew, and Michelle and I text sometimes. It's one more thing about losing Duke that makes everything hard, but we'll be okay." She took a sip of her beer and then leaned back in her chair. "And I didn't come here to talk about my family."

"Amen to that," he said, tipping his mug toward her before taking a drink. She felt a flash of annoyance at his tone, but then he winked at her. "I came here to see how many beers it takes to get you to go in the store room with me and show me what you're wearing under that shirt."

"I would actually throw up before I drank enough beer to have sex with you in the store room of a bar."

"Even this bar? They're practically family. And it's really clean back there. You'd be surprised."

She laughed at his earnest tone. "Even this bar, no matter how clean it is."

He leaned close to kiss his way up her neck to her earlobe. "You've had a good time, right?"

"Yes, I have."

"Can we go home and have a better time now?"

She shivered, though she wasn't sure if it was his breath against her ear or the fact he'd said *home* instead of *my place*, but the answer was definitely yes. "Let's go."

There was some whistling and hooting as they waved to the crowd as a whole and headed for the door, but Cait didn't mind. There would have been polite goodbyes if they hadn't liked her, not laughter as Gavin lifted his middle finger in the air in a final farewell bird.

"I like them," she said when they were out on the sidewalk.

The smile he gave her warmed her, despite the cold night air. "They liked you, too. Believe it or not, they were mostly on their best behavior, so the more you're there, the more comfortable they'll get saying stuff they probably shouldn't."

"I'll probably just say questionably appropriate things back to them."

He laughed and two women on the sidewalk ahead of them turned to look. Cait tugged him closer as they walked, and the women resumed their pace. This guy was all hers, she thought, and she was a lucky woman.

And, judging by the heat in Gavin's eyes when he looked at her, she was about to get a whole lot luckier.

Chapter Fifteen

Cait decided cuddling on the couch with Gavin, watching action movies from the 1990s, was her new favorite thing. Other than naked cuddling in Gavin's bed, of course. Even a sweaty Bruce Willis couldn't top that.

Naked cuddling had already happened, though, so now they were half-naked cuddling in front of the TV. She had on a T-shirt and he had slipped on sleep pants, and they had a fleece throw over them.

It was pretty damn perfect.

The entire last month, since Valentine's Day, had been pretty damn perfect, actually. When they weren't working and her family didn't need her, she was with Gavin. Whether they went out or stayed in, she never got tired of his company. She'd even learned how to play pool at Kincaid's fairly well, although she suspected the other guys were going easy on her for Gavin's sake.

She'd had dinner with his parents twice, and they seemed to like her a lot. The second time, Jill and her family had also been there and they'd continued bonding over teasing Gavin. Carter had played ball again with the guys, though he said it wouldn't be a regular thing because he didn't like getting up that early. And Gavin had eaten dinner at her mom's house a couple of times.

Her mom was definitely struggling with her daughter

not being around as much, but Cait was doing her best to try to balance her family's needs with her own. It wasn't easy, but it was worth it.

"I need food, but I don't know if I can get to the fridge," Gavin mumbled against her hair.

"I thought firefighters were tough."

"I was tough enough to get through my shift. It was the sex this morning that wiped me out. Also, if I'm starving, I think you have to provide me with food for my medical well-being. It's literally your job."

"No, my job is literally to keep you alive until we hand you over to the ER staff." She decided to switch tactics. "A gentleman would get food for his lady."

When he groaned, she knew she was winning. "Oh, you play dirty, ma'am. What do you want?"

"Something that doesn't require too much effort to eat."

She had to move to let him up—which he did with a melodramatic amount of groaning—and then she flopped over on the couch to await his return.

They'd both been on yesterday—with Cait taking a later shift than usual—for the utter chaos that was St. Patrick's Day in Boston. There were a few days every year in the city that meant nonstop running for all the first responders, but St. Paddy definitely brought the most drunken idiots.

They'd crashed for a few hours, and then woken up and made love. Now they were just killing time until they could take a nap.

When Gavin returned with two bananas, she laughed. "I could probably have managed a *little* more effort."

"Potassium. It might give us the strength to make a real meal."

She sat upright until he was settled again and then

leaned against his shoulder while they ate their bananas and watched guys with guns spout corny one-liners on the TV. Once they'd tossed the peels onto the coffee table, she snuggled back into her comfy spot against his chest.

When he kissed the top of her head, she smiled.

"We don't usually talk about work much," he said, "but I've been wondering something. Are you happy being an EMT?"

She didn't even have to think about it. "Yes. Are you happy being a firefighter?"

"I can't imagine doing anything else. During the summer I do some landscaping with a buddy of mine on my off days and I enjoy that, but I hope to retire from fire service when I'm an old man. But, you know, eventually I'll start trying to test up the rank ladder so I can get a cushy desk job someday."

"People often assume I want to go to nursing school or try to become a paramedic," she said. "I've thought about it but, honestly, it's a lot of time and money, and I actually *love* what I do now. Yes, being a paramedic would make me more helpful in the field, I guess, but there's always a need for EMTs, too."

"I think that's awesome, Cait. It's good to not only love your job, but to be able to resist pressure to do more if you don't want to. EMTs are invaluable."

"Thank you. Firefighters are pretty awesome, too." She smiled, and then felt his chest heave under her as he took a deep breath and let it out slowly.

"What about a family? Do you hope to have kids someday?"

It would have come off as a casual question if she hadn't felt him take that bracing breath before he asked it. The answer mattered to him. And that might mean he was starting to think long-term when it came to their relationship. They'd been together almost two months, so it was definitely serious, but talking about kids was *very* long-term.

So she gave him an honest answer. "Someday, probably. I can't even think about starting a family while mine's still a mess. What about you?"

"I definitely want kids. And you can't put your life on hold forever, you know. It seems like the longer you're a crutch for your mother, the more she's going to get used to leaning on you."

It was Cait's turn to take a deep breath, not wanting to mar their day by snapping at him. "I'm not her crutch. I'm her daughter. And she's getting stronger. I've been spending a lot of time with you, even spending the night, and they're fine. And she and Carter are communicating a lot better."

He stroked her arm, his fingertip running from her elbow to her shoulder and back again. "But they're still a factor in your future hopes and plans."

"It's not so much them as the timing, I guess. By the time I find a place of my own and get settled—while still checking in to make sure they're doing okay—it'll be a while. I'm not saying ten years. I just want the ducks I have to be in a row before I start adding more ducks."

"Quack."

"Not you." She elbowed him. "I meant baby ducks."

He chuckled. "So I'm already considered part of your pond of unruly ducks?"

"You're definitely in my pond." She frowned when he laughed, shaking them both. "I guess that sounded weird."

"A little bit. But I'm glad I'm in your pond."

"Me, too." Cait kept her gaze on the television, but she

wasn't really paying attention to the bad action movie anymore.

It was the closest they'd come to a conversation about their future together and, even though she knew it was inevitable, it still made her nervous. They enjoyed being together so much and there was no mistaking how important they were to each other.

It made her afraid of changing it. They lived their lives *almost* together, but still separate enough so there weren't discussions about bills and plumbing problems and whose family they were having Sunday dinner with.

Right now she was pretty damn happy with the way things were, she thought as she snuggled deeper into his embrace. It was almost perfect.

Gavin sat on the bench, rolling his hockey stick back and forth between his hands. He still had his skates on, but he was tired. And when Aidan and Scott were in a competitive mood, rink time became less about blowing off some steam while getting some exercise and more about checking each other against the boards.

After a few minutes, Grant joined him. "We should all go home and let those two duke it out."

"Hard to believe they're best friends sometimes."

"Yeah. They say it's all in fun, but we don't have refs with whistles and after that last hit, I thought it was 1973 again."

Gavin laughed. "You weren't even here for 1973 the first time around."

"Yeah, I just picked a random year." He took a swig from his water bottle, and then both winced when Aidan and Scott ended up in a tangle of arms, legs and sticks that collided with Danny in the net.

Gavin was surprised the words coming out of Danny's mouth didn't melt the ice in front of him.

"How are things with Wren?" he asked Grant, realizing he hadn't gotten an update in a while.

"Good. Things are good, I guess."

Gavin waited, expecting more. Grant was always the talkative type, but especially when it came to women. But now that he thought about it, his friend hadn't had a lot to say lately.

"What's going on?" he nudged.

"Sometimes I want to tell her I love her."

Whoa. "The *L*-word? Sounds serious."

"Yeah."

"But only sometimes?"

"Lately, it's been all the time. And not just when we're in bed or getting off the phone, like most people say it. I want to tell her all the time. Every time I open my mouth, I'm afraid I'm going to say it."

Gavin almost made a smart-ass remark out of sheer habit, but now wasn't the time. The heaviness in Grant's voice, along with the pinched mouth and slightly hunched shoulders, told him Grant wasn't happy about a situation that should be making him *really* happy.

"I gotta ask," he said. "Why are you trying so hard *not* to tell her?"

"It's hard to explain."

"I'm not even going to pretend I know jack shit about true love and all that, but I think if you really love a woman, you should say it."

Grant shook his head, looking down at his hands. "I think she'd push me away."

"I'm not gonna lie, dude. I'm a little worried about you with this woman."

"Why?"

"Well, for one thing, I haven't met her. Forget everybody else. *I* haven't met her and you've been talking about her since before Cait and I started dating."

"She gets anxious about meeting everybody, and we're taking it slow."

"Have you done a Google search on her? Facebook? Anything?"

"There was nothing, really. And she doesn't have a Facebook account."

"That right there is sketchy enough. How many women don't have a Facebook account?"

"She's really private." Grant tapped his hockey stick against the toe of his skate. "I know it sounds weird when we're talking like this, but it's not when I'm with her. She's just really private and she's skittish about our relationship. She's warming up to me, though. You'll see how awesome she is when you meet her."

"I'd like to. Especially if you're thinking about dropping the *L*-word."

"Have you ever said it to a woman?"

"No." Gavin paused, then lifted one shoulder. "I mean, back in school, maybe. When you're young, you fall in love every week. But since I grew up and it became more about finding somebody you want to settle down with for the rest of your life and less about getting to second base? No, I haven't said it."

"What about Cait?"

What about Cait? It was a question he asked himself a lot. "We're getting there. Pretty quickly."

"Good. I think you guys are the real deal."

"What makes you think that?"

"I don't know. Just seeing you together." Grant shrugged. "It's obvious you're into each other, and it's just natural.

Like you *get* each other and you fit. It's hard to explain. Gut instinct, I guess."

Gavin wished it was that easy. He wished there was a way to simply *know*, without a doubt, that he and Cait were meant to be together forever. He was starting to believe they might be, but he felt himself holding back. If he started pushing her for more, would she feel as if he was pulling her away from her mother?

If he thought about it too much—and he did—he always ended up frustrated by his inability to know the right thing to do.

"I *was* thinking about asking her to move in with me," he said.

"No shit?"

"No shit."

Grant started to grin, but then it faded. "What do you mean *was*?"

"We were talking about whether we wanted kids, like in a vague way, and she said by the time she found her own place and got settled enough to think about a family, it would be a while. So I guess she's not in the same place I am in that regard."

"Maybe she was giving you an opportunity to say, 'Hey, you don't need your own place because you can move in with me' and you blew it. Again."

Gavin hadn't really thought about that possibility, but he didn't think that was the case. Thinking back, there hadn't been any sense of hinting or nudging in her voice. Just a statement of fact. "I don't know. I'll probably bring it up again soon, though, since I think about it pretty much all the damn time."

"What about her family?"

"I don't know. I'm hoping Diane's in a place where she can handle it and, to be honest, she has to see it coming.

Cait spends as much time at my place as she can, and she's been spending the night more often."

"That sounds promising."

"Yeah, I guess it does." He grinned at Grant. "Maybe we both found the right ones this time."

"Lucky bastards."

"Fucking right."

"Hey," Scott called from the ice. "You two gonna play hockey or do you want to start knitting some shit over there?"

Grant looked at him and then at Gavin. "First one to take him to the ice gets a free beer next time we hit Kincaid's."

He snorted. "You recognize the irony in that, right? Since it's his family's bar?"

"Just makes it all the sweeter."

"You're on."

Chapter Sixteen

Cait wasn't accustomed to having company for her first cup of coffee in the morning, since she got up earlier than her mom and her brother, but on Friday Carter had a meeting with his guidance counselor before school started. He was bleary-eyed and clearly unhappy to be awake, but he still managed a quick smile when he saw her.

"I can't believe you get up this early every day."

"Do well in school and go to college, and maybe you can get some fancy office job with bankers' hours."

"Ha ha." He grabbed a soda from the fridge and popped the tab while Cait winced. The only thing worse than liquid sugar in the morning was carbonated liquid sugar. "Hey, there was a fire on the news when I walked by the TV."

Frowning, she took her coffee and went to sit on the couch. She set her mug down to pick up the remote control since she always turned the volume down to a murmur in the morning.

"Crews are still battling an early-morning fire at this hour," the news anchor announced, before they cut back to the live scene.

It was a massive fire, and it looked like it had originated in one triple-decker before jumping to the one next door. The middle of the night and early-morning hours were the worst time for residential fires, she thought sadly. Most families were sound asleep when they started.

"Do you think Gavin's there?" Carter asked, startling her. She hadn't realized he was standing behind the couch, and she turned sideways so she could see both him and the television screen.

"He's there." She didn't need to seek out the information or try to see the numbers on the apparatus on the screen. She knew he was on shift, she knew the building's location and she could see the scope of the response. Engine 59 and Ladder 37 would be on scene.

"It looks dangerous."

She heard the underlying tension in his voice and it pretty much matched the tension she herself was feeling. She probably would have changed the channel if she was alone in an attempt to fool herself into thinking she'd stop worrying, but Carter's gaze was so glued to the screen, she wasn't even sure he'd blinked.

"I know it looks like chaos," she said, "but it's actually very organized. There's a guy in the command area who has a magnet board where all the trucks and firefighters are accounted for. And they're all very well trained."

"But things go wrong."

Cait didn't want to talk about that. Just the thought of something going sideways twisted her stomach into knots and made her throat ache. But just the fact Carter was so intent on the screen and the conversation—phone forgotten next to him—told her how much he cared and she didn't want to discount that.

"Sometimes, but not often. You hear more about the few times it turns ugly than you do the thousands of times it doesn't. There's a lot of experience and training on that scene. And if they think it's unsafe, they'll pull everybody out."

Carter only nodded, and then Cait watched him tilt his head, craning his neck as if he could see around the news anchor to identify the firefighters in the background. It was sweet and she found herself smiling at the back of her brother's head.

She'd done enough fire standbys so she could make sense of what she was seeing, but she had to admit this time was different. The worry she usually felt for the first responders—many of whom she knew on at least a passing basis—was amped up and, like her brother, she couldn't stop herself from trying to pick Gavin out of the crowd.

Then a new camera view picked up Ladder 37. She didn't need a close-up to know it was Gavin at the top of the ladder. She just knew.

A woman and a little girl were in the window, screaming as the flames closed in on them. The ladder was moving and she could see Gavin yelling to them and see his body language. She didn't need audio to know he was telling her it was okay. That he'd get them.

The woman shifted the girl in her arms and Cait knew she was going to throw the child to Gavin.

"Jesus," she whispered as her stomach knotted.

The camera cut away, going back to the front of the scene. Cait didn't move—she couldn't move—as she realized the emotional toll it would take on Gavin if the mother threw the little girl and he didn't catch her.

"Cait?"

"You need to get to school," she said, more sharply than she intended.

"Are you okay?"

"Yes, I'm okay. And so is Gavin." She forced herself

to look away from the TV and paste a smile on her face. After taking a sip of her coffee because her mouth was dry, she stood up and walked around the couch to give him a quick hug. He wasn't a fan, but he accepted it. "If you don't go, you're going to be late for your meeting."

He slung his backpack over his shoulder, but didn't move. "But if Gavin's there, maybe they'll interview him."

She shook her head and shoved him toward the door. "It'll be a while before anybody does an interview. And only the officers do interviews, so you won't see Gavin, anyway."

Once he was out the door, Cait noticed the time and realized she needed to get a move on. But she couldn't stop herself from looking at the television one last time.

The scroll on the bottom of the screen changed to *Fatal Fire* and Cait felt her eyes well up. Nothing said the fatality was the woman or her little girl, but her gut told her it was. She swiped at her eyes, and then she made a few phone calls and, for the first time in a very long time, called in sick.

It wasn't really a lie. Her stomach hurt but, even more, her heart ached.

Gavin sat on the curb, his elbows propped on his knees and his hands dangling between his legs. Head bowed, he stared at the disposable coffee cup that had slipped from his fingers, losing its lid and steaming contents when it hit the pavement. He didn't care.

He could hear the little girl crying. The screaming for her mother had abated to sobbing and to pleading with the EMTs. She just wanted her mommy.

But her mommy was gone because Gavin hadn't been

able to catch her. Fifteen seconds. Maybe even ten. But if she'd just waited fifteen more seconds...

Gavin knew all the right words. He couldn't save them all. He'd done all he could. That was the job. Blah blah blah. He knew all the correct words and he'd even had to say the words to others once or twice, but right now they offered no comfort. It would probably be a long time before they could overpower the memory of the little girl screaming for her mother.

A hand closed over his shoulder and squeezed. Gavin closed his eyes, hoping whoever belonged to the hand—probably Jeff, judging by the grip—didn't say the words to him right now.

After a few seconds, the hand lifted and Gavin opened his eyes to see boots moving away from him.

The cold radiating from the pavement to his already chilled body was starting to hurt, so Gavin finally pushed himself to his feet. Their tour was over. They were returning to quarters and then he'd go home. Maybe he'd sleep or maybe he'd lie in bed and listen to the little girl screaming in his head, but for now he followed the others to the trucks.

Jeff was limping, favoring his knee, but he wasn't surprised when he waved off the EMT who approached him. It wasn't an injury, but a chronic problem Gavin suspected was getting worse and the cold didn't help.

Nobody spoke on the ride back. Utterly exhausted and with the pall of a fatality hanging over them, they simply stared out the windows until the trucks were backed in and they could robotically go through their checklists before handing everything over to the next shift.

Gavin didn't bother to shower. He just wanted to go home, and he didn't speak to any of the guys on the way out. Derek Gilman, who was on his way in, slapped him on the shoulder, but they didn't exchange words.

As he stepped through the firehouse door, a car pulled up to the curb and it took him a few seconds to realize it was Cait's.

Something shook loose inside of him and he took a deep, shuddering breath. Then he opened the door and slid into the passenger seat and closed the door. She didn't say anything. She just reached across to hold his hand and pulled back onto the street.

"Don't you have to work today?" he finally asked, realizing his voice sounded hoarse from screaming. *Don't jump. I'm almost there.*

"I called in sick."

"Thank you."

Cait didn't ask him any questions. She seemed content to just drive and hold his hand until they parked in front of his building. He knew if he talked about it, she'd listen, but he couldn't do it. Not yet.

Once they were inside his apartment, he turned to her, though. He wanted a hug in the worst way, but he looked down and realized he must stink of sweat and smoke. But when he looked up again, she was moving toward him, her arms apart.

He buried his face in her neck as she squeezed him tightly. "Did somebody text you?"

"I saw the fire on the news. The camera cut away because I think the camera person realized the woman was going to throw her daughter to you. A few minutes later they changed the headline scroll to fatal fire."

"I caught the little girl." Barely, and he'd almost gone off the ladder himself. "The mother...if she'd waited fifteen seconds. I told her to wait and she didn't, Cait."

"You saved her little girl." She squeezed him tighter. "You did everything you could."

"I was yelling at her to wait. And then…she jumped. I thought maybe there was a chance she'd survive. People fall three stories and survive, but she didn't."

"I'm sorry, Gavin."

Her arms around him helped. She was so calm, and her firmly spoken belief he'd done everything he could eased some of the tightness in his chest. After a long moment, he kissed the side of her neck and pulled away.

"I'm going to take a shower."

"Okay."

Once he'd washed away the grime and smell, he toweled off and pulled on his favorite pair of sweatpants. He went into the bedroom, intending to crawl into his bed and stay there until sleep finally came, but Cait was waiting for him.

"I knew you'd come this way. Come sit down and eat first."

"I'm not really hungry."

"I know. It's not much, but you need something in your stomach."

He sat on the couch, noting that she'd already changed the television channel from the local station, which might show the news, to a random cable channel showing repeats of a crime drama. And when he looked at the paper plate sitting on the coffee table, he actually smiled.

"What is that?" he asked, looking at what appeared to be a slice of toast smeared with peanut butter, with sliced bananas spread over it.

"It's a light meal, but with good stuff to help you get your strength back while you're sleeping. My mom always made it for us when we were sick or too upset to eat."

"What about you?"

"I ate mine while you were in the shower. Now eat."

He did as he was told, and was surprised by how good it was. He'd had peanut butter on English muffins before, but the banana twist was new. And she was right. It did settle his stomach a little, having food in it. She'd also gotten him a small glass of milk, and he drank it all.

Then, instead of going and crawling into the big bed, he laid down on the couch and put his head in Cait's lap. She stroked his hair and he closed his eyes, letting himself relax under her touch.

When her phone chimed, he was surprised to realize he'd been on the verge of sleep. He thought it would be hours before his mind calmed enough to let him drift off.

She reached across him to the coffee table, and he watched her flip the switch to silent before she leaned back and resumed stroking his hair.

"It might be Diane or Carter," he said, unable to keep his voice from sounding flat. "Your mom might need you."

"*You* need me."

He closed his eyes, holding back the words. *I love you.*

He didn't want to say them now, in this moment. Today was dark with loss and sorrow and guilt. When he told Cait how he felt about her, he wanted nothing but happiness on that day.

Maybe he'd take her back to the beach, he thought drowsily. Walking the rocky beach had been one of their favorite dates and it was a perfect excuse to go back. He could picture her with her hair blowing in the ocean breeze. Her cheeks rosy from the cold, but her eyes sparkling with joy.

I love you, Cait.

I love you, too.

Chapter Seventeen

Cait's phone rang at the usual time, which was shortly before she would leave for work. Unless he was busy, Gavin always called her in the mornings. To keep her company while she drank her coffee, he said.

"Good morning," he said when she answered. "It was probably too late to call when I had a chance last night, but how was your shift yesterday?"

"Busy. Pretty much nonstop."

"At least you don't have to shovel snow."

She didn't have to shovel, but a weird March snowstorm had definitely kept EMS on their toes. It had been a heavy snow, due to the warmer temperatures, so they'd been chasing back injuries and cardiac calls all day. "It seems stupid to shovel. It's going to melt, anyway."

He snorted. "I can't even count how many hydrants we shoveled out yesterday. It was somewhere in the area of not-sure-I-can-lift-my-arms-this-morning, so I'm just hoping I can climb into my truck."

"Poor guy. Do you want me to make you breakfast?"

"You're not working?"

"No, we switched things up to accommodate a few sick days across the shifts, so I'm off today."

"I was going to soak in the tub, too."

She didn't blame him. Soaking in that tub was heaven,

and the only thing missing when she did it was Gavin. "Is that a refusal or an invitation?"

"Oh, it's an invitation. Or more like a desperate plea worded badly."

"I'll be there in a little bit, then."

"My day's looking better already."

She was smiling when she hung up. It had been a week since the fire, and Gavin was mostly himself again. She still caught glimpses every once in a while of his sadness and guilt, but she probably would for a while. At least he was laughing again and he'd sounded okay before his shift started yesterday. Going in Tuesday had been tough, and she'd had to resist the urge to call him periodically throughout the day.

But he was enjoying life again, and that's all that mattered to her.

I love you, Cait.

She was very sure Gavin didn't remember saying those words, or that he'd said them in his sleep. And he didn't remember her whispering "I love you, too" back to him.

But Cait remembered, and everything had changed. Now when Gavin looked at her, she knew he loved her and she knew she loved him. There were no hypotheticals anymore. Unless it all went horribly wrong somehow, he was going to be the man she shared her life with.

But first they had to do the *I love you* thing while fully awake and lucid.

And two hours later, when they were naked and up to their shoulders in hot water and scented bubbles— because she liked them and he assured her he was man enough to handle smelling like fruit—she had to admit it was a very nice life. No matter how much time they spent together, even fully clothed, she never got tired of him.

"I love your tub," she said. "I think it's ruined regular bathtubs for me forever. I just settle for showers at home now."

Gavin blew at the bubbles over her shoulder, which never failed to make her laugh. He always tried to blow the bubbles away from her breasts so he could see her nipples, even though it never worked.

"You know," he said, and then paused to kiss the side of her neck. "This could be *your* bathtub, too."

She didn't catch his meaning for a few seconds, but when the words sank in, she stilled. Or maybe she wasn't catching his meaning. He couldn't be asking her to move in with him already. It was too soon.

Sure, she spent as much time with him as she could. And she'd spent the night a few times. Rushing to get home in time to get ready for work was tough on the rare nights she fell asleep in his bed on a work night, and she'd been thinking about the possibility of leaving a few things at his place. Not a lot. Some toiletries, underwear and a uniform, probably.

But moving in with him? That was a big step.

"It makes me nervous when you don't talk," he said, and he tried to be teasing, but she could hear the nerves.

"I'm just trying to wrap my head around what you're talking about."

"I'm talking about you moving in with me."

"It's a big step." She wished they weren't having this conversation in the tub, with his naked body cradling hers and his breath tickling the wisps of hair that had escaped from the messy knot on top of her head.

She wanted to see his face. And she wanted to be able to move and think clearly. Her current state of languid relaxation wasn't ideal for making a huge life decision.

"I know it's a big step," he agreed. "But I like waking

up with you. I like sharing my day and making meals together and I want to come home to you instead of calling you. Not that I don't like talking to you on the phone, but I like talking to you like this a whole lot better."

She did, too, but there was so much to consider. And not only her mom and Carter, though Gavin would probably assume they were first and foremost in her thoughts.

Living together changed a relationship, and she liked what they had right now. Maybe it was selfish, but she liked her time with Gavin being free of things like bills and arguing over big purchases and a million tiny aggravations that added up. Other than a stroll through the mall on a rainy day, they hadn't even shopped together.

You didn't just move in with somebody you hadn't even gone grocery shopping with.

She knew they'd have to navigate those changes as their relationship progressed and it would be a part of making a future together. She just wasn't sure she was ready to make those changes yet.

"I like this, too," she finally said. "But I don't want to rush into that kind of decision and mess things up between us. Do I get to think about it?"

"Of course you do." He chuckled, his breath warm against her chin. "There's no pressure. I just wanted to throw it out there."

She knew him too well to believe it was just a random idea he was tossing out on a whim. But she appreciated that he was willing to give her the space she needed to consider it. And that he didn't question whether or not her need to think about it was because of her mom, even though he probably suspected it.

His hand skimmed over her arm before sliding over to cup her breast. "How about we get out of the tub and, after we dry off, I'll take you out to lunch. I'll dry your back and you can dry mine."

"I don't know. Are you sure you have the strength to thoroughly dry me off after shoveling all that snow?"

He growled and nipped at her shoulder. "Oh, I'll be thorough. Don't you worry about that."

Gavin stood on the doorstep of Diane's house, waiting for somebody to answer the door. Maybe he should have felt at home enough to simply knock and then walk in, but he didn't feel comfortable doing that yet.

When her brother opened the door, he grinned. "Hey, Gavin."

"Hey, Carter. Long time, no see."

They'd been together that morning, playing some basketball. The kid wasn't a regular, by any means, but sometimes he managed to drag his nocturnal teenage self out of bed in time to shoot some hoops.

"Come on in. Mom and Cait are in the kitchen arguing about something."

"Maybe I should wait outside," Gavin said, only half-joking.

But Carter gestured for him to get in the house, so he did. He couldn't hear any yelling or crying, so hopefully their disagreement wasn't too bad. He'd grown up with a sister, so he knew mother-daughter fights could be really unpleasant to witness.

But then Cait was walking toward him, smiling, and he figured no tears was a good sign. "Hi, gorgeous."

She kissed him hello, but it was a quick peck on the lips in deference to her younger brother being in the room. Gavin felt the quick rush of pleasure he always felt when he first saw Cait after being away from her, even for only a day.

He wondered if that would ever stop happening, and really hoped it wouldn't.

"Everything okay?" he asked, and he tipped his head toward Carter when she looked confused. "I heard there was an argument in progress."

"Oh, that. It wasn't really an argument. I forgot to tell her you don't like onions because it never really came up in conversation, and now her life is ruined."

He chuckled. "I'm not a fan of onions, but it won't kill me to eat them. Or I can pick them out and hide them in my napkin when she's not looking."

"She made a New England boiled dinner, and even though I told her she didn't have to, she just finished picking and straining every last bit of onion out and putting it in a separate dish." She laughed at his expression. "Don't worry about it. She likes you."

That was good news, so he shrugged off his worry about Diane being upset. "Did your brother tell you I kicked his ass on the basketball court this morning?"

Carter snorted. "As if. I ran you so ragged on that court, you probably couldn't lift your foot high enough to reach my ass even if you could catch me."

"Kid, I'm faster than you while wearing gear that's half your weight."

The friendly trash talk came to end when Diane walked out of the kitchen. "I thought I heard your voice, Gavin. I'm glad you could make it."

"Thank you for inviting me. It smells delicious." He pulled a candy bar from the pocket of his coat and held it out to her. "Cait told me these are your favorite."

"They are and thank you. That's so sweet." Then she gave him what Gavin thought of as the affectionate-but-slightly-admonishing mom look. "You don't have to bring a gift every time you visit, you know."

He did if he didn't want his dad kicking his ass and, unlike Carter, his old man could actually do it since Gavin couldn't fight back. "It's the least I can do when you're letting me share meals as good as yours with you."

Diane blushed and waved a hand at him before going back to the kitchen. "Carter, pour the drinks, please."

Carter rolled his eyes, but disappeared after his mother. Gavin turned to Cait, who was watching him with a bemused look on her face. He grinned and after shaking her head, she did, too.

"I think charming mothers is your superpower," she said quietly.

"Just one of them." He raised his eyebrows at her. "I have a few."

He caught her hand and tugged her forward for another kiss. Since he'd been waiting all day for it, he let his mouth linger on hers, but not for too long. If it was time for Carter to put drinks on the table, one of them would pop out of the kitchen any second to tell them it was time to eat.

"It sounds like you and Carter had a good time this morning," she said, taking his coat to the closet near the front door to hang it up.

"He fits in well with the other guys. I like having him there."

"And he likes being there." She smiled. "It's good for him, too. He's always in a good mood when he gets home."

Gavin nodded, even though he didn't want to talk about Carter. Or onions or anything but the question burning in his mind.

It had been a week since the day he'd brought up the subject of moving in together and, other than catching

Cait looking at him thoughtfully sometimes, it felt to Gavin as if the conversation had never happened.

Not that he'd expected an instant answer, especially since he'd brought it up while they were naked in his tub, but he'd thought they'd talk about it a little. It wasn't just a matter of them both being on the same page as far as their relationship went. If she was considering it, there would be details to work out. Financial discussions. Closet space. Which brand of toothpaste they'd finally compromise on because having two separate tubes sitting side by side on the vanity was dumb.

The fact she'd said nothing at all made him wonder if she was as invested in making a future together as he was. And rather than rock the boat, he was keeping his mouth shut. Until she was ready to be his full-time, having her part-time was better than not having her in his life at all.

But as they sat down for dinner, Gavin felt restless and the vibe was slightly off. He wasn't sure what, if anything, had happened while they finished putting supper on the table, but Diane and Carter were going out of their way to avoid speaking to each other all of a sudden. And it wasn't his imagination because Cait's gaze kept bouncing back and forth between the two.

And Gavin was a little put out by how much like "company" he still felt. He knew it had nothing to do with the hospitality and everything to do with his frustration at not knowing where he stood with Cait, but he couldn't help it.

They made it almost all the way through dinner before things started going sideways. Carter's mood had been going downhill and the more sullen he got, the more upset Diane got. Her cheerful tone was obviously forced and Cait was doing a lot more moving food around with her fork than eating.

"The carrots are mushy," Carter mumbled, and Diane set her glass down with such a thump they all jumped.

"Feel free to leave them on the plate, then," she said. "Don't be rude in front of guests."

So much for almost being part of the family, Gavin thought, taking another bite of his dinner. The carrots were softer than his mom usually made them, but they were far from mushy. And her seasoning was perfect, though he recognized now wasn't the time to tell her so if he ever wanted Carter to speak to him again. He kept his mouth shut and chewed.

"Whatever," Carter mumbled and, judging by the way his body jerked, one of the women kicked him under the table. He'd bet on it being Cait.

"They're planning the company picnic for next month," Diane said when the next few minutes drew out in uncomfortable silence. "I told them you'd both be there."

"Great." How Carter packed so much unpleasant tone into one word was beyond Gavin, but he had a knack for it.

Luckily, it looked as if everybody had eaten all they had appetites for and Gavin could start counting the minutes until he and Cait could get out of there.

Diane ignored Carter and smiled at her daughter. "Unless you have a date planned with Gavin for that weekend, of course."

It was the word *date* that finally did it. To his mind, it implied a casual relationship and it felt as if Diane was trying to maintain a distance or disconnect between him and Cait. He was tired of it.

And before Cait could say anything, he opened his

mouth. "Hopefully she doesn't have a date planned with anybody *else*, since I asked Cait to move in with me."

He'd intended for the words to sound light, almost joking, but they didn't come out of his mouth that way, and he knew when he heard Cait's sharp intake of breath that he'd made a critical mistake.

"You're moving out?" Carter asked his sister, his fork frozen halfway between his plate and his mouth.

"I…I had no idea," Diane said, and her expression when she looked at her daughter didn't bode well for the rest of the night.

"We're just talking about it, Mom."

That wasn't really true, Gavin thought. He'd been talking about it. Cait had been silent on the issue since he brought it up, and she was carefully avoiding looking at him right now.

"I didn't realize it was that serious," Diane said in a trembling voice. Tears shimmered in her eyes and Gavin felt a strong pang of regret and guilt. "I… That's wonderful."

"Mom, I think—"

"We'll be fine, of course," Diane continued. Her words were rushed, and Gavin got the impression she was talking more to herself than to Cait. "And Carter's doing so much better in school and everything. He'll be okay, too, I think."

"Thanks, Mom," Carter said, his voice twisted with sarcasm again. "It's good to know you have faith in me."

"Maybe you should give me a reason to," she snapped, and he heard Cait's long sigh.

"It's not like you give me a chance to do anything. You have Cait to do everything for you, so what the hell do you need me for, anyway?"

"Watch your language. And at least your sister doesn't make my life any harder than it already is."

"Whatever." He stood so abruptly his chair fell over backward. After picking it up and slamming it onto its legs, he took his plate into the kitchen and they all winced at the sound of it clattering in the sink.

Diane burst into tears.

Cait tipped her head back and stared at the ceiling for a few seconds and then stood, while Gavin just sat there and tried to figure out how the hell to make everything better.

After Diane stood and walked quickly to the kitchen while trying to hide her face from him, Gavin stood. "I'm sorry, Cait. I should go."

She said nothing, her lips pinched together, as she walked to the front door with him and retrieved his coat from the closet.

"I can't believe you did that," she said finally, anger practically radiating from her body.

"She was talking about not knowing if you have a date planned with me. We're well beyond just dating, Cait, and she needs to know that and accept it."

"She just meant that she didn't know if we had made plans together for that day. Calling it a date was an easy word to sum it up, and she didn't mean anything by it."

"You hadn't talked to her about it at all." He didn't bother making it a question since he already knew the answer.

"About what?"

"About the fact I asked you to move in with me. It's kind of a big deal. Or at least I thought it was." He ran a hand over his hair, trying to calm down. "You've been downplaying our relationship to her, haven't you? So she wouldn't think you're pulling away from her."

"I haven't downplayed anything. I just don't talk about my private life a lot. And you should have respected that instead of going around me to my mother, as if I'd give in because we were in front of other people."

"Give in? Jesus, Cait. I was asking you to share my life with me, not be my hostage."

"You know what I mean."

He didn't, actually, but he heard a door slam and was reminded they weren't alone. "Look, why don't we go to my place so we can sit down and talk about this privately?"

"I'm not going anywhere with you, Gavin. I have to stay here and deal with the fallout from you making them believe I'm moving out."

"You've gotta be joking." Even though he knew he'd spoken out of turn, he couldn't keep the anger at bay. "We need to talk about this, Cait, and we can't do it standing in front of your door."

"You saw what's happening in there and, trust me, it only gets worse from here."

"What *I* saw was a mom and her teenage son being a typical mom and teenager and you trying to mediate instead of letting them hash it out."

"You know how my mom is—"

"I don't think it's your mom. It's you, Cait."

He regretted the words as soon as they left his mouth, even though he didn't think he was wrong. Her face paled and her eyes widened with hurt before narrowing in anger.

"Who the hell are you to judge my family?"

"Just the guy trying to be part of your life." Since he'd started it, he might as well get it out there. "Your mom didn't just scare Carter when your stepfather died. She scared you, too, and you're not moving past that fear. You can't go forward with your own life until you get past it."

She stared at him for what seemed like an eternity, her face pale and her lips tight, and then lifted her chin. "I guess if you don't think I'm moving forward, there's not much sense in you hanging around then, is there?"

"Cait, don't—"

"It's time for you to leave." She tossed him his coat and nodded her head toward the door. "Don't make it any worse. Just…just go."

A minute later, he was sitting in his truck, staring at the door she'd practically slammed behind him and unable to bring himself to move. Maybe it would open and she'd run down the steps. He could tell her he was sorry. That he was an asshole and he never should have said anything to Diane about asking her to move in with him.

But he didn't know what to say about the words he'd flung at Cait. He knew they'd hurt her, but he wasn't sure he could bring himself to take them back. No matter what happened now, he still meant them. Cait couldn't look forward to a future with him while living in the past.

With a hand that was shaking a little, he put the truck in gear and backed out of the driveway.

It was an argument. They happened all the time. Even the happiest of couples fought sometimes, and then they worked through their disagreements and moved on.

Cait stared at her ceiling, ignoring the light shining through the window and the sounds of moving around elsewhere in the house.

It was just a fight, she told herself again, wondering how many times she'd have to think it before she actually believed it.

It hadn't felt like the argument of a happy couple. It had felt more like a breakup.

She rolled onto her stomach, burying her face in her pillow, as somebody—presumably her mother—tapped on her door. She didn't want to talk to anybody right now.

But the slight squeak of old hinges told her whoever it was didn't care if she wanted company or not. "Honey, are you awake?"

"I have a headache, Mom. I just want to be left alone."

But, of course, the bed dipped as her mom sat on the edge of it. A second later, she felt a hand on her shoulder. "You need to eat something."

She'd just throw it up, if she could even get it past the lump in her throat to begin with. "I'm not hungry."

"I'm sorry, Cait. I really am. I didn't mean to ruin dinner."

"You didn't do anything wrong. He blindsided you, talking about me moving in with him, but we've only talked about it once."

"And I should have been happy for you. Instead, your brother and I got upset and ruined everything."

Cait really didn't want to have this conversation. Not now. Not in an hour. Maybe never. It was like a never-ending loop she wanted to stop. She rolled onto her side and looked at her mom.

"If he can't deal with a family who's not 1950s TV perfect, that's his problem. We're doing okay."

"You should go talk to him, honey."

"There's not much to say."

"Of course there is. Every couple fights and you know that. Duke and I were very happy together, but we still fought sometimes."

"I know." She'd spent the night telling herself that.

"But this one's been simmering between us for a while and maybe we didn't have a strong enough foundation yet."

"This is how you build a strong foundation. You find the cracks and you work together to fix them."

Cait didn't have the heart to tell her she couldn't see a way to fix their cracks. Gavin wanted her to be sure moving in with him was the right thing to do and she wasn't. She wanted to be, but look what had happened when he brought it up.

Every time her mother got upset like that, Cait remembered the fear in Carter's voice the night he'd called her. She relived trying to get her mother—limp and sobbing—up and out of the bathroom because she was afraid she might actually take her own life. She'd put her in bed and then climbed in beside her, afraid to let her out of her sight.

Cait knew they'd come a long way together, but she still remembered that fear and utter helplessness when the tears started. She knew how bad it could be. Gavin didn't.

Her mom would take that on herself, though, and beat herself up some more, so she just smiled. "Maybe. We'll see how it goes."

"No, you don't wait and see how it goes. If you want to keep Gavin in your life, he has to know that. And it goes both ways. The only way a relationship survives the ups and downs is if both of you want it enough to fight for it."

Her mom's words stayed with her throughout the long, miserable day, and that's how she came to have her phone in her hand later that afternoon. Can we talk?

The response took a few minutes, and they felt like the longest minutes of Cait's life.

I'm home. Or I can meet you somewhere.

I'll come there.

Whenever you're ready. I'll be here.

By the time he'd buzzed her up to his apartment, Cait's stomach was tied into so many knots, she was surprised she could stand up straight. And when he opened the door, all of those knots twisted.

He was wearing his favorite sweats—which were so worn, he probably couldn't get away with wearing them out of the house—and an equally threadbare T-shirt that bore a faded and cracked logo from the fire academy. They were his comfort clothes, which let her know he'd had as miserable a night and day as she had.

"I'm glad you're here," he said as he closed the door behind her. "All day I've been wondering if I should call, but I didn't know if you'd answer."

"I would have," she said quietly. She didn't know what to do with herself, so she finally pulled out a chair and sat at the table.

What she wanted to do was throw herself into his arms, but that wouldn't be enough. She wanted them to be *okay* again because while hugging him now might be a comfort, it was hugging him tomorrow and every day after that that mattered.

He pulled out the chair across from her and sat down, scrubbing his hands over his face before he spoke. "I'm sorry about last night."

"Me, too." She was twisting her fingers together, so she clasped her hands together and set them in her lap.

"I did a lot of speaking before thinking and I shouldn't have."

"And I am sincerely sorry I told your mom I asked you to move in with me. It was stupid and I shouldn't have done it. I should have let you tell her when you were ready."

"Or when I thought *she* was ready." When he looked away, she knew she'd struck a nerve. "Oh, that's right. You already decided she's ready and that it's me who's not."

"I'm not saying it won't be an adjustment, for all of you. But I think you're not even giving her a chance to make that adjustment. You're just assuming she can't hold things together without you."

"You saw how it went last night."

"And again, I saw a teenager have an attitude with his mother and she got upset. You can't stop that from happening, and they need to figure out how to communicate with each other without you in between them. It's not only wrong for you, but it's not doing them any favors, either."

Coming here so soon after the fight and on little sleep had been a bad idea, she thought. She didn't want to hear any more of this. Knowing he'd been judging her, even blaming her for enabling the situation that was tearing them apart, was too much. But she knew if she walked out the door right now, she might never cross his threshold again.

"You're always doing stuff for your family," she said, very carefully keeping her voice calm. "How is that any different?"

"Because my family also does stuff for *me*. Yeah, I'm always there for them if they need me, but they're also there if I need them. When's the last time anybody was there for *you,* Cait?"

"If I need one of them, they'll be there for me."

"You do need them. You need for them to tell you that they can handle living in a house together without you." He ran his hand over his hair and she tried not to notice the way the cowlick refused to stay down. "Family's supposed to be a give-and-take thing but when it comes to yours, I see a whole lot of taking from you and not much in the way of giving, because you've made it a pattern."

"So is it them or is it me? Make up your mind."

"It's not that simple. No, she's not coping with things like she could be, either. She doesn't *have* to, Cait, because you do it for her and you can't see that she doesn't need you to."

"This was a mistake." She stood up and so did he, but he didn't move around the table toward her. "It doesn't matter how much we talk about this, we're not going to agree."

"I'm not trying to make you choose between your family and me. I'm really not."

"It's not about you at all, Gavin."

"No, it's not about me. It's about *us.*" He blew out a breath. "I don't think your family situation has changed much since we first got together and I…I want us to move forward together and I don't think you can do that right now. And based on how hard you're pushing back at me, I don't know if you will be anytime soon."

Her skin prickled with heat as she heard what he didn't say. *And I don't know if I can wait.*

"I'm going to go," she said as she walked toward the door, feeling numb. She couldn't give him what he needed from her. "I don't want to do this anymore."

He caught her arm. "Cait, don't leave like this."

"There's no sense in staying here and dragging it out. We're talking in circles and we're not going to get anywhere and it hurts too much."

His hand fell away and, in that moment—when he let her walk out the door—Cait knew what true heartbreak felt like.

Chapter Eighteen

One second Gavin was standing on the edge of a roof, and the next, Jeff's knee buckled and he fell sideways and Gavin was holding on to the small lip of the roof, with one arm, while scrambling to get his other hand up.

Then he felt a hand close over his wrist before other hands grabbed the back of his coat and hauled him back onto the roof.

Pride be damned. He stayed there for a minute, breathing hard and trying to process what the hell had just happened.

"Holy shit, Boudreau," he heard Danny say.

"Yeah, that," he said and there was some weak laughter.

It wasn't even a fire. The maintenance man had gone on the roof to check the equipment, smelled something weird and called the fire department.

The weird smell turned out to be an employee of the building smoking pot on his lunch break and, after reporting that info to the building manager to do with as he saw fit, they'd taken their time up on the roof. The sun was shining and spring was around the corner.

Danny had been telling a funny story about his kid and then, bam, Gavin was dangling four stories over the sidewalk.

It was Jeff who hauled him to his feet. "I'm so fucking sorry, man. So fucking sorry."

Gavin mustered a grin and slapped him in the shoulder. "You tripped, man. I should have been fast enough to get out of the way."

Jeff looked like he was going to say something else, but then he just shook his head.

Maybe Gavin's reflexes would have been enough if his head had been in the game, where it belonged. But then Danny started talking about Ashley and Jackson, which made Gavin think about Cait, and he hadn't been able to dodge the gut punch he got every time he thought about her.

He missed her. Every second of every day, he felt her absence. He even dreamed about her, so not only was there no respite in sleep, but he started every day with a renewed sense of loss.

Back at quarters, Gavin went about the regular routine of the firehouse, trying not to think about Cait and only managing to think about her more. The other guys were giving him a wide berth and he wasn't sure if they were giving him space after his brush with being sidewalk art, or if his grief was actually surrounding him like some kind of invisible force field of emotion.

It wasn't until they'd all gathered in the kitchen to eat that he saw Jeff again. He'd seen Jeff's wife earlier and figured she'd stopped by for a quick visit, either coincidentally or because Jeff had told her what happened. He'd seen her leave a little while later, but Jeff had stayed in the bunk room.

Now that he really thought about the sequence of events, it was weird and he spooned pulled pork from the slower cooker onto his bun with a feeling of trepidation. Sure, he'd almost accidentally killed Gavin, but shit happened. Hell, Grant had knocked his first LT unconscious with a ladder his second week on the job and put him out of commission with a concussion.

Gavin wasn't the only one who felt it coming. Even once the meal was done, nobody left the kitchen. They all lingered, restless and waiting for the shoe to drop.

"I talked to Cobb," Jeff finally said, and they all got quiet. "And my wife. I'm putting in my papers."

Nobody spoke. They shifted in seats and fidgeted with napkins or whatever was at hand, but Gavin didn't know what to say and apparently neither did anybody else. Only Rick didn't look surprised.

"My knee is done, boys, and so am I. It's one thing to push through the pain for a little while, but it's not getting any better. Lately it's been even worse, and I knew there would come a day it gave out on me and every day I got more terrified it was going to happen on the job. When lives are depending on me. It gave out on me today and that's why I fell into you, kid."

Gavin couldn't say he was surprised—he spent way too much time with the man to miss the signs of his knee's deterioration—but he wasn't prepared for the swell of emotion he felt.

"I've been having nightmares about it for a while," Jeff continued. "And after today... I know I just can't do it anymore."

"Today was a fluke," Grant said, and Gavin wasn't surprised he pushed back. They might work different trucks, but the Ladder 37 and Engine 59 crews were a team. A family. They worked together and lived together. They rolled out together. "There's always the potential for an accident, but we got through it. You pulled him back up."

"But with me out there, the potential is stronger and

we—or at least *I*—can't discount what happened today. It's just plain luck that Gavin caught himself. I almost killed him today and I can't brush that off. And you guys shouldn't let me."

Gavin didn't say anything. Not because he'd been the one who almost got hurt. It wasn't the first time he'd almost bit it on the job, and it wouldn't be the last. But he was watching the others, and when Rick leaned back against his seat with his mouth set in a grim line—not saying a word—he knew Jeff was really leaving.

If Jeff was just in a mood because of the day's events, Rick would be telling him to sleep on it. He'd offer to take him out for a night on the town, or at least a beer or two at Kincaid's. But it was obvious the LT thought Jeff was making the right decision, and a lot of pressure from the rest of them was only going to make Jeff feel shittier than he already did.

"It's not just about you guys, though, or Gavin," Jeff continued when the silence became heavy. "I'm pretty much maxed out on over-the-counter meds to get through the day. In this fucking cold weather, it's not enough and I…I know a guy who said he'd hook me up with some prescription stuff under the table."

"Shit," somebody muttered under his breath, though Gavin knew they were all thinking it.

"I got kids," Jeff said. "I have a wife and my kids and I can't do that to them so I said no, but I considered it and that was a wake-up call. The best thing for my family is for me to find work that isn't physical. If I take some of the stress off my body, I can ease off the medications and take care of myself and them the right way."

"You've gotta make the decision that's best for you and your family," Chris said, nodding. "It'll hurt like hell to see you go, but not as much as seeing you lose your family because you get hooked on drugs."

They all nodded, and Jeff cleared his throat. His eyes glistened and he had to try two more times before he could speak again. "When I say this is the best way I can take care of my family, I mean you guys, too."

There was a *lot* of throat clearing and sniffling then, so Rick stood up and spoke. "It's effective immediately. Medical leave until the paperwork processes and all that crap. Anybody here have a problem with Derek Gilman?"

Nobody did. He was pretty well liked throughout the community, but especially in his own house. They'd all worked with him a few times when guys got shifted around to fill in for sick or vacation days.

"We're going to reach out and see about bringing Derek in to fill Jeff's spot. Get him off Saturdays since he gets his kids every other weekend."

And that was that. A floater arrived to cover the rest of Jeff's shift, and they all tried to keep things light as he packed up his things. The goodbye was excruciating, though. Even though they knew they'd see him around, it would never be the same again.

When Jeff was gone, Gavin chose to skip watching TV or working out and went to his bunk. Stretching out, he put his hands under his head and wished he could talk to Cait.

She read him like nobody else, even his mom, and knew when he needed a hug or if he'd rather have a laugh. She listened to him and she always seemed to know the right thing to say or do.

Jesus, what a week. He'd lost the love of his life, almost died and said goodbye to a member of his crew. And he couldn't turn to the only person in the world he wanted to talk to right now.

Gavin put his forearm over his eyes and blew out a breath.

He had no fucking idea anymore how he was supposed to get through life without Cait.

Cait was not in the mood to deal with anybody's crap today. She'd slept badly and she had her second teen boy in three days from the same rink in her ambulance. The first had taken a puck to the face. This one had been gashed by a skate blade.

She'd enjoyed watching hockey until she became an EMT.

She'd also hated knowing Gavin played sometimes, but he was a grown man who made his own choices. And it really wasn't her problem anymore.

Missing him every minute of the damn day *was* her problem, though. She couldn't count the number of times she'd picked up her phone to call him or send him a text message, only to remember they were over.

Over.

Even that simple word hurt. It had been almost a week and it was still as painful as the first night she went to bed knowing there would be no Gavin in her life tomorrow.

Once they'd transferred their patient to the ER staff, Tony gave her a look. "You need to work on your bedside face right now, Tasker. I think you scared that poor kid more than the blood did."

"Yeah, I just… I know. I need to get my shit together."

"Maybe we can sneak an ice cream cone before the next call. A twist with jimmies makes everything better."

Cait didn't know if it would help, but it wouldn't hurt. She nodded and shoved the stretcher toward Tony to push before turning toward the exit.

And it was just her luck that, across the other end of the department, she saw Gavin. He was with Grant, who had an ice bag held to his head, but was laughing.

Seeing Gavin at the end of the hall hit her so hard, she couldn't breathe for a few seconds.

"I'm going to the restroom," she said, stopping so abruptly that Tony almost rammed her with the stretcher as she turned her back to the other two guys.

But then he must have spotted Gavin because the confusion turned to anger—the kind of big-brotherly anger that could cause a problem.

"Do you want me to go kick his ass?" Tony asked, not taking his eyes off Gavin.

That startled a laugh out of her, and she shook her head. "Trust me, if I wanted his ass kicked, I'm more than capable of doing it myself."

"Okay. Do you want me to at least threaten to kick his ass? Wait, scratch that. *Can* I threaten to kick his ass? Please? I can be scary."

"I'd rather we just avoid him altogether, to be honest." She tried to sound like she didn't care, but her heart was breaking and Tony must have heard it in her voice. His expression softened as he looked at her, and that just made Cait feel even worse. She did *not* want to cry in the ER, dammit. "Don't say anything to him. I'll be right back."

Once she was alone, Cait filled her hands with cold water from the sink and lowered her face to it. It wasn't cold enough to shock her out of her current emotional state, but she didn't think even sticking her face in a bucket of ice water would do it. She just wanted to keep the threatening tears at bay and make her eyes look less puffy.

But she knew every minute she was in the bathroom

was a minute she was leaving her partner outside with his anger on her behalf and no supervision, so she dried her face and hands and gave herself a hard look in the mirror. She could do this.

Sure enough, when she opened the door to leave the restroom, she could hear Tony's voice, and he sounded pissed.

"What the fuck did you think you were doing? Do you know what she's been through with her family? If you couldn't handle it, you should have left her alone."

"Pretty sure my personal relationships are none of your fucking business, pal."

"If you two intend to do something stupid, take it out to the parking lot," Karen Shea barked at them. "I don't have time to deal with your mess."

Great. Now they had *everybody's* attention, she was sure. And even if they didn't name her, bystanders would see an EMT and a firefighter in a verbal pissing match and then see the EMT's partner was a woman. Two plus two.

"Look, I know you're just watching out for your partner," she heard Gavin say to Tony, "and I get that. But if there's any chance at all that we can work things out, you and I having a beef won't help that any."

Cait's heart skipped a beat. *We can work things out.* Hope burned through her, but it fizzled almost as quickly.

Nothing had changed. Their situations remained the same.

"No, it's you being a self-centered asshole that won't help any," Tony responded, no less heated than before.

Cait winced and decided enough was enough. They weren't going to get anywhere but written up and she wasn't going to spend the rest of her life hiding from Gavin. Their paths crossed too often for that.

She stepped out and walked to Tony's side. There was no way around looking at Gavin, so she forced herself to meet his gaze. "Hi, guys."

"Hey, Cait," Grant said, while Gavin said nothing.

He looked as bad as she felt, Cait thought. Tired and sad, with his mouth set in a grim line. She wanted to go to him and hold him, comforting him until he smiled again. Until they both smiled again.

Forcing herself to look away, she pointed at Grant's head, because she couldn't shut off friendships any more than she could shut off her feelings for his best friend. "What happened to you?"

"Oh, you know, on the job. Being a hero." He shrugged. "Firefighter stuff."

Gavin rolled his eyes. "MVA. He tripped on a line and hit his head on the edge of the open car door."

"Was I or was I not on the job at the time?"

"I would have let it slide if you hadn't added the hero part. The only heroic thing about it was how many curse words you were able to string together before repeating one when you were lying in the street."

Cait found herself smiling at their familiar banter, but then her gaze locked with Gavin's again and her amusement died before it became actual laughter. She couldn't do this, but she couldn't just walk away.

"What about your helmet?" she asked Grant when the silence stretched on between her and Gavin.

He shifted his weight from one foot to the other and, after looking at Gavin, rolled his eyes. "I had my helmet off because I thought there was a bug in it, and I was trying to check it quick. And that's why I tripped in the first place."

"Concussion?"

"Nope. Just hit my head and as long as I don't develop any weird symptoms, I'm good to go."

"Good." None of them seemed to have anything more to say, so Cait mustered a fake smile. "We've gotta run. Take care."

Then she turned and walked away, with Tony pulling the stretcher at her side. She wasn't even sure she was going the right way, but it was a hospital. There were a ton of exits to choose from and she'd find the ambulance bay eventually. Or Tony would.

"I'm sorry, Cait," Tony said when they were out of earshot. "He saw me and instead of walking away, he wanted to ask me how you're doing. I lost it a little."

"It's fine. I just want everything to stay professional because we're going to run into him sometimes and I just want to…"

The words died as her throat tightened around the knot of unshed tears. She just wanted to wake up and find out this entire mess was nothing but a nightmare and she was still in Gavin's bed, with his body curled around hers.

When the seemingly endless shift was finally over, Cait turned down Tony's invitation to join him and Rob and the kids for dinner in favor of going home, pulling her covers up over her head and crying some more.

But her mom gave her a long look when she walked in, and Cait's heart clenched at the sadness she saw there. She didn't have room in her life today for more pain—no matter whose it was. "You okay, Mom?"

"No, I'm not."

Shit, please not today. Cait wasn't sure she could take much more. "What's the matter?"

"Let's sit on the couch and talk for a minute."

Cait wasn't sure what to make of it, since if her mom

was upset, there were usually tears by now. But her mom's eyes were dry. "Where's Carter?"

"He went to his friend's for dinner. They're having a barbecue just because it's finally warm enough, according to them, and I said he could go because he needs to spend more time with friends."

So it wasn't about Carter. "What's going on, Mom?"

"I talked to a family therapist today. I made some appointments."

Cait felt her eyes widen. "What changed your mind?"

"You." She said it so matter-of-factly, Cait recoiled. "I refused to see a therapist because I didn't see anything wrong with not being able to let Duke go. But there is something wrong with not being able to let *you* go and it cost you Gavin."

The one-two punch of his name and the sudden tears in her mom's eyes were almost Cait's undoing.

She was tired of being strong. She was tired of people needing her. When was it *her* turn to go to bed and stay there for days, sobbing her heart out?

"You didn't cost me Gavin," she said. "I cost myself Gavin. And he cost himself me. We just aren't ready for the same things and—"

"You *are* ready for the same things Gavin wants. *I'm* the reason you think you're not ready."

"Mom, it's *not* your fault."

"You need to go live your life, Cait. And I need to live mine."

"Even if I packed my stuff and left right now, it doesn't change what happened between Gavin and me, Mom."

"Only if you get stubborn about it." Her mom sighed. "Listen, honey. I don't know how to explain it. It's… Look at it like this. I've been swimming my entire life, but I almost drowned once and you pulled me out of the water. And now you've been swimming with me because I remember what it felt like to almost drown and having you rescue me. And you swim with me because you're afraid I'll almost drown again. But I *can* swim, Cait. I won't drown and I won't take your brother down with me."

Tears slid over Cait's cheeks. "I know you can swim, Mom. And Carter can swim, too."

"It's time for you to go, honey. And I hope to God you can work things out with Gavin because he loves you and I know you love him. But even if you don't, or if it takes a while to get back there with him, you need to go find your own happiness."

Cait laughed through her tears. "Are you throwing me out?"

"Yes." Her mom made a sound that was part laugh and part sob and reached for the box of tissues on the end table. "Not right this minute, obviously. But it's time to start planning what you're going to do."

It was, and Cait knew it now, but she couldn't picture herself moving on with her life without Gavin in it. It hurt too much to even try.

Her mom said it was time to find her own happiness, but Cait knew she'd already found it and she'd thrown it away. But she didn't know if she had the strength to show up at his door again only to find out there was no chance of getting back what they'd lost.

"You should go home."

Gavin looked at Aidan, who was leaning on his pool cue and scowling at him. "I'm waiting for my turn."

"You're not here to shoot pool. You're looking for a fight, so that beer's going to be your last."

"It's my first." And it wasn't even half gone, despite

his urge to chug it and keep chugging another and another until he was so shit-faced he didn't think about Cait anymore.

"And your last. Lydia's not going to give you another one and, if you bust this place up, Tommy's going to toss you out on your ass. Or I will."

"So you marry the owner's daughter and now you're king shit around here?"

Aidan chuckled, though it wasn't really a humorous sound. "It's not going to be me who takes a swing at you, kid. It's going to be those guys at table four you've been giving the stink eye for the last half-hour."

"Fuck them."

"Waking up tomorrow with a hangover, all busted up, with pissed-off friends isn't going to make it feel any better."

It wasn't the words that broke through. It was the concern in Aidan's voice, and Gavin's awareness that he'd been there himself and he was just trying to help. The fight went out of him, and he took a sip of his beer to give himself a second or two so his voice didn't crack.

"My apartment feels so fucking empty," he finally said.

"I know what that feels like and it sucks."

"Grant's out with Wren and I didn't want to put my shitty mood on my parents or Jill and the kids, so I thought it would be better to hang out here." He shook his head. "But you're right. Being an asshole won't make me feel any better tomorrow."

"I can go home with you, if you want. Watch a game or something."

"Thanks, but I'm just going to go. I'll put something boring on and hope I nod off on the couch or something."

"Reach out if you change your mind."

Gavin saw the concerned look Lydia gave him as he walked toward the door, so he mustered up a reassuring smile and waved goodbye.

He'd walked to Kincaid's—not wanting the temptation of his truck if he tried to drink Cait's memory away—and he thought about calling a cab, but maybe the fresh air would do him good.

It was a chilly night and he kept a good pace. It wasn't as if his thoughts were good company, anyway. Just a constant loop of beating himself up for losing Cait and then trying to figure out some way to fix it. It couldn't end this way.

Gavin refused to believe there was nothing left but awkward interactions when they crossed paths on the job. He could fix it. He just needed to figure out how.

He was jogging up the front steps, pulling his keys out of his pocket, when he realized somebody was sitting on the top step.

He stopped abruptly, wondering if he was going to have a problem, before he realized it was Cait.

"Jesus, Cait. It's freezing. How long have you been sitting here?"

She pushed back the hood of her sweatshirt and stood up. In the light, he could see the signs she'd cried recently, and his heart twisted in his chest. "Not long. Your truck's here, so I thought you were home but I buzzed and got no answer."

"I was at Kincaid's. You should have called. Or sent a text."

Her mouth twisted in a sad smile. "I didn't want to give you the opportunity to tell me not to come over."

"Never." The word popped out of his mouth without thought because it was the truest thing he'd ever said. "I'll never not want you here with me."

Her eyes welled up again and he jogged up the last few steps so he could pull her into his embrace. She wrapped her arms around him and squeezed, her face pressed into his coat.

He held her close, feeling her body shake. He kissed her hair as their arms tightened around each other even more. "I've missed holding you."

Cait nodded against his shoulder and it felt as if the crushing weight that had been suffocating him was lifted. This was all that mattered.

"Let's go inside," he said after a few minutes of holding her. "You must be freezing."

"Not anymore," she said, using the sleeve of her coat to mop at her face as she pulled away.

Once they were inside his apartment, they made quick work of taking off their coats and boots, and Cait grabbed a paper towel to wipe her eyes again.

"We need to talk," she said.

"Can I hold you while we talk?" He didn't want to let her go and some part of him felt that as long as they were touching, they could talk through anything.

She walked straight into his arms, though this time she rested her face against his chest instead of burying it in his shoulder. "I've missed you so much."

"My life's broken, Cait," he admitted, since he knew there was no more holding back from her. "Without you, it's not whole anymore. And slapping emotional duct tape on the cracks isn't going to heal them. Those pieces aren't going to knit back together no matter how much time I give them."

When she pulled back to smile up at him through her tears, he felt hope for the first time since she walked out of his door. "Emotional duct tape?"

"That's what it's felt like since you left. Like my heart

and my life are breaking apart and I keep slapping duct tape on the cracks, but it's not enough." And with her looking up at him with those dark eyes, he went all in. "I love you, Cait."

"I love you, too."

And just like that, he could breathe again. The ground was no longer shifted under him and everything would be okay. "From now on, no matter what, that's all that matters. We love each other and we can figure out anything else together."

"You were right before," she said quietly, "about me being a crutch for my mom and enabling her to lean on me when she didn't need to. I didn't want to face it, I guess, and rejecting that meant rejecting you and I'm so sorry."

"I'm the one who's sorry because whether it was true or not, that's your relationship with your mother and I had no place butting into it."

"You did, though. If we're going to make a life together, there are no *places* or butting in because we're totally each other's business and sometimes taking care of somebody means helping them face truths they don't want to. I'll do better at being taken care of."

"I want to make a life with you. I want to take care of you and I want you to take care of me. And together we'll take care of our families and, when the time is right, take care of our own family."

"I want that, too. I don't think I knew how much until I thought we were over. I thought I lost you."

The thought of her hurting almost killed him. "I'm going to spend the rest of my life making sure you never feel like that again."

She smiled, and this time there were no tears or shadows in her eyes. This was his Cait and he had her back. "Never?"

"Never." He ran his thumb across her bottom lip. "Do you trust me?"

"Completely."

"I'm going to love you for the rest of my life, Cait."

Epilogue

Two months later

"See? I told you the secret to the neighbors not complaining about the noise is to invite the neighbors to the party," Gavin whispered in Cait's ear.

"I've never seen so many people in this backyard before."

"We've got a lot of people who love us." He shrugged, which she felt since she was tucked under his arm, leaning against the fence. "And the neighbors."

Their parents had insisted on a joint family event to celebrate Gavin putting an engagement ring on Cait's finger after a romantic walk on the beach, but they'd managed—with his dad's help—to contain the two moms to a barbecue. Diane's backyard was bigger, so it and the small cape were full of family—including their coworkers—and friends. It was noisy, but Cait was loving every minute of it.

Gavin's hand strayed down her back toward her ass. "How long do we have to stay?"

"Until the end. Can you imagine us getting out of here without either of our moms noticing?"

"Didn't you have a bedroom here?" He bumped his hip against hers, making her laugh.

"One, I'm not having sex with you in my mother's house. And Michelle and Noah are staying in my old room."

Across the yard, she saw her sister chasing her young nephew, who'd managed to snag a cupcake from the table. Her brother-in-law hadn't been able to get the leave time, but when Michelle had told her there was no way she was missing her engagement party, Cait had burst into tears. They'd had a good cry together via FaceTime and were closer now than they'd been in a long time.

"I guess I'll make it until we get home," Gavin said, his voice heavy with exaggerated sorrow. "And there *is* cake."

"I know which bakery your mom ordered the cake from and, trust me, we want to stay." She tugged at his hand. "Come on. Let's go mingle before you talk me into doing something we'll never live down."

It wasn't easy to keep track, but Cait did her best to make sure they talked to everybody at their party. Derek, who'd fit right into the Ladder 37 crew, was there with his kids. Grant was also there, of course, but this time he'd brought Wren with him. She was a pretty blonde who was reserved, but seemed friendly.

"Grant wanted her to meet everybody, but Kincaid's isn't really her thing," Gavin whispered to her as they watched Grant handing Wren a soda.

"He looks happy." It was harder to tell with his girlfriend.

"Not as happy as I am."

She slapped his arm. "Not everything's a competition."

"Wrong," Scott said as he walked by them carrying a plate of food. "I don't even know what you're talking about, but everything's a competition."

"And someday you'll win one," Aidan called from a few feet away.

"Cait!"

She heard her mom calling her name and finally spotted her on the back deck. She was sitting in a lawn chair next to Gavin's mother and, if she had to guess, she'd say the two women had nailed down 70 or 80 percent of her wedding plans since setting out the fruit punch.

"I'll be right back," she said to Gavin, who was deeply involved in a six-way argument with the other guys about who'd done a better job of manning the grill.

As she walked, she watched the two women with their heads together, over-talking each other in their excitement. Yeah, she thought. Definitely wedding plans.

She didn't mind. Her mom was happy. Carter had achieved average teenager attitude. They still had rough patches and Cait still got phone calls. But she'd learned she could talk them through things and rarely had to show up in person. Gavin encouraged them constantly and now that they only called her when they really needed her shoulder to lean on, he was a lot more patient about it.

She knew the family therapist was a huge help, but she also suspected Carter showing up to Saturday morning basketball had also made a difference as he and Gavin grew closer. Nobody could ever replace Duke, but having a solid brother-in-law in his life would help.

"What are you two whispering about up here?" she asked when she reached them. After pulling a chair up next to her mom's, she sat.

"Okay, we know it's a *little* early yet," Gavin's mom said, "but we were talking about wedding gowns and we might have been looking at them on our phones and…"

"We don't know what kind of wedding you plan to

have," her mom finished. "I know you don't like dressing up, but you're not going to do the courthouse thing on us, are you?"

"I always thought I'd be happy to have a small wedding and maybe wear a skirt or something." Cait laughed when their faces fell in unison, and then she looked across the yard to her future husband. He was looking back at her and he winked. "But I remember the look on his face when he saw me in that red dress on Valentine's Day and I want to see that again. I want that look on his face when he sees me at the end of the aisle."

"Oh, thank goodness," Gavin's mom said, while her own mother actually clapped her hands together.

"Mom, you know what suits me better than I do. You two can dress shop to your heart's content and once you've narrowed it down to a few choices, we'll have a girls' day out—us and Jill, if she can make it, and maybe Michelle by FaceTime—and try them on before we splurge on desserts and wine."

"You're definitely going to be my favorite daughter-in-law," his mom said, and they all laughed.

Tony's kids went running by, screaming and waving water guns in the air, with Carter on their heels.

"Carter," Cait called, stopping him in his tracks. "Tell me you didn't put water in those."

He just grinned and took off after the kids again, just in time to hear a high-pitched yelp from somewhere in the yard.

"It's just water," her mom said when Cait started to get out of her chair. "Let Carter be a kid with the little ones for a while. People will dry."

Thirty minutes later, the moms decided it was time for cake. Gavin's mom smiled at her, before holding up her hands in an *I don't know* gesture. "When I said I ordered the cake, what I really meant was that I ensured that ordering the cake was checked off the list by giving the name of the bakery and the number of guests to Grant."

"Oh, no."

Sure enough, Grant was looking pretty smug as he and Aidan carried the huge sheet cake out to the table they'd set up for it in the yard. Cait met Gavin there, sliding her hand into his as she looked at the cake.

Grant—no doubt with urging, if not outright help from the other guys—had blown up the Snapchat photo of Gavin checking out Cait's ass and had it printed on the surface of the cake. He'd removed Carter's original caption, though, and now it read *SHE SAID YES.*

"This is why you never put a firehouse crew in charge of the cake," Gavin said when the laughter had died down.

"I love it," Cait said, pulling his face close enough for a kiss.

"Never mind," he said when she broke it off. "Good job, crew."

There was more laughter, and then cake and more laughter. Cait couldn't remember the last time she'd been so happy, but she was ready for the party to start winding down. It had been a long day and unseasonably warm, and she was looking forward to a nice soak in their tub with her future husband. Or a quick shower and straight to bed. She was okay with either.

"What are you thinking about right now?" Gavin asked, turning his body so nobody could see the hand he ran down her back to cup her ass.

"Getting naked with you."

His eyes lit up and he put his free hand on his stomach. "I don't feel so good, so we should go. Right now."

"I'm an EMT, so you're in good hands." When he

laughed, she raised her eyebrow at him. "I'm pretty sure I can think of a way to make you feel better."

"You think so?"

She cupped his face in her hands. "Do you trust me?"

Heat flared in his eyes and he grinned. "Oh, yeah."

"You keeping smiling at me like that and people are going to think we're up to no good."

"I can't help it. I'm the happiest fucking guy in Boston right now."

She slid her hand behind his neck and kissed him until cheers and a few whistles broke out in the crowd around them. "And we're just getting started."

* * * * *

To read more from Shannon Stacey,
visit www.ShannonStacey.com.

Author Note

The processes and organizational structures of large city fire departments and emergency services are incredibly complex, and I took minor creative liberties in order to maintain readability.

To first responders everywhere, thank you.

Acknowledgments

Thank you to the Carina Press team for all of your hard work in bringing my stories to readers. And a special thank you to my editor, Angela James, for helping me make those stories the best they can be.

*Read on for a sneak peek of the next book
in the* BOSTON FIRE *series*

UNDER CONTROL

*coming September 2018 from
Shannon Stacey and Carina Press.*

*What would have been a random incident with an
attractive stranger becomes something more when a
charity event brings them back together. They're from
different sides of the tracks—literally—with friends,
family and careers to consider. But as Derek and
Olivia are discovering, chemistry doesn't allow for
plans, and love doesn't bother with logistics.*

Chapter One

Nothing made a guy feel conspicuous like walking down the hall of an office building in full turnout gear.

Or he would if anybody actually noticed him, Derek Gilman thought as he shifted to the right to avoid running into a woman looking down at her phone. How people navigated the hallways with their eyes glued to their screens was beyond him.

One guy actually looked up from his phone as he brushed by, and then did a startled double take. "Should I be evacuating?"

"You can evacuate if you want," Derek said, "but there's no reason to. We're just doing some high-rise training."

Which was a fact everybody in the building was supposed to have been made aware of before they arrived. They didn't have much in the way of glass skyscrapers in their neighborhood, so the crews of Engine 59 and Ladder 37 had schlepped across Boston on what should have been a day off to hone their skills.

Remembering to bring everything they needed from the apparatus was apparently *not* one of their skills, and, as the newest guy on the Ladder 37 crew, Derek had been sent to retrieve the paperwork Rick Gullotti—their

lieutenant and the guy in charge of paperwork—had forgotten.

A woman stepped out of an office ahead and turned,
walking ahead of him in the same direction. She was
notable for two reasons. One, she wasn't looking at a
cell phone. That in itself was enough to make her stand
out in this crowd.

But it was her looks that captured Derek's attention.
He only got a glimpse of her profile before she turned,
but she had delicate features and dark blond hair drawn
up off her neck in a loose bun. Her navy suit looked as
if it had been tailored specifically for her body, and the
jacket flared slightly, accenting the curve of her hips.
Her legs were long, and his gaze lingered on her calves
before sliding up to the soft spots behind her knees that
were playing peek-a-boo with the hem of her skirt.

And he'd never realized how sexy the click of high
heels on a marble tile floor could be. When he was a
kid, he'd hated the sound because the high heels usually
belonged to an angry teacher he was following down
the hallway to the principal's office. But following *this*
woman as she walked down the hallway with long, confident strides was a hell of a lot more enjoyable.

Of course, she reached the elevator just as the door
opened and a man stepped out. Because he'd slowed to
leave enough space to appreciate the view, Derek knew
there was a good chance the door would close before he
reached it, and there was no way in hell he was taking
the stairs if he didn't have to.

"Hold the door, please," he called as the woman
stepped in and pushed a button on the panel.

She looked up at him and he saw the hesitation in her
body language. She didn't want to, but he watched the
fact he was a firefighter register, plus it would be rude

to pretend she hadn't heard him after making eye contact. He smiled as she hit the button to hold the doors.

"Thank you." The button for the lobby was already lit, so he stepped back as the doors slid closed.

She only nodded and pulled her phone out of the back pocket of the leather journal she was holding, which was stuffed with notebooks and paper from the looks of it. But Derek could see her reflection in the highly polished metal door and she was looking at him. And not a quick glance to make sure the stranger was staying on his own side, but a lingering look.

He should say something, but he wasn't sure *what* to say, since women wearing power suits in the Back Bay were way out of his league. The floors were ticking past like seconds on the clock, though, and he was running out of time.

She was taking a step forward, probably in anticipation of reaching the lobby level soon, when there was a grinding sound and the elevator lurched to a stop. Off balance, she stumbled and—thanks to good reflexes and maybe some good luck—he ended up with an armful of beautiful woman.

Apparently he was getting an extension.

She tilted her face up to him, and he saw the distress in her pretty greenish-blue eyes. "What's happening?"

"We stopped," he said, hoping she'd find the obvious answer funny. In his experience, humor relaxed people. She didn't even crack a smile, and he cleared his throat before continuing. "There are a few reasons it could happen, but the system probably has a problem or a malfunction somewhere and it shut the elevator down to be safe."

"This is not safe." She wasn't in a full-blown panic, but her anxiety practically crackled around her, and she was clutching his arm so tightly he could feel her grip through the heavy bunker coat. "And what do you mean by a malfunction? So something could be *more* wrong than the fact we're not moving anymore?"

"Everything's fine." He had to let his arms fall away from her as she backed away, wincing a little. "Are you hurt?"

"No." He wasn't reassured by the quick way she said it, as if it was a reflex and maybe not the truth.

He pulled out his phone to send a quick group text to Danny Walsh—Engine 59's LT—and Rick Gullotti. Elevator's stuck. Why? Then he peeled off the heavy coat and tossed it on the floor, dropping the helmet on top of it while she sent a text message of her own to somebody. "We're okay in here. Just try to stay calm and we'll be out in no time."

"Stay calm," she muttered as her phone vibrated and she sent another text. "That's easy for you to say. Being brave in the face of death is part of your job."

That was a little dramatic, but she wasn't *totally* wrong. About his job, anyway. "You're not facing death. I promise."

His phone vibrated with a response from Walsh. Working on it. Stand by.

The woman's face was slightly flushed. "Shouldn't you... I don't know. Go up through the ceiling hatch and climb up the cable or something?"

Derek managed—barely—not to laugh outright at her, but he couldn't hold back a short chuckle. "I'm a firefighter, not John McClane."

"Who's John McClane?"

Oh, she did *not* just ask that. "The greatest action hero of all time? The guy from *Die Hard*?"

"I've heard of those movies, but I've never seen any of them."

If he'd needed any more of a definitive sign this woman wasn't his type, that was it. "You're missing out. So, what's your name?"

"Olivia."

"Pretty name." Classic and elegant, and it suited her. "I'm Derek."

"Can you pry open the doors?" she asked, clearly not in a place to be distracted by small talk.

"With my bare hands?" He held them up, showing off his lack of tools. "I work out a little, but not that much."

Her gaze flicked over his body, and he stood up straighter and sucked in his gut. Not that there was much to suck in, but he wasn't in his twenties anymore. Hell, he was barely still in his thirties. "You work out more than a little."

Her tone of voice made it sound like just an observation, but he didn't miss her gaze lingering for a second on his chest or the way her eyebrow lifted as her mouth curved into a hint of a smile. She wasn't flirting, but she liked what she saw and he'd take the win. He'd need all the ego boosting he could get once the other guys started giving him shit for having to rescue him from an elevator.

Then she shifted her weight and, when she winced again, Derek gave her a stern look. "You're hurt."

"No, I'm not. I twisted my ankle a little when the elevator stopped."

"You need to get those shoes off and let me look at it."

She laughed and shook her head. "I don't care how nice this elevator is, I am *not* touching the floor with my bare feet."

Derek picked up his coat, letting the helmet roll free, and—with a flourish—spread it over the floor in front of her. "Your carpet, milady."

* * *

Olivia McGovern didn't have time to be stuck in an elevator today. Her schedule was so tight the Lyft driver who was probably outside waiting for her would determine the fate of her punctuality streak, and she hadn't been late to a meeting in the three years since she'd officially hung out her McGovern Consulting shingle.

But none of that seemed to matter when she looked into the warm blue eyes of the firefighter smiling at her right now. It had been the smile he gave her as he stepped onto the elevator that first caught her attention. That smile that was just a little friendlier than a polite "thank you" and radiated warmth had been sexy, she had to admit. His helmet coming off to reveal tousled dark, dirty blond hair, along with the Boston Fire T-shirt showing off a very nicely built upper body, hadn't hurt, anyway.

But it was the boyish grin he gave her as he spread his coat out like a gentleman in a story that really kicked her heartbeat into high gear.

As did putting her hand on his arm to steady herself as she stepped out of the heels. The first time she'd clutched his arm—after she'd been thrown into his arms—he'd been wearing the coat she was standing on. But now she could feel the firm muscle and the warmth of his skin through the blue cotton.

"Thank you," she said in a slightly choked voice. Her ankle really wasn't that bad, but being out of the shoes for a few minutes would definitely help.

Then he dropped to his knees in front of her and she sucked in a sharp breath. His hands closed around her ankle and she pressed her lips together so she wouldn't make any sort of a sound when he ran them up over her calf muscle and back to her ankles. He pressed gently with his thumbs, and maybe it was her imagination, but it sounded like the deep breath *he* took shuddered just a little.

"No swelling," he said, pushing back to his feet. "It doesn't look bad, but you should elevate it while we're waiting. You can sit on the coat."

Getting into a sitting position on the coat while wearing a skirt was a challenge, but Derek had turned away to retrieve his helmet so she did it as quickly and with as much modesty as she could. She assumed he was going to use the helmet to prop her ankle up, but he simply set it right-side up and then sat down at her feet.

An unexpected rush of heat flooded her when he lifted her foot and shifted so he could rest it on his thigh, and she hoped it didn't show on her face.

"It really should be elevated more, but we don't have a lot of options," he said. "Is this okay?"

His hand was massaging her ankle and she didn't trust herself to speak, so she nodded. He had callouses and his hands weren't abrasive, but just rough enough so a shiver went through her.

"Are you cold?" he asked, his thumb brushing over her ankle bone.

"I'm fine," she forced herself to say, but she was struggling with the awareness that for the first time in her life, she was very tempted to make out with a total stranger in an elevator.

Before she could say anything else, his phone chimed and he checked the message before sending back a brief reply. "They're going to pry the door."

It was utterly ridiculous that disappointment would be her first reaction to imminent rescue, but it was. Followed fairly quickly by the awareness of how much time had passed since she sent an update to Kelsey.

"Does that take long?"

"Shouldn't. They've probably already cut the power to make sure it doesn't start moving again at a bad time, so it won't take long to bypass the door restrictors and get the doors open. How's the ankle feeling?"

"Better, thanks." The ankle was better, but now the rest of her body was a little hot and achy. "I think I can get up."

He helped her, of course, taking her hands and pulling as she pulled her legs under her so she was on her knees and then got to her feet. And he didn't let them go once she was standing. They were close—so close she had to tilt her head back slightly to see his face—and for a few crazy seconds, she thought he was going to kiss her.

And she wanted him to.

"Can you put weight on it?"

This time she knew the blush was visible because she could feel it on her face. He was holding her hands because of her ankle. "It's fine. It really wasn't that bad and sitting for a few minutes helped."

As did his hand massaging her ankle, though she didn't say so. And she managed to stifle the sigh of regret when he released her hands. Then she heard sounds on the other side of the metal doors and realized they wouldn't be in the elevator much longer.

She sent a quick text message to Kelsey. They're getting ready to open the doors. Find a car for me ASAP, please.

On it.

Olivia told herself she should be happy when the doors finally opened and another very attractive firefighter looked down at her from the opening. *They should do a calendar*, she thought, and was very thankful she hadn't said it out loud.

"Hi there," he said. "I'm Aidan Hunt, with Engine 59. We're going to get you out now."

"Took you guys long enough," Derek told him, even as Olivia silently wished it could have taken just a little longer. Then he turned to her. "You ready to get out of here?"

She nodded, but didn't move to the front. "I… They can't line up the doors with the floor?"

"The elevator's still stuck, so that would be a no. This is as good as it gets, but I'll give you a boost up."

A *boost*? Olivia wasn't sure what that meant, but it implied him picking her up, and maybe having to hand her up to Aidan, which might involve Derek's hands on her butt. Not that she'd mind that very much, but she was in a skirt.

"That doesn't sound very graceful," she pointed out. "Or modest."

"I think we skimmed over being graceful at the fire academy. But, tell you what. To make it easier, I'll get on the floor. If you step up onto my back and take Aidan's hands for balance, I'll get up on my hands and knees and you should be high enough so one of the guys can get you under the arms and lift you out with no problem."

"You don't mind?"

"Trust me. It won't be the worst thing that's happened to me on the job."

Her gaze flicked to the scar that ran down his jaw, but she didn't ask. Instead, she walked to the opening and handed her leather notebook up to Aidan. "*Please* don't lose that or drop it down the elevator shaft or anything. It's my entire life."

"Don't lose this, Scotty," Aidan said, handing the book

over to another firefighter. Then he took Olivia's shoes from her and set them aside. "I'm going to lay on my stomach so I can reach out and give you something to hold on to while you step up on Derek. Then Chris here is going to get you under the arms and lift you so you can reach the lip. You ready?"

She nodded, and Derek got down on the floor as if he was going to do some push-ups. This still wasn't going to be all that graceful, she realized as she stepped onto his back. "Am I hurting you?"

"Nope. You ready?"

She reached up and Aidan grasped her hands. "Okay. But no looking up."

His chuckle vibrated through the bottoms of her feet. "I won't. I promise."

His back muscles flexed and she barely had time to register his strength as he lifted himself—and her—before somebody grabbed her under the arms and lifted her. She got her knees onto the lip, but they didn't let her go until she was on her feet and several feet away from the elevator shaft.

"Lieutenant Rick Gullotti," one of the older of the group said to her, and she shook his hand. "Are you injured at all? Do you need medical attention?"

She wouldn't mind Derek's hands on her some more, but she definitely didn't need an ambulance. "I'm not injured. Thank you—all of you—for getting me out."

He nodded and then turned back to the elevator. She stepped into her shoes, thankful her ankle didn't offer up more than a slight twinge. And the firefighter who'd been called Scotty handed over her journal. "Thank you."

Her phone chimed with the tone set for Kelsey Harris, her assistant. I found a car service in the area but if you can't be outside in two minutes, he has to leave.

Olivia hesitated. She wanted to stay and thank Derek. Maybe she'd work up the nerve to ask his last name or give him her business card.

But if she got in the car right now, she could still salvage her day. Rescheduling one appointment was bad enough. Depending on traffic, she could make the next one and maybe not even be late. And it was a big client she'd been trying to land for a while.

Coming now, she messaged to Kelsey.

"I really have to run," she said, "but thank you for everything."

"All in a day's work," Scotty said.

She looked at the elevator, hoping Derek would be out already, but Aidan was in the process of pulling Derek's coat and helmet out of the elevator. "Tell Derek I said thank you, too."

"You sure you can't wait a couple more minutes?"

She wanted to. She really did, but she shook her head. "I have a meeting. But tell him I said thank you."

She walked toward the front door as fast as her sore ankle allowed, feeling a little like Cinderella fleeing the ball.

Once she was in the back seat of the black SUV, she knew she could check her email account and see if anything needed her attention as she always did while in transit from one appointment to the next.

Instead she leaned her head against the leather and closed her eyes, regretting her decision already. Not that leaving was the wrong decision. Success came from making a plan and executing it, and right now her focus was 100 percent on her business. Dating was *not* part of her plan yet.

She opened her eyes as the SUV pulled away from the curb and she caught a glimpse of two fire trucks parked down a side street as they passed by. It would be a while before she forgot her firefighter, she knew. His laugh. His eyes. The feel of his hands on her skin.

And now she'd probably never see him again. Sometimes making the right decision really sucked.

Don't miss UNDER CONTROL
from Carina Press and Shannon Stacey,
available September 2018.

About the Author

New York Times and *USA TODAY* bestselling author Shannon Stacey lives with her husband and two sons in New England, where her two favorite activities are writing stories of happily-ever-after and driving her UTV through the mud. You can contact Shannon through her website, shannonstacey.com, where she maintains an almost daily blog, visit her on Twitter, Twitter. com/shannonstacey, and on Facebook, Facebook.com/ shannonstacey.authorpage, or email her at shannon@ shannonstacey.com.

To find out about other books by Shannon Stacey or to be alerted to new releases, sign up for her monthly newsletter at bit.ly/shannonstaceynewsletter.

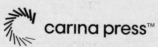

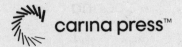